Born in 1960, Ravi Shankar Etteth is the Deputy Editor of *India Today* magazine. He is also a political cartoonist and graphic artist. A collection of his short stories has been published in India, and he is also the author of two novels, *The Tiger by the River* and *The Village of Widows*, both of which are published by Black Swan. He lives in New Delhi, with his two dogs, Boski and Guru.

Acclaim for *The Tiger by the River*:

'*The Tiger by the River* dazzles with its intricate plotting and stylish prose'
David Davidar, author of *The House of Blue Mangoes*

'A heady mix of mythology and myth-making . . . A rewarding, atmospheric read, laden with ghosts'
Time Out

'Full of stories and overlapping voices, teeming with history and myth . . . Etteth negotiates the cultures of west and east and the narratives of folklore and modernity with a rare and appealing skill'
Sunday Herald

'An outstanding first novel . . . beautifully handled in poetic, mystical and symbolic prose. From the first there is a sensation of being safely in the hands of a talented story spinner. This sad yet uplifting novel continues to haunt long after the book is back on the shelf'
Historical Novels Review

'A majestic novel of love and loss'
Books magazine

Also by Ravi Shankar Etteth

THE TIGER BY THE RIVER

and published by Black Swan

THE VILLAGE OF WIDOWS

Ravi Shankar Etteth

BLACK SWAN

THE VILLAGE OF WIDOWS
A BLACK SWAN BOOK: 0 552 77078 7

First publication in Great Britain

PRINTING HISTORY
Black Swan edition published 2004

1 3 5 7 9 10 8 6 4 2

Set in 11/13.5pt Melior by
Falcon Oast Graphic Art Ltd.

Black Swan Books are published by Transworld Publishers,
61–63 Uxbridge Road, London W5 5SA,
a division of The Random House Group Ltd,
in Australia by Random House Australia (Pty) Ltd,
20 Alfred Street, Milsons Point, Sydney, NSW 2061, Australia,
in New Zealand by Random House New Zealand Ltd,
18 Poland Road, Glenfield, Auckland 10, New Zealand
and in South Africa by Random House (Pty) Ltd,
Endulini, 5a Jubilee Road, Parktown 2193, South Africa.

Printed and bound in Great Britain by
Cox & Wyman Ltd, Reading, Berkshire.

Papers used by Transworld Publishers are natural, recyclable
products made from wood grown in sustainable forests. The
manufacturing processes conform to the environmental
regulations of the country of origin.

For Kavita
who is my story

Acknowledgements

My gratitude and affection to my agents Martina and Malcolm for putting up with my endless questions, my editor Simon Taylor for telling me about editor's block, to Pramod and Kiran Kapoor for the use of St Asaph's where, undoubtedly inspired by the resident literary ghost, I was able to finish seven chapters in fifteen days. Special thanks go to my dear friends Deputy Inspector General of Police Shiv Sahai and Captain Hunney Bakshi of Military Intelligence for their stories on Kashmir, where they spent years fighting the Mujahedeen. Thanks to Supriya Bezbaruah for teaching me about genetics and murder, to Carin Fischer for the first read, and to Prasannarajan for suggestions about the big picture. My gratitude too, for all their help, to Sapna Kapoor, Kamal Goel and Kishore. And above all, I am indebted to my father, Etteth Gangadharan for gently reminding me every day that I am a writer.

CHAPTER ONE

The murderer awoke suddenly, thinking of the blood smoking on the marble. The architect had chosen fine stone from Rajasthan for the floor: milky white with subtle shades in it, smooth like first sleep. The reflection on the floor of the giant jacaranda outside the gabled window appeared as a hazy inky colander of branch and foliage, through which the blood had spread and congealed. Parts of the floor were wet with the water that had mixed with the blood; fuchsia blotches sugary with broken glass from the carafe the killer had tipped over.

He lit a cigarette. On the bed, his lover shifted, moaning in a cloudy dream. The murderer reached out and stroked the familiar cologned cheek of the man curled beneath the white satin sheets. The last of the moonlight glimmered in the dawn, oxidizing the skin of the sleeper's cheek. His mouth was open, full and deep-lipped, and his hair was sweaty. The steam of sleep escaped through his lips, a dissipating heat that reminded the murderer of Radama Zafy's blood.

The blood had flowed down the carved leg of the rosewood chair upon which Radama Zafy had sat. His chin was crushed against the red leather of the table top before him, arms akimbo, face twisted to the left towards the locked door and wearing an expression predominantly of shock. The glowing screen of his laptop computer was spattered with bloody vomit, the haemorrhage glistening between the keyboard spaces. As the murderer leaned across to switch the machine off, the cursor kept blinking, its green palpitation an electronic indifference to death.

The weapon had entered Zafy from the back, pushing its way past the skin along the edge of the spine through the ribs and the soft, unresistant mass of muscle and tissue, crushing first the heart, puncturing a lung, and almost breaking a rib. The force of the blow had driven Zafy forward to hit his cheek against the table, the leather padding muffling the sound. The killer unconsciously felt his right fist, recalling the touch of the weapon: one that he had so carefully fashioned for its purpose. Zafy's blood had splashed on him, and his skin trembled as it remembered the steamy, warm splat on his chest and abdomen. The killer had been naked, as Zafy had expected him to be. He had also metamorphosed into a monster, as Zafy had not expected him to be. Radama Zafy had been waiting for him while reading his email and going over the details of his various Cayman Islands accounts. The murderer was in the small basement downstairs, stripped and lean.

'Go and bathe first,' Zafy had said, kissing him

lightly on his mouth as he had come in. 'Yesterday you smelled.'

Radama's own breath had a trace of peppermint in it, and he noticed the frown on his lover's forehead. He smoothed it with slim, expert fingers.

'Bear with me, my darling, humour an old man, who has loved you for many years.'

So yesterday the killer had gone down to shower in the small basement, with its home gym, billiards table and the deep freeze, which stored, among other things, Zafy's favourite zebu burgers that were flown in from Madagascar. Though Radama Zafy was only First Secretary at the Malagasy mission in New Delhi, he was also a royal of Madagascar and a direct descendant of King Andrianumpoinimerina and the bloodthirsty Queen Ranavalona. The French had turned Madagascar into a colony in the nineteenth century and abolished its monarchy, but there had been enough time to spirit away bullion and treasures worth billions of francs.

Didier Ratsiraka was now President, but the ruling elite of the Malagasay still enjoyed privileges that were subtle and not easily discarded. And it was this wealth that beckoned the murderer in his youth to enter Radama Zafy's employment in his Toamasina villa by the sea. He recalled the first sight of his benefactor, sitting on the huge bamboo chair on the patio overlooking the beach, seagulls cawing and swooping down the waves glinting in the African sun.

On a table beside him were the remains of a meal, which he recognized as *koba* – a banana and rice pâté. Zafy must have noticed the sudden glint of hunger in his eyes. A small, secret smile had appeared on his lips. He, for his part, had met Zafy's gaze steadfastly,

11

his soft brown eyes fringed with dark cocoa lashes. Radama extended his arms, and he went into them like a small boat rowing into a large, calm harbour.

Radama Zafy had been his benefactor as well as his lover; sending him to school during the days and sleeping in his arms at night. The large French windows were open to the sea and welcomed the breeze in, to cool the sweat of their skins and allow the vapours of his uneasy dreams to dissipate. Zafy had used his connections to educate him in private schools, visiting him in his rooms whenever he was hungry for his creamy Creole skin. It was Radama Zafy who got him into the Malagasay government service. For Zafy, he was a privilege, a lover by right, something owned as part of a habit, an ancient practice.

It was this claim to ownership over him the murderer had sensed when he had walked down the marble steps that led to the basement, having been commanded to have a shower. The marble was not overly smooth, unlike the Italian kind that so many fashionable Delhi architects chose for their wealthy clients, and this helped him to carry out his task without slipping or losing his balance. For silence and balance were so important: he had to be like the fosa, the most lethal cat in the world, whose hunting grounds were the impenetrable forests of his island. He had to come up behind his prey in absolute silence; when he drove the weapon with all his strength into Radama Zafy's muscle and bones he had to remain steady on his legs, with the centre of his gravity shifting effortlessly from the balls of his feet to his toes and then back again. In the basement he had slowly stripped off his clothes while idly looking around, the dark idea possessing his mind: how to be free of Radama Zafy and make his riches his own. As the water pricked his body with small nips of heat, it opened up alleys in his brain that he never knew existed.

The murderer stretched on the bed, drawing deeply on his cigarette. He felt free. He had repaid his debt to Zafy over and over through the years, with the loneliness of a unacknowledged concubine, with his mouth and fingers, and with a million caresses of an ageing, ever unsated skin.

He was not a murderer by habit.

'Who is?' he wondered, stubbing out his cigarette in the crystal ashtray beside his bed.

He felt in a philosophical mood. Murderers are not as a rule, he thought, like Jack the Ripper or the Son of Sam – men with a ravenous incubus devouring their insides that could only be calmed temporarily with the spilling of blood. Murderers were usually ordinary men, and they only became killers by chance, when they were protecting something that was threatened, or were deprived of an innocence that could never be restored. It was just a temporary shift of planes, like a maimed secret fleeing through a hidden door into an intense, private night that was brilliantly lit up by the final moment of violence – a violence so absolute and ultimate that it was pure and godly. That light also cleansed the evil and redeemed the murderer. But its recollection lived as a perverse mascot forever in a small, unforgiving grotto inside, a dragon who could be summoned any time with a whisper of fire.

'I'm not a monster,' the murderer murmured tenderly to himself, running his soft palm along his own familiar cheek, the tips of his fingers touching the fringe of his unruly hair, playing with the corner of his lips that were still sore from his lover's kisses.

No, he was definitely not a monster, he told himself again, in a soft and reassuring whisper – a breath of words in the early dawn of that winter's night.

He was just a man, protecting himself and the one he loved. Now, with what he had taken from Zafy, he and his beloved would be free to live their lives together.

They would not return to Madagascar immediately, he thought, but go to Greece first, then Italy and Portugal. Just like Radama and he once had, when there had been love between them. He remembered the warmth of the sun on his bare skin and how the Mediterranean heat had felt like a golden bath, as he lay on the pure white sands of Naxos while Zafy slowly kneaded the muscles in his back with olive oil.

Zafy had plundered the early years of his adolescence with his greedy mouth and urgent, demanding fingers – a mentor and ally at first, until the day he wanted to become his eternal master.

'No,' the killer snarled into the dawn, as it stealthily lit the branches of the *gulmohur* in the front yard of his apartment. The sandstone sides of the nameless Mughal tomb in the park across the street began to turn pale as the sun rose.

'No-one will be my master, ever!' he swore, and certainly not Zafy, who now sat dead in his own blood inside his private chamber at the Malagasay embassy in Chanakya Puri, Delhi's diplomatic enclave.

He remembered that most of the blood which had poured from Radama Zafy's back, drenching his shirt, had been soaked up by the chair cushion. The rest had flowed down in small rills, chasing the disappearing heat. In the room that was turning cold after the killer had switched off the heating – which he had to do in order to escape – Zafy's blood began to smoke.

As he had walked towards the basement door, he had turned and looked at Radama Zafy taking the last few breaths of his life. An old man, bent over his computer, his cigarillo smoking in the crystal ashtray on the table, a silk scarf thrown carelessly over the back of the chair. The electronic safe in the alcove underneath a portrait of Didier Ratsiraka was open, the light inside it illuminating the few papers it held. The codes would be there, the murderer reasoned, which would help him transfer Zafy's millions into his own Zurich bank account. The lamplight reflected on the planes of Zafy's face, and a fit of sudden affection overcame him. He rushed to the old man and put his strong, muscular arms around his neck.

'My old bear,' he crooned in French, 'without you, where would I be?'

At that moment, if Radama Zafy had returned his embrace, or stroked his hair the way he did when they once lay together on a Naples bed, nibbling slices of a juicy red apple dipped in honey, he would, perhaps, not have died. But Zafy wriggled his neck in his lover's embrace, squinted up at him, and answered with a sharp laugh, 'You would have been in the gutter, pimping your mother on the west coast. Now go and bathe, and come to bed. I have to meet the Ambassador early tomorrow morning.'

And so the murderer had quickly walked down the steps and undressed, throwing his clothes upon a bench placed on a gym mat. He had taken the weapon out from where he had put it the day before, feeling its weight and solidity again, holding it out before him carefully. He did not bathe, there would be time for that afterwards. He stole up the stairs naked.

He had watched Zafy die, twisting spasmodically where he sat, feet encased in Bally shoes, drumming out of tune on the Moroccan rug. His hands jerked against the sides of his trousers each time he convulsed, producing a flapclapping sound which made the murderer giggle.

'Clapping to his own murder,' he laughed low, 'Radama the dead.'

The force of the blow was so strong that the weapon had broken and was scattered on the floor near Radama. Part of it stuck in his back, showing through the bloody mess of bone and mangled muscle and tissue. Turning up the heating to full, he had walked – still naked – to the safe and sat down to examine the papers.

The codes were there, as he had seen previously, and he went across to the computer, humming softly. He picked up Zafy's silk scarf that was draped on the chair and carefully wiped the blood that had splattered onto the screen and the table top. He scanned the files one by one: details of investments, stock holdings, kickbacks and money transfers. He transferred them onto diskettes. The watch showed the time as a quarter to eleven.

He knew that the servants would have retired by now. If Zafy wanted dinner to be sent up, he would have telephoned down to the kitchen before nine thirty. Usually, if the First Secretary wanted a snack, he would go down to the basement and fix himself a zebu sandwich or put a precooked *foza sy ken-kisoa*, a stir-fried pork and rice dish, in the microwave. Or sometimes Radama would ask his lover to fix a meal for just the two of them, and open a bottle of Chablis.

He would go down to the little kitchenette, take chicken from the deep freeze and warm it for a minute in the microwave. First he would sprinkle it with salt and extra pepper, hot the way Zafy had liked it. Then he would cut tomatoes into small cubes and squeeze milk from the desiccated coconut in the refrigerator. As he heated onions and ginger and the tomatoes and chicken in the frying pan, Zafy would shout from above.

'Ah, you are making my favourite *akoho sy voanio*! I am hungry, my young bull, hungry for both the food and you!'

Zafy had let him into the embassy compound unseen, knowing when the late evening guard shift changed. He had not brought his car with him; they would not note what time he left. Zafy's private chambers opened out into a small, high-walled garden with its own private door, which surely must have been a passageway for some of the old man's other lovers as well. He knew there was only one key to that door, a heavy iron key that never left Radama, always strung on a chain fastened to his belt. The garden gate opened out into a small hillock of wood and rough shrub. All he had to do was to cross the outcrop and slide down the narrow gravelly path, which would lead him to the lane towards Sardar Patel Marg. He had parked his old Volkswagen Rabbit at the Maurya Sheraton and entered the hotel lobby through a side entrance; he could always nonchalantly walk out of the glass doors and ask the liveried doorman, a fake Rajput warrior in red, gold and white, for his car to be brought to him.

All he needed was Zafy's key to the gate. That would be easy.

17

The murderer remembered walking down the steps to the basement, his lover's blood drying on him. He had switched the heating off, and by the time he came up after his shower it would be cold again. That too was necessary; the key to his escape, he thought, and grinned.

As he closed his eyes to the drumming of the water on his face, he remembered the rain of the Krindy forests. An incessant, cleansing rain that carried with it the smell of wet herbs and leaves. He remembered the clean blue sky. He felt the blood of the murder leave his body as if in ablution, his skin regaining a life that had the freshness of strange new freedoms. He thought of Radama Zafy sitting in his blood-soaked chair, growing cold and stiff, and wondered who would find him first.

It would almost certainly be the Ambassador. They would first knock, try to call on the internal telephone line, then bang on the door, and then finally break it down. The Ambassador would rush in, and there would be phone calls to be made: first to the President himself, because Zafy was an important public figure, and then to the Counsellor for Public Affairs, who had to deal with the police and brief the press.

The murderer, working at Public Affairs, knew Delhi's police well. A bunch of overworked, underpaid, tired men who were notoriously corrupt. And he knew their officers, who mostly drank whisky they could not afford on their salaries and jockeyed in Delhi's government circuits to hold onto their city postings.

Who would be put in charge of the case, he wondered briefly as he towelled himself dry. In all probability it would be that new Deputy Commissioner, Anna Khan.

A woman, he thought with contempt.

He remembered meeting her when a diplomat's car had been reported stolen, and she had received him in her room at the Deputy Commissioner's office. A slim woman wearing a purple silk sari, which was wrapped around her shoulders and made her skin look pink; her hair was long and black and tied in a plait that reached down to her waist; her eyes were black and calm. She had offered her hand to be shaken, and he had brushed her fingers with his own hastily, concealing his dislike of touching a woman's flesh. He noticed the faint white mark of an absent ring upon her middle finger and wondered if she was divorced. She had been posted in Kashmir before coming to Delhi, and fought the Mujahedeen and Kashmiris that were bent upon secession. How would she have tackled the jehadis, he wondered, those tough battle-scarred monsters left over from the Soviet–Afghan war, now fighting to liberate Kashmir from India?

But she had found the car in Doda a few weeks later, smuggled across to Kashmir from New Delhi, where stolen vehicles were used as car bombs and for suicide strikes.

She was clever, the killer admitted, but terrorists were one thing and a private murder was another. As far as terrorists were concerned, she could rely on an unholy alliance of informers, criminals and fences who lived in an uneasy truce with the police.

But there were no informers to help solve the murder of a diplomat, no network of spies to tap into. So what would they say about who killed Radama Zafy?

A *kinoly*, perhaps? An *angatra*, a vicious Malagasy ghost? The Malagasy were terribly superstitious, and when they finally discovered Zafy dead inside a locked room, with his back torn open and no weapon to be found, they would most certainly say that it must have been a *kinoly* – one which had savaged him with its long fingernails. He remembered a story his mother had told him once while he lay in her lap in the afternoon sun under a ravenala tree. The story of a man who met a *kinoly* in the forest.

'Why are your eyes so red?' he asked the ghost.

'Because God passed by them,' the evil one answered.

'Why are your nails so long?'

'To tear out your insides.'

The murderer began to laugh.

He knew that the police would go over the rooms with every device available to them. They would use forensics experts, sniffer dogs, fingerprinters, and the non-diplomatic staff would be interrogated endlessly and not allowed to sleep – the rest would claim immunity. A murder in an embassy would be Priority A for the Delhi police, but he had taken all the necessary precautions. He had spent an hour going over the entire room, carefully recalling the places and objects he might have touched, wiping them clean. He scraped the bathroom floor and cleaned it with large amounts of phenyl and acid. The killer knew the police would find the total absence of evidence suspicious, but he didn't want to leave any signs of his presence in Zafy's rooms. As a final gesture, he had tipped Zafy's favourite crystal water jug onto the floor, the noise of it breaking sounding like eerie laughter. The floor should be wet when they found the body, he thought. One must be a perfect artist to commit the perfect crime. He knew they would keep the murder a secret from the Indian press. The Ambassador would bring pressure on the investigating officers by speaking to the Foreign Office, and perhaps there would even be questions from the Prime Minister himself. Maybe President Didier would demand urgent action – after all, there were rumours that Zafy had handled the President's overseas funds.

He was confident that the police would come up with nothing.

But if everything failed, he knew that the Ambassador would turn to another man for help: an old friend, a tall, inscrutable man called Samorin.

'Samorin.' The murderer spoke the name softly to himself, almost like a question.

Would Samorin be able to find anything where the police had failed? He had seen Jay Samorin once or twice briefly, at diplomatic dinners and Delhi's cocktail parties where he himself kept to the background: an impeccably dressed man with a mysterious smile, usually dressed in dark colours. The murderer had also noticed Samorin's long, restless fingers, always appearing in internal communion with some private god of caricature, creating the impression that he drew in his mind a distorted picture of whoever he spoke to. The man had once been a famous political cartoonist, and had retired a few years ago. In a magazine interview he said he could not draw politicians any more because his eyesight was failing. 'Thankfully,' Samorin had told the interviewer. The interview also revealed that Samorin lived in a house on a hilltop a few miles from Delhi, part of a small private estate. He discouraged visitors. How Samorin came to be associated with crime was a mystery; few knew him as anything but a retired artist of independent means.

But the murderer knew. He kept his ear to the ground, it was part of his job. He knew that the British High Commissioner had involved him in the Masterson affair and the Austrians in the Lignite scandal. He had seen him once escorting Patricia, the British High Commissioner's daughter, to a party thrown by his own ambassador, and could only make wild guesses.

A private detective with secret contacts? A wealthy man with a hobby? A dark profiler who studied evil in the laboratory of his own disillusioned mind?

But would Samorin succeed where the policewoman was bound to fail? And would she allow him to interfere?

The muted arguments of birds from their nests among the great branches of the *gulmohur* sounded through the closed windows of the bedroom. The tomb in the park shimmered in the thin February mist, washed in the cold morning light; a dome of rose and gold. The sleeper on the bed stirred, opened his soft dark eyes, their pupils like grapes, and smiled drowsily at him. On his mouth was the faint red of dawn.

The murderer kissed the rosy lips and closed his eyes to the sound of his own heartbeat. When he opened them to the sudden peal of the telephone, morning had arrived in its blunt brightness, glistening on the luscious, starry red flowers of the *gulmohur*. They looked carnivorous, drunk on blood.

CHAPTER TWO

Jay Samorin sat in front of the black stone idol of the goddess in the *kalari*.* He had anointed her with the sacred oils, doused her stone tresses with unboiled milk, and gently applied crimson to her smiling, severe mouth.

Kali, Mahakali, the goddess of warriors, we worship thee.

He did this just as his ancestors had worshipped her when they went to war, before strapping their gleaming blades to their red cummerbunds. This was how his day always began, ever since he had been a child.

The *kalari angam* was a quadrangular structure at the sunset side of his house on the hillock, whose northern windows opened out into the plains beyond which lay the beginnings of New Delhi. When

* *kalari*: secluded arena where martial arts are practised.

Samorin had bought the twenty-seven acres a decade ago, the area was mainly jungle and rocks inhabited by hyenas and foxes, a place where rich *jat* farmers came to shoot rabbit and woodcock. To the north of his land were the Sohna sulphur springs, converted by a tourist-hungry government into a picnic spot. Developers had moved in, building apartment blocks in the middle of the barren land, clearing the trees and bulldozing the rocks, and soon there were housing colonies named Malibu Town and Sun City.

Someone had made a golf course for the Japanese who worked in the Government's Maruti car factory, and companies hoping for collaborations had already started to set up units in and around. But Samorin's house was tucked away from the satellite townships and its arterial networks. It was always hot in summer and misty in winter, and February's fog smoked in the mustard fields and wove around the harsh trees of the Aravalli plateau. The private road through Samorin's land connected with a long black road to Delhi that ran desultorily through the Haryana countryside, dipping and rising as it lost itself among the stony outgrowth and the fog. Anyone coming up that road could not see the house in which he lived, and the turn into the private drive was partially hidden by thickets of bamboo and two huge banyan trees.

The land was enclosed by a barbed-wire fence twelve feet high, strung along an inner wall of silver oaks planted close together, a druidic line of tall trees that turned into ivory and tinfoil in the moonlight. The house was built in the conservative tradition of Malayalee architecture: two-storeyed with attic windows hidden by gables, sloping down to corners and carved out of dark *veeti* wood. The red tiles of the roof gleamed in the northern sun and the only deviation from tradition was a covered veranda, which formed a jacket of white brick around the four sides of the house, interrupted by evenly spaced arches. A stucco barrier wall covered with wistaria concealed the front patio's slender wooden pillars and gargoyled rain-corners.

Samorin had lit the *nilavilakku*, the great many-tongued lamp, which had belonged to his family for generations. From it, he then lit a small hand-lamp and in prayer circled it thrice across the face of the goddess. In the flickering of illumination and smoke, she seemed to be smiling lazily – Kali the goddess of warriors, who had presided over the training of count-less fighters. The goddess of Samorin's *kalari*.

The four walls of the *kalari* formed a square cloister, with the temple at the northern end. Samorin had built it to the exact specifications of the *kalari* of his house in Manali. In the centre was the enclosed *angam* – a flat yard covered with soft sand, where warriors trained. The *kalari* itself was constructed according to *tachusastra*, the feudal science of Kerala's original architecture, with dark wooden rafters and a gabled, tiled roof. Ancient portraits hung on the walls, images of severe-looking men who had fought and died in the long-forgotten battles of Kerala centuries ago, and whose blood had changed into the syllables of folk songs. Antique swords and spears were mounted on the white plaster, while a mural of a *kalari* battle in progress took up the whole southern wall. Two warriors were locked in combat; one was in the middle of a leap, his teeth bared in a grin of powerful hatred, a shield thrust out in one hand while he held a long, gleaming sword in the other. His opponent's head was turned to avoid the blow as he pivoted on the ball of his left foot, while kicking a plume of dust in the face of the leaping warrior.

The mid-air leap. Higher and higher . . .

Samorin steeled himself, forcing his concentration away from the image that suddenly appeared within.

The gallows in the mist. The figure that swayed from it . . .

His imagination was suffused with the grey morning light and he was suddenly vaulting towards the brooding sky, soaring to rise above the scaffold, above the small jail courtyard with the dwarf tree in the windless corner, above the enclosure where traces of the last energies of doomed men lingered with forfeited footfalls – those who had mounted the ramp wet with morning dew to place the first steps of their last moments.

Father, walking across the square laid with dusty, red brick, looking up at the dark wooden pillar that was his final destination.

Was there fog that morning? Closing his eyes and feeling the familiar, small coldness within him, seeing the fog that rose from the swamp at the foot of the Palghat hills, breathing its way across the earth's wet crimson face, across the damp grass and little flowers, lifting as the wind rose and swayed, falling softly from the misty sky which would be warm with the sun in a while. What did Father see as he walked to his death?

Higher, trying to leap higher: as a boy, digging the balls of his feet into the earth as the moment of lifting came, the tightening of the calves learnt with patient calibration, the curling of thigh tendons, the gathering speed within him clenching and pumping down at the moment of final impact: trying to leap higher than Father's death, higher than the thick black frame of grainy wood from which the gate to death was built.

'The boy flies,' the *kalari* Gurukkal had told his aunt. 'He is like an eagle. He soars.'

Aunt could be seen dimly through the billowing curtains of the great bay window as he practised under his ageing warrior-teacher. Her gaze followed his every movement as he leaped against the glistening sun, her presence a quiet consciousness and part of all his learning movements. As he became familiar with the intricate manoeuvres of the ancient martial art, his young body oiled and kneaded with the foot of his guru, turning his muscles supple and taut and his bones pliant, Aunt would be there at the end of the day to soothe his bruises, to massage his sprains, and to make him laugh at the wounds he had received in the course of his training. He was instructed in the science of the *marmam*, those vulnerable nerve centres in the human body, on which just a gentle application of pressure would render an opponent immobile. He was taught to fight blindfolded, to use a stick as effectively as a sword, and the master imparted to the child his own special knowledge of armlocks and angles of strikes which could fell a full-grown bull in one movement. And through the years of his training, Aunt's touch was rarely far away from him.

He recalled her fingers on his hair as he sat leaning against the wooden walls, his body covered with sweat and oil, panting as if he had run a long way.

'My little warrior,' she would say in that soft, slightly dry voice of hers. 'My eagle.'

The warrior in the picture, hand raised like Jatayu's

wing, the mythical bird who challenged the evil
Ravana to combat in the sky . . .

'*Puzhikadayan*,' Aunt would point at the cloud of
dust in the picture, 'an act of cowardice, not meant for
real warriors. That was how the great warrior
Aaromalunni was tricked.'

The trick was to kick dust into an opponent's eyes,
temporarily blinding him, while one went in for the
kill.

'It is not a true warrior's ploy,' Samorin remembered
Aunt's voice. 'For a true warrior never wins by
treachery. I always want you to remember that.'

The painting had hung on the wall of the *kalari* at
Samorin's childhood home, where he had been
brought up by his aunt after his parents died. Whenever Samorin remembered his childhood, it was
always set in an atmosphere of height and white space.
The great villa with its vast terraces and cool verandas,
the huge whitewashed rooms with French windows
and polished teak doors opening into small corridors
and ante-rooms always made him feel as though he
was in a friendly, pale maze. It became the quint-
essential idea of home. As he grew up with the
loneliness that his mysterious past had wrapped
around him like a transparent, untearable gauze,
Samorin communed with the ghost of the house's
architect. It taught him the austerity of space, the
white beauty of empty, vast walls. The only picture
Samorin ever remembered seeing in the precincts of
the house and its grounds was the painting in the
kalari. There were never any photographs of his
parents in the house he had grown up in, and Aunt
always hushed him when he asked about them.

It was not until many years later that he had the

opportunity to go through the newspaper files in the municipal library of Palghat. It was the first time he had looked upon the faces of his parents.

Father had a long face with a strong jaw, and even in the grainy black and white of a photograph taken nearly four decades ago, Samorin recognized from where he had inherited his eyes. It was a clear, calm gaze, which held his in a steady scrutiny. Father's hair was swept back from his wide forehead, and he wore a half-smile. Mother resembled her elder sister, and Samorin gently touched the lower lip, which was fuller than Aunt's, and the thick black hair which was plaited and worn over the front of a sari.

The headlines about the murder and the trial were in thick bold type. He flipped through the pages, seeing more black-and-white pictures. There was a full-length studio portrait of his parents taken by the local photographer and bought by an enterprising correspondent: Father in his pilot's uniform with Mother standing against him, fingers twisting one edge of a silk sari. In another photograph, taken just after the trial was over, Father was looking back at the photographer as he was being led away from the court-room by grim, apologetic-seeming policemen – his eyes appeared amused by some small secret. Samorin looked closely at the grainy, blurred faces behind Father, and among them he recognized the unsmiling face of Aunt, whom for a moment he mistook for his mother.

Aunt, a severe woman who always wore white as a sign of her widowhood, rarely smiled. She was Mother's elder sister, who had been married young, barely at the age of ten; her husband had perished in a smallpox epidemic even before she had reached puberty. Custom then forbade her to marry again. Aunt was lucky. If her father, who had been a barrister at the Inner Temple when India was part of King George's empire, had not intervened, she would have been banished to the widow's village at the outskirts of the little principality of Manali, of which they were once the *naduvazhis*. These were chieftains of feudal Kerala, who administered small fiefdoms, and who owed their allegiance to a king. Samorin's grandfather claimed descent from the Zamorins of Calicut, and family stories said that he had left the palace after an argument with the king, long before it was burnt down by the English, and was granted a fief by the king of Palghat.

Samorin did not know his mother or his father; they were very hazy recollections, belonging to the shadowland of another time. It was Aunt who was his guide and protector, who was always at his side when he fell and was hurt in play, and who fed him when he was hungry. It was she who had taught him how to pray to the *kuladevi*, the goddess of the clan. She wove garlands of white jasmine for the deity to wear, stringing the fragrant flowers with nimble fingers. She was forbidden to enter the premises of the temple, because she was a widow. He had often come across her in the evening, sitting on the white sand and leaning against the tall wooden pillar of the veranda, humming the *njanapana* hymn softly under her breath and looking across to the sanctum of the goddess.

The *embranthiri* priest would have lit the evening lamps, and the goddess appeared golden and her skin lustrous through the fragrant smoke of joss sticks. Samorin would sit down beside her, and take her hand in his, and she would give him a garland to place at the feet of the idol.

'I cannot go,' she would say with soft regret, 'I am not clean.'

'It doesn't matter,' he said one evening, 'to me you look like the goddess herself.'

The wind, which blew into the paved courtyard of the house, was a tide of a million odours. Rushing down the mountainside through teak and sal, it carried the tender scent of the tea gardens, growing thick and green on the neighbouring mountains, and the ancient smells of spices and herbs. The great house was a Victorian villa built by an English tea planter at the foot of the youngest mountain in the range. It stood with its back against a rockface that rose steep and uninterrupted for nearly forty feet before flattening out into a ridge, topped by the forest. The mountain seemed to be a gigantic palm held over the house as if in benediction, and when the sun tipped over the catafalque of rock above, the great shadow of the stone was like a violet hood deepening with the night.

From the veranda of the bungalow, Samorin could see the plains as a palette of emerald hues shot through with clusters of mist and cumulus, the horizon itself lost in an arch of blue and silver. The Bharatapuzha river was a shining waistband that ribboned its way along the paddy fields and the grave foliage of hermit trees, lazily nudging the village of Manali, which thrived along its banks. Between the malachite of the fields and the little hamlet that fringed them, the young Samorin could see the gleaming, forbidden mirror – Lake Spicewater. And Cardamom Hill, too, which was part of the family estates – a small hilly island in the middle of the lake. The lake's waters were as clear as a widow's tears. Legend said that it was created when Gandhari had died of grief: Gandhari was the mother of the Kauravas, the evil brothers of the *Mahabharata* who were slain by the five Pandavas. She died cursing Krishna and the victors, and the lake was born out of her tears.

In reality, the lake was an offshoot of the Bharatapuzha which flowed down to the Arabian Sea – a body of clear green water trapped by the Palghat foothills. The Malampuzha dam, built in the 1950s further nourished the lake, and the Samorins were grateful to it for keeping Cardamom Hill's soil ever fertile. The boy's sleep was often redolent with the distant scent of cloves and cardamom, and the wind that came in through the open windows insinuated into his dreams the smell of a thousand spices.

Aunt forbade him to go to Cardamom Hill.

'But I want to see the old mansion that Great-grandfather built for his wife,' he complained one day to her.

'Whoever told you there was such a mansion?'

'Chami, the fence-maker's son.'

'Rubbish. There is no mansion there, only a huge forest full of leopards and wolves.'

But after that day, Chami no longer came to play with him. He missed his games with the dark, half-naked boy, pretending to be Robin Hood and King Arthur, tying Chami to the trunks of coconut trees like Porus had been bound by Alexander's soldiers. Sometimes he was Pazhassiraja fighting the British and sometimes he was the warrior Aromalunni attacking the venal Chandu, and Chami's squeals of mock-terror were deeply satisfying. When his friend failed to appear, Samorin asked Aunt where Chami had gone. But she dismissed him with a vague reply about harvests and tamarind yields. One day, un-expectedly, he saw his truant playmate passing the mango orchard behind the house. When Samorin called out to him to stop, Chami turned and looked and broke into a run.

'Wait! Stop!' He ran after him, jumping across the break in the bamboo fence which was tied over the crumbled walls, but Chami only quickened his pace. Samorin was faster, and he caught up with the boy near the haystacks and wrestled him down to the ground.

'Why do you run away from me?'

'The widow's curse.' Chami's voice was trembling. 'Father said if I played with you, the widow's curse would fall on me and I would be turned into a *napumsakam*.'

A creature without limbs, a live ball of flesh, which could only moan and scream.

'What widow's curse?'

'Your aunt!' Chami said, and Samorin loosened his grip, taken aback by the fierce fear in his playmate's voice. Chami saw his chance and darted away through the huge bales of hay into the darkness of the mango orchard beyond. Samorin did not pursue him.

'What is a widow? Is it a bad thing?' he asked Aunt in the evening.

They were in the old library. It was a favourite place where Samorin and his aunt would sit before dinner, after he had shut his schoolbooks for the evening, bathed and got ready to listen to stories. It was a large room dominated by laden bookcases. Beside the window that opened out into the courtyard was Grandfather's desk and his wingbacked chair up-holstered with red velvet. Behind the chair was a vast bookcase that contained all his law books. It had been locked up the day he died. Aunt's rocking chair was placed on a small Afghan carpet. There she would sit, waiting for him to join her so that he could continue his education in the way she had planned for him. For Jay Samorin did not go to school until he was nine years old.

One night he had overheard a conversation Aunt was having with someone in the library. Peeping through the keyhole, hearing voices, all he could see was Aunt. The room was dark except for the reading lamp which, as always, cast its circle of light on her white linen lap, obscuring her features and shoulders, backlighting her thick black hair, a book open on her lap, held by long, slim fingers. The young Samorin had woken from a disturbing dream in which crows were pecking at the eyes of a dead man floating weightlessly in the air tides, the corpse's mouth forming words lost in the noise of breath escaping his lips. He had stumbled across his room in the night, seeking the comfort of Aunt's lap, when he realized that the door to the library was locked from the inside.

'You know I cannot send Jay to school here after what happened,' Aunt was saying.

He was astonished. What had happened? Besides, Aunt never received visitors inside the house. Even Narayana Menon, who was the steward of the estates and whose family had served the Samorins for five generations, was only allowed into the small visitors' room in the east wing. Here Aunt went over the accounts of the estate with him and settled payments for the labourers and the purchase of seeds and fertilizers. And Samorin was shocked that someone was inside the library with Aunt at such a late hour.

The stranger said something in a low voice, which the boy couldn't catch.

'I am teaching him more than any school can.' The boy was amazed at Aunt's voice; it had taken on a vibrant undertone, one he would have never associated with her. 'And when he is ten, I will send him off to boarding school, in Sanawar or Doon. But he has to master the *kalari* first, learn the classics. And I have discovered with gladness that a boy as young as he has developed a taste for Jonathan Swift.'

The stranger said something, and Samorin was startled at hearing Aunt's answering laugh.

'Widows make better men of children, as you will see one day.'

He knocked on the door with his little fist, and suddenly there was silence.

'Who is it?' he heard Aunt ask, and he replied that he was frightened.

He heard her steps approach the door, expecting it to open, so that he could see who was in the room with her. But it remained closed.

'Go to sleep,' she said gently from inside, 'it is all right.'

'I'm afraid.'

'Warriors are never afraid. Tomorrow I will tell you the story of the wise king Vikramaditya, who bested the riddle-crazy vampire.'

He walked away reluctantly, back into his night, and he could not sleep. He asked Chami the next day about vampires and riddles, but the only vampire his friend knew about was the white woman of Cardamom Hill. This woman, with hair that turned into black serpents, sat in the hooded shade of the frangipani tree near Spicewater Lake and combed her hair. Even the poachers, who quietly rowed across to Cardamom Hill for rabbit and deer, ceased their expeditions after two of them were set upon by wolves, seemingly obeying the vampire's commands. The boy told Samorin about how the vampire woman suddenly appeared out of the darkness, her face invisible, her white garments fluttering behind her in a wind that seemed only to arise around her. Then the wolves leapt out of the darkness behind her, gigantic silver beasts, tearing at the throat of one man while the other dropped his country-made musket and ran to the water, screaming for help, flinging himself into Spicewater's cold embrace with the hot breath of the demon beast at his heels.

'But why didn't the wolf get him? Can't wolves swim?'

'Of course wolves can. But these were demon wolves, you see, and all creatures from hell are afraid of water.'

They were silver wolves, who could not be killed by any arrow or bullet, and served the vampire of Cardamom Hill, Chami informed his playmate. The vampire woman was a widow, who had drunk her husband's blood during full moon many centuries ago, performing the dark rites of *koodotram** in search of immortality. So the goddess of darkness turned the widow into a vampire, and she lived on the blood of the beasts of Cardamom Hill and added their lives to hers.

'Why is she never seen in Manali then?'

'I told you she cannot cross water,' Chami explained impatiently. 'After she killed her husband, she became evil. And evil cannot cross water.'

* *koodotram*: South Indian black magic.

36

Samorin thought about the widow who lived on blood, trapping leopards and deer with her spells, guarded by silver wolves.

'Widow? What does it mean?'

Chami looked at his friend strangely.

'Hasn't your aunt told you?'

That evening, Aunt looked up from the book she was reading, and her gaze was full of shifting dark curtains.

'A woman whose husband is dead,' she answered. 'Why do you ask?'

'Did you curse Chami?' he continued.

Aunt laughed under her breath, a low mirthless sound.

'I spoke to his father and asked him to send Chami to school, instead of hanging around and telling silly stories about mansions in spice forests, and vampires,' she said.

'So you know about the vampire!'

'Just Chami's father and his crazy stories,' she replied with a small laugh. 'I'm sure he was the second poacher, who got away. The other one must have been mauled by some bear he had wounded. Silver wolves indeed!'

The young Jay Samorin was silent.

'Was it Chami who told you about the widow's curse?' She leaned over to him and lifted his chin with her slender little finger.

He nodded.

'Being a widow is a curse,' she said gently, as if to herself, 'but it could be worse.'

He looked up at her, sensing a sudden defiant shift in her voice, and he would always remember her posture as she sat on her father's armchair, head upright, profile outlined in the lamplight, her black hair streaming over her slender shoulders like deep silk at night. The wind rose from the dried arroyos of the ghats and hurried through the wooded slopes of the island hillock, and Aunt went across to the window and raised her arms to the monsoon sky. The spicewind billowed on her garments, her white cotton sari swept out from her shoulders like a dove's wing, her hair alive in the wind. She turned around suddenly, hands at her back clasping the window frame, laughing.

'Yes, my son, it could be worse.'

It was the first and last time he had ever seen her laugh. She looked like a fierce Madonna, her eyes large and black, mesmerizing him, and her usually pale lips were suddenly red and wet. It was then that the vague fog of suspicion began to form in his mind: a suspicion without a name or a face, a foreknowledge that Aunt possessed a secret that she held tight as if it were the crown jewel in a tiara of sorrows. And it would be many years before he uncovered the secret of the Widow's Curse. As his childhood opened through the moist, golden Malabar days, he sensed that Aunt's secret was interlinked with his own destiny, the revealing of which could change everything.

Aunt's rules were somewhat eccentric: he was not allowed to leave the estates unless he was accompanied either by her or Narayana Menon. She rarely left the grounds of the house, but twice a month would drive out in the big black Studebaker chauffeured by Menon. In the first week of the month, her expedition was always a visit to the Widow's Village on the outskirts of town. She would sometimes take her nephew with her and they would drive through a breaking dawn crowned with mist, along an old tarred road the width of a single lorry. The planters had built this road around the mountains, hewing its space from the rock and the stubborn soil, clearing old trees and hostile bush. The road ran down into the valley, meeting up with a cinnabar path fringed with clusters of sibilant bamboo and rustling palmyras heavy with scented purple fruit, the hedges pungent in the breeze. The Widow's Village was a single street of houses built wall to wall along half a kilometre, ending in a small, open square at the edge of marshland. The mist obscured the facades of the dwellings, whitening the great hermit tree that stood at the edge of the marsh; on the brick platform around it were picayune idols of the snake gods and a solitary *sivalinga*.

When they drove there for the first time, Samorin was surprised by the ethereal quality of the place: it was as if the darkness of verandas and doorways rose up in greeting, interrupted by flutters of white. Each subsequent visit, the car would stop at the foot of the giant tree, and Narayana Menon would open the boot and take out gunny sacks of rice, spices and flour. He would place them along with bundles of vegetables and plantain sheaves on the stone steps leading to the brick platform.

'The poor women will come and get them after we have left,' Menon would tell Samorin.

'Why can't they come now?'

Menon's eyes opened wide in shock.

'It is bad luck to look at a widow.' His voice sounded horrified.

Only later did he realize that Aunt was a widow, too, and one day he asked Menon how he could look at Aunt and not be cursed for it. But Menon said that

Aunt was a *thampuratti**, and the only administrator of the fortune of the Samorins. This somehow made her different from other widows, and he could understand the economics of it only very vaguely.

Aunt always left him sitting in the car when she went inside the houses to visit the widows. There was one house she always called on first. It was built slightly away from its neighbours, its bamboo fence almost riding into the marsh. The breath of the marsh swam across the face of the house, as if it wore a separate, wispy garment, the stone steps leading to the veranda glistening dew-wet and black. The mist robed the deep ochre pillars, further deepening the gloom. Aunt always took a special offering with her – new *kadali* plantains fresh from the farm, a small basket of golden mangoes from the orchard, a small *bharani*[†] of venison pickle.

Standing by the door stained by time and dawn, she was a wraith from another era. A creak would come from one of the windows, as if in regret, and a small yellow patch shone upon the wall as someone inside lit a lamp. A slender, white hand with a golden gleam would appear at the edge of the door, but Samorin never knew who lived there, or why Aunt always visited that house first. Each time he would become aware of a depth within the darkness, of an intense gaze challenging him with open scrutiny. He would try to return that gaze but he could not meet the eyes of this morning watcher. All he was aware of was the look. He would be piqued by its refusal to embody itself, and force an unspoken challenge into his own

* *thampuratti*: aristocratic lady.
† *bharani*: earthen jar used for pickling.

eyes. But then he would hear the soft thud of a door being closed and realize that he hadn't watched it open: the gaze had rubbed out the small space of time in between, banishing everything else, the rattle of chain bolts and the grating of wooden bars, the window closing. Aunt would swiftly run down the steps and walk briskly towards the other dwellings.

When the low murmur reached him and became louder, he would know that she had entered the porticos. It looked as if the shadows that were lying in wait, attached to the walls and the spaces in the rafters, had detached themselves to swarm around her. Aunt's face was lost in their assault and as she stooped towards them, the hair knotted at the nape of her neck suddenly came untied to hide her face. She seemed like a headless white ghost surrounded by forms in the fog. It was only later, much later, that he realized what the shadows were – they were the children of the widows, who rushed out to greet their benefactress. They retreated to hide behind the pillars, watching the car as it passed them on its return journey. The young Samorin tried to glimpse their eyes in the gloom by staring into the translucent darkness, smiling at the unseen faces he knew were watching him.

But the memory of the disembodied gaze, challenging him from the solitary dwelling on the edge of the marsh, travelled with him into the morning, now opening pale and fragrant around them as they wound their way back home – the beginnings of birdsongs, a rooster crowing in the distance, a bullock cart with its spoked, painted wheels and wooden chassis clattering on the stony road, a sudden wind sweeping into the car with its drowsy bouquet of cardamoms and the damp, not unpleasing smell of vegetation. Aunt was warm, her skin fragrant with soap and cologne, her palm gentle on his cheek as he leaned his face into her lap, the thin fingers stroking his hair. He felt the memory of the look grow distant. There was something different about the children in the Village of Widows, something which separated them from Chami or the ones he saw in the town. It was silence, he realized. The children of the widow's village never made any noise.

And once a month Aunt would drive her nephew to the Indian Coffee House in town on Gandhi Bazaar Road, for mutton cutlets and fruit salad with vanilla ice cream. The waiters were always dressed in white Arabian suits with red bibs, and crimson turbans that fanned out behind their heads, bordered with filigree. Many of them had fierce moustaches and white smiles, and they treated Aunt and him obsequiously. He became used to these eccentric forays into the outside world with Aunt. Sometimes, while walking with her along the grassy hillocks of Tipu Sultan's fort, his small hand sweaty in hers, she would give him history lessons with the panache of a natural storyteller.

As they drove past houses in the town, the laughter and cries of children at play would reach him in snatches and he would long for the company of others his own age. He glimpsed children on the streets walking with their parents, skipping or running, crying, picked up and comforted, and naked urchins with wild hair and clear eyes swimming in the temple lakes, calling out to one another while they dived. Then he thought of the silent children of the forbidden village, and wondered what their play would be like. A pantomime of childhood, in a landscape without fathers.

Sometimes, as the twilight swam up through the orchards, the boy at the bay window would look up from a fading daydream. Far away, beyond the mango groves and palm clusters and farmers' huts, he could see bordering the lap of the western foothills a long rim of dancing paddy, clear and golden with light. It was as if the day refused to die there, and the night when it came was kept at bay. It was a fringe of immortality, a frontline of light that separated the mountain night from the twilight. And from across that twilight, trance-inducing distance, Samorin felt someone was watching him. As the days passed into months and then years, he felt his life itself was being overseen by an invisible guardian. He often prayed to this saint of the distances without Aunt ever knowing, demanding little signs of compliance and commitment. Sometimes he found strange gifts in unexpected places: a model aeroplane – 'A Stuka bomber,' Aunt called it with surprise in her voice – strung from the lowslung branch of the jackfruit tree that grew in the backyard. A repeater watch under his pillow, which woke him up with an alien whirr in his ears, a Swiss army knife hidden inside a hole in the trunk of the mango tree, upon which he had built his small tree house as the Swiss Family Robinson had. Aunt said that the gifts were left for him by the Prince of Children, since he was a good child and did not make any trouble for her.

As he grew older, he guessed it was Aunt herself who had left these erratic tokens for him, as part of his strange and rich education. He had discovered a talent for drawing, while idly doodling on the margins of his

43

notebooks. The first picture he drew was of a face hidden among foliage – a face with slanted, hooded eyes and a smile that merged with the detail of leaf and branch. It was the watcher, he told Aunt while showing her the drawing in the buttery light of the reading lamp in the library, who always looked at him from afar – the Prince of Children, who kept a distant eye on him.

Jay Samorin rose slowly from the bamboo mat, legs bent and ankles crossed, his hands clasped together in front of him in a *namaste* to the goddess of warriors. His eyes were closed, but he could see everything around him, inside him. It was part of what he had been taught in his childhood; 'the mind sees more than the eye' was an old dictum of his guru. It was a training reinforced when he came home for holidays from his school in the Himalayan foothills, and had become part of his daily routine ever since.

As the school slept, he would sneak down the ancient wooden staircase of the dormitory without waking up the housemaster or the other boys, and practise the familiar moves in the semicircular lawn of the school courtyard, ringed with tall pines that stood sentry. Unseen to anyone in the Himalayan dawn, Samorin was the boy-warrior for whose esoteric discipline the empty basketball court and the deserted football grounds were an outlandish theatre. During dark winter mornings, stripped to the waist, immune to the mountain wind that whipped the pine boughs and screamed up the slopes, his mind instructed his body to banish the cold, telling it that the wind was something outside him: only if he let it touch his skin would it enter his mind and turn his bones to ice.

'Turn the wind into your movement,' he commanded himself, 'for when one moves, all of one's self is given to that movement, until one becomes the movement itself.'

'As you move forward, you become length, and pure length only,' were the master's words. 'See it in your mind. You are uninterrupted, flowing length with a purpose. As you leap, you become the height, and as you descend for the kill, you become the depth. You are the longitudes and latitudes of the earth, its axis, its revolution, and you are nothing but what you are doing at that particular point in time.'

It was while he was this phantom in the cold, the warrior of winter aware of the great dimensions around him – the height of the mountains, the depth of the ravines, the width of the dark sky – aware of his power and his solitude, that he suddenly knew he was being watched. The straight torso sank slowly back on sinewy thighs, one leg stretched out, the fists held in front like half-claws coming down, suddenly tilting to the left, shifting the weight of the upper body to his palm on the cold earth while his upflung legs pirouetted in the air, moving sideways in the crab pincer move, to tighten his leg around the neck of the form hiding behind the mossy cedar. There was a stifled gasp, the body hit the wet grass, and Samorin was on top of his victim, one hand clasped around his mouth, the other raised to strike.

'Dhiren,' Samorin hissed in recognition. 'What are *you* doing here?'

Dhiren Das, the long-haired boy with cold eyes, who looked too big for his age, who always sat at the back of class behind Samorin. Many times he had felt a prickling sensation on the back of his neck, only to turn to meet Dhiren's intense look.

The boy on the ground now wriggled. 'I've seen you sneak away from dorm many times,' he said, 'I thought you were meeting some girl. Then I see you doing kung fu in the volleyball court.'

'It is not kung fu,' Samorin said with disgust, 'and next time you sneak around me, you may not be so lucky.'

'If the housemaster finds out, neither will you be.'

Samorin turned and looked at his classmate.

'Dhiren, the next time I catch you, I will kill you.'

Dhiren gave a small hysterical giggle, backing away from Samorin. 'I am not afraid of you,' he said, 'I know what your father did.'

He turned on his heel and walked back to the school building.

'Wait!' Samorin shouted, but Dhiren did not look back. Later, whenever their paths crossed in the school corridors or the playground, he saw the amused, enigmatic smile in the other boy's eyes. *I know what your father did . . .*

It was that memory of Dhiren that suddenly ambushed Samorin as he practised his *dhyanam* in the *kalari*. He rose to his full height, a little under six feet, his hands now moving forward from the *namaste* to a rigid sword of muscle and bone, the lower edges of the palm held tight against each other, one raised leg slowly stretching away from the body as he swung in a graceful circle. Samorin bowed to the idol as he turned, took two steps forward and leapt into the air, drawing the sword of his forefathers from his waistband, a gigantic falcon dark against the sky for a long, slow moment . . .

Higher, and higher, the gallows now reducing to a small black dot in one corner of the brown quadrangle, the little figure seen from a great height, jerking in sudden earthlessness, the sword arcing through the air and severing the rope, flying higher and higher, beyond the Sun and Neptune and Pluto and the exploding supernovas, Father in air, Father without earth, flying . . .

Samorin landed in a crouch on the ground of the *kalari*, panting. His black hair with its single streak of silver was pasted against his forehead with sweat.

Inside the house the telephone was ringing.

CHAPTER THREE

Somewhere inside her house, Anna Khan's telephone was ringing. She was standing in her bath, the shower needle fierce on her body as the steam glided and rose like a fever in a dream, breathing up from the white tiled floor and opening the pores of her skin. She felt Irfan's arms around her, strong and sinewy, his palms flirting with her belly and her hips, his thumb playing circles around her navel, his hands moving up to caress her heavy breasts. Anna shivered, caught in a brief spindrift of memory – she was turning towards her husband, raising her thigh along his hip, opening herself to him, then the phone was ringing, and suddenly there was only the fall of water on the tiles, the familiar rustle of rain. Snapping awake, she shouted for her orderly Surender to pick up the telephone, but he was already on the line, answering the caller.

That sudden wakefulness was now second nature after three years of policing in the Kashmir Valley. It was as if a hidden sister had one day risen up inside her, an unseen warrior sensitive to the merest changes in atmosphere. This ninja-woman was the watcher within as she patrolled the crowded markets of Srinagar in her bulletproof police Gypsy. Her route took her past ancient mosques in whose doorways bearded Moslems stood glaring at the machine-gunner scanning the crowd from the roof of the moving Jeep. The watcher within Anna readied her for the bomb that would tear through the metal and glass any moment, or the sudden star of bullet impact webbing the windscreen. She automatically searched for the concealed pattern of a concerted attack, the geometric shift in formation that meant a *feyadeen* suicide squad was preparing to attack.

'Kashmir is not a place for a beautiful woman, even if she is tough,' she remembered Irfan telling her, stroking her hair, kissing away the small droplets of love sweat on her upper lip.

'Wherever you are, that is the place I want to be.'

'My warrior princess,' he laughed. 'Anyway, we have only eight more months to go in this damned state. After that we get transferred to Delhi where we can party every night. We won't need protective clothing then.'

'Memsahib, it is the Commissioner,' her orderly's shout reached her, 'it is urgent.'

The hot shower had beaten the tiredness out of her skin and muscle. She stepped out of the bath and wiped the mirror with her wet palms. She was a smear of eyes and hair and skin through the vapour. Before, Irfan would have wiped the mirror with his towel, and

49

they would have stood for a long moment looking at themselves. Even in the mirror, it was her face Irfan would seek with his gaze, and she would answer the reflection of his eyes with the smile she kept only for him.

'I'm coming,' she shouted to her orderly, 'ask him to hold on.'

Deputy Commissioner of Police Anna Khan came out of the bath wrapped in her terry robe and took the call on an extension in her bedroom.

As she listened to the Commissioner's rasping voice her immediate thought was the man needed to lose weight and quit smoking. He was a political appointee, as most of Delhi's police commissioners were – a seasoned chess player in the secret matches that took place in the Ministry of Home and Internal Security. But she had to admit, for a political appointee, he was a surprisingly astute policeman. She had not encountered the superciliousness of most senior male officials in the Indian police service, the patronizing concern that accompanied their offers of soft postings like traffic and industrial security to women officers.

'A rather strong record,' the Commissioner had said, looking at her as he lit a Rothman's. Her file was in front of him, the only papers on his large desk with its shining glass top. A cardboard policeman, she had thought then, who depended on his juniors to do all his paperwork. It was only later that she realized that he cleared files faster than he could shoot.

'Fifty-eight terrorists killed in the seven months of operations you have led in the Valley,' he said, 'but a low capture record. Only three arrests.'

He winked. She did not smile, looking back at him

with her face composed and eyes clear, thick long hair tied up in a bun below her beret. Her lipstick was all but invisible.

'You must miss your husband,' the Commissioner said, his eyes locking with hers. It made her throw her head back for an instant, but she met his gaze.

'I don't see what that has to do with anything, sir.'

'You had requested a transfer to Srinagar when your husband's brigade got posted to Kashmir,' the Commissioner blew out a smoke ring that lingered in front of his eyes and then dissipated in a sudden shiver, 'but now you want an extension in Kashmir for another three years.'

'I am a good cop, sir,' she said woodenly.

'That you are. Perhaps too good,' the policeman said softly.

Sunlight falling in smoky strips through the pines, the hillside crunchy with fallen needles. Singling out one falling pine cone among the noise of pine cones falling ahead of them, the watcher within awakes, automatically analysing every sound, every shadow, every change in light that could mean the difference between life and death. Slowing her gait, Anna raises her hand, and suddenly the flat chatter of an AK 47 is a stitch across the mountain silence, and her face is stung with a spray of pine needles. Two men burst out from the trees ahead, their dark *pherans** billowing behind them as they run down the slope towards the dense forest. Anna fires after them, breaking into a run. One of them turns and lets loose a short burst in her direction. Ducking instinctively, she weaves out of its path, but the inspector behind her coughs and falls.

* *pheran*: robe worn by Kashmiris.

51

The other policemen – her squad – are running, too, firing downhill, and one of the figures ahead stumbles and falls. The other stops, turns, drops his gun and raises his arms. An eagle is riding the thermals under a clear blue sky. Reaching the man, Anna kicks the gun away.

'You shot first, didn't you?' she asks quietly.

He is a young Kashmiri, with a long face and a black, sparse beard. His face is unscarred, unlike the Afghan Mujahedeen, who have infiltrated the Kashmir Valley to wage *jehad* against the Indian government.

The boy nods, then smiles. His lips are soft and pink.

'Sorry,' she says, finger tightening on the trigger of her pistol, 'you fired first.'

The others did not meet her eyes, and she did not bother to explain. 'Encounter,' she wrote in the file, 'killed in combat.'

One more for Irfan. Many more to go.

'I am turning down your request, Anna,' the Commissioner's voice was gentle, almost regretful, 'I am posting you to Delhi. The diplomatic district.'

A soft posting. Cloak-and-dagger crises to be handled with pens rather than guns. The disgust on her face showed.

'Kashmir is too personal for you, my daughter,' the policeman said. 'It's time you gave your gun arm a rest.'

Anna got up and saluted. She would wait. After three years in Delhi, they would have to send her to Kashmir again; it was her cadre after all. Time was meaningless, as long as one had a purpose to fulfil. She didn't care about dying, if she was all that mattered. But she had to live for Irfan.

'Thank you for not arguing with me,' the Commissioner continued. 'I don't want to lose a good cop to a bunch of demented, suicidal Afghans and Chechens.'

In Kashmir she had always worn uniform, her 9mm semi-automatic pistol kept in a front holster, the AK 47 always within arm's reach. When she appeared at her Chanakyapuri office to take charge, she was wearing a peacock-blue Benares silk sari, its free end wrapped around her upper body, concealing the shoulder holster. She was the only woman in the capital's police force who carried a gun even when not in uniform.

After the Commissioner rang off, she chose a pink salwar kameez with loose tunic sleeves and a pinched waist. She buckled on her holster, pulled on a light brocaded linen vest to hide the straps at her back, and draped her *chunni* loosely around her shoulders to cover the slight bulge the gun made against the side of her breast.

'Be discreet,' the Commissioner had warned. 'A murder inside the Malagasy embassy is bad enough but when it's the First Secretary, a man rumoured be close to their President . . .'

The Malagasy embassy was a low red structure built into a rocky hill, affording a raised view of the city. Two police Gypsies were parked inside the Embassy, and a handful of armed officers stood looking rather lost.

'Discretion, Anna, the press should not get wind of this at all,' had been the Commissioner's orders.

The lobby of the embassy was large and sunlit, the day coming in through the bevelled glass doors. There were expensive rugs on the cool, smooth floor and in a corner, with the light shining on it, was a huge display board that read 'Embassy Activities'. Anna's eye caught a poster from which the familiar face of a bearded man stared out with an intense, dark gaze, reminding her of Rasputin. Dhiren Das, the artist. She owned a painting of his – bought before he became too expensive – of a small crow sitting on the rump of a bull. It hung in her sitting room and had been a favourite of Irfan's. She paused to look at the poster. *Madagascar Landscapes by Dhiren Das*, it said in bold type. She made a mental note to go along. Someone coughed at her elbow. Anna turned and saw a man who also seemed familiar. Slim-waisted and broad-shouldered, his hair was curly and his skin the colour of light honey.

'You will like his paintings, he is terrific. But that is not what you are here for, I know. We have been expecting you.' He came forward, taking both her hands in his. 'This has been an awful business. Shall we see the Ambassador now? He has been told you would soon be here.'

'Who told you I would be coming?'

The man spread his hands out in an elegant gesture, his soft smile abruptly secretive.

'It is a delicate matter, and we have to be careful,' the diplomat spoke softly, mincingly. 'Ambassador Tsiranana spoke to both the Home Minister and the Police Commissioner this morning.'

A discreet job, the Commissioner had said early in the year, needs a woman's tact.

Then Anna remembered.

'We have met before,' she said, 'at a reception at the French embassy a few months ago. You are Philibert Stansi, right? The Press Secretary.'

He bowed. But his eyes were wary.

'You have a fantastic memory, Commissioner Khan. I am the Counsellor for Public Affairs. Now, if you would come with me, the Ambassador is waiting.'

'The body first,' Anna said brusquely, suddenly disliking the man.

'I'm afraid that will not be possible. Protocol, you see. The Ambassador himself wishes to speak to you first.'

'It may be protocol, but it is also murder.'

'Yes, murder,' Stansi sighed. 'But you are inside our embassy and this is a diplomatic area. It's Malagasy territory you are standing on, madame.'

Anna stared at the man wordlessly, and he met her eyes with a polite smile. She took in his grey Armani suit, the tailored blue cotton shirt, the silk tie and the handmade shoes. She noticed that he had a habit of using his tongue to moisten the corners of his soft, full lips. He had typical Creole skin and dark hair, and there was an air of obvious feminity about him. Must make a note to check on him, using the grapevine, she told herself. Maybe his name would come up on the gay network.

Anna nodded her compliance and followed him to the Ambassador's chambers. Must check up on the dead man through the grapevine, too, she thought, It's amazing what floats to the surface when the sewers are dredged.

The embassy was richly decorated, finished with glazed stone and a lot of glass. Flutings of green soapstone curved in arches above polished walnut doors. The floor was malachite marble with brass inlays criss-crossing at right angles, and light came from crystal lamps on the walls as well as the skylights that interrupted the smooth ivory of the ceiling. Ahead of Anna, Stansi stopped and knocked on a huge, polished mahogany door. Then he opened it, and stood aside for her to enter.

There were two men in the room. They stood up as she walked in, and the man behind the gleaming desk extended his hand towards her. His cuff was like a verge of fresh snow against dark cashmere.

'Ambassador Tsiranana.' His voice was low and pleasant. 'It's a pleasure to meet you, Commissioner Khan.'

Anna shook his hand. Stansi had brought a chair for her.

'You may leave now, Stansi,' the Ambassador said brusquely without looking at the diplomat. Anna glanced at Stansi's face and noted the brief lash of anger that twisted across his features. Then he smiled and bowed.

'I shall remain outside Radama's door until you come.'

The other man in the room had walked across to a low Rajasthani table beside the window, upon which *shatranj* figures were arranged. He was framed by the light that came in through the square windows, and Anna's immediate impression was one of fluidity and strength. He was dressed in dark colours, and as he bent down to take a *shatranj* piece and place it on another square on the board, she noticed his hands, long fingers below strong wrists. There were two crystal tumblers with amber liquid in them. The Ambassador offered her a drink. She refused.

'I would like you to tell me what happened,' she said, 'and then take me to the scene. I need to get the forensics people here as soon as possible.'

56

'There is always time for a good malt whisky, isn't that right Samorin?' the Ambassador laughed, glancing across the room.

The man beside the window turned with an answering laugh and nodded. Anna looked at him, and saw that he was clean-shaven, with long black hair brushed back to fall loose over his shoulders. His eyes were clear and grey, somewhat like a cat's. Anna felt an irrational irritation towards him.

Throwing his personality around, she told herself, as if he were someone privileged.

'This is Samorin,' the Ambassador introduced the other man. 'Jay Samorin.'

'Excellency, this is an official investigation,' Anna said. 'If we could be alone, I would very much like to be briefed on the murder.'

'Mr Samorin is here at my invitation,' the Ambassador replied. 'He represents the interests of the Malagasy mission in this investigation.'

'I do not wish to be in your way.' Samorin's voice reminded her of woodsmoke, and the annoyance flared again in her, without obvious reason.

'We'll see about that,' she retorted sharply. 'This seems to be a *fait accompli*. I don't like it at all.'

'I confess I don't like it either,' Samorin said. 'Ideally, I would have liked to spend my time with Ambassador Tsiranana playing *shatranj* as usual, discussing the merits of single Highland malt and non-roasted tobacco, or how raunchy Chaucer really was. But today, there is a dead man in a room not far away from here.'

'That doesn't explain your presence here,' Anna said, 'in the middle of police business. Are you a private detective?'

'God forbid,' Samorin said with a smile. 'God forbid I should spend my time hiding in smelly automobiles, spying on fat businessmen and their mistresses or chasing bank clerks who have disappeared with yesterday's deposits.'

'Samorin is a consultant with a special gift,' Ambassador Tsiranana said gently, 'and he is my friend.'

'A crime consultant?' Anna raised her eyebrows sarcastically.

Samorin's eyes were suddenly serious.

'I am a student of evil,' he said in a bantering tone that robbed the statement of any melodrama, 'and its profiler.'

Suddenly, memory flooded back. She remembered a magazine article somewhere about the political cartoonist who had become a recluse.

'A retired cartoonist now chasing evil,' she laughed, the spite in her voice surprising herself. 'Sounds like Batman. What are you, Inkman?'

The Ambassador coughed.

'You will not insult my guest, Commissioner Khan,' he said, 'or I could ask for another investigating officer as a replacement. I am sure the Home Minister would humour the request of a friendly country.'

'I am not offended, Charles,' Samorin said, chuckling. 'Inkman, indeed! Very cute.'

He came across the room, drew his chair to one corner of the desk and sat down, lighting a cigarette.

'The murder, Charles, tell her about it.'

'The victim is Radama Zafy, an ex-royal and First Secretary, friend of President Ratsiraka,' the Ambassador began. 'He had an appointment with me in the morning. He was half an hour late, which was itself odd, since Zafy was a meticulous man and scrupulously punctual. My secretary called his house. It seems he had not returned home for the night, and his housekeeper said his bed had not been slept in. We tried his cellphone, but there was no answer.'

'We will need to question the housekeeper,' Anna said.

The Ambassador cleared his throat, and fidgeted with the knot of his necktie. Then he nodded.

'You should of course interview the housekeeper,' he said, 'but the interrogation will have to be done in the embassy premises, in my presence.'

Anna looked hard at the Ambassador, who returned her gaze with a frown. His eyes were hostile. Better to pursue this later, she thought. If the embassy wanted to be involved in every part of the investigation, they must have suspicions that the murder could open doors that better remained closed; she smelt scandal.

'Didn't the guards at the gate see the murder victim leave?' she asked.

'Zafy had some privileges other diplomats here didn't have,' Tsiranana said. 'He had a private entrance, which let him out of the embassy without having to go through the main gate. And the only key to it was always on his person. He handled many sensitive government affairs, and President Didier himself gave him instructions sometimes even I wasn't privy to.'

He made a small grimace.

'Was that a problem, Mr Ambassador?' Anna asked softly.

'Perhaps,' Tsiranana said. 'But not one serious enough to kill him.'

'So, where was the key?'

'In his pocket. We telephoned his chamber on the intercom, shouted for him, and banged on the door. Eventually one of the security agents climbed onto the roof, and was lowered by a harness to look in through Zafy's window. Then we had to break open the door.'

'The door was locked after the murder?'

'That is the odd thing, Commissioner. The door was locked from the inside, and it is one of those big, custom-built ones which are not easy to pick. And it does not lock itself automatically when you close the door behind you. You have to turn the key in the lock. And the only key was in the dead man's pocket.'

'What about the private gate?'

'That too was locked from the inside. The same lockmaker, the same type of lock. And the key,' Tsiranana shrugged, 'was in Zafy's pocket.'

'Isn't there any other way the murderer could have got out?'

'There are grilles on the windows which are sealed for maximum air conditioning, or heating. The basement downstairs has only two windows, each of which houses an air-conditioning unit and which haven't been removed for months.'

'A locked-room mystery?' Samorin whistled. 'I thought they only happened in Agatha Christie.'

'What do you know about murders?' Anna turned to Samorin.

'That they are usually boring,' Samorin's face was serious, 'unimaginative, brutal, bloody affairs without apparent motive and revealing a marked lack of intelligence. Or something cowardly, like a poisoning husband after his wife's wealth.'

'How was Mr Zafy murdered?' she asked.

'Stabbed through the back,' Tsiranana replied, 'with

what seems to be a huge sword, or some similar pointed weapon. It tore through his back, crushing ligament and bone at first sight, to come out through his heart on the other side.'

'And the weapon?'

The ambassador spread his hands. His face looked haunted.

'Nowhere to be found. It has disappeared. If you look at the wound, it is impossible that a weapon of that size could disappear into thin air, or could be carted away concealed. It simply doesn't make sense.'

Anna and Samorin followed the diplomat into Radama Zafy's room, stepping gingerly over the shards of wood on the marble floor from the broken-down door. Stansi stood in the doorway, leaning against the wall, a blank expression on his face.

'I can't come in and see him like that,' he said in a small voice.

'No-one is asking you to.' The ambassador's reply was curt. 'Your job is to make sure that this does not get out prematurely. The fewer people who know about this the better.'

Stansi bowed his head and walked away, announcing that he could be reached in his office. Anna watched him go, noting his mincing walk, and frowned. Samorin caught her frown.

'Maybe you suspect Stansi and Zafy of having been lovers,' he said softly. Tsiranana frowned.

'Perhaps they were,' Anna said. 'It will come out in the questioning.'

The Ambassador looked worried.

'That could create a major problem in our diplomatic service,' he said. 'It's something we cannot afford.'

'There was no housekeeper at Zafy's house last

night, was there?' Anna asked. 'My bet is Stansi was waiting for him.'

The Ambassador glanced at her sharply.

'A guess?'

'I'm a cop. I am trained to guess. Let's investigate first, maybe there was something the murderer forgot.'

She noticed that Samorin was looking around the room, moving slowly across the floor, as if he was in a trance. He went across to where the body of Zafy lay slumped across his desk, standing at a distance behind the police photographer who was taking pictures. The smell of blood filled the room, along with the dry odour of death. The victim seemed to have shrunk, as if the mass of muscle had condensed within itself, leaving the skin to sag. Anna felt the dispassionate pity she always did for a human being in death, and an accompanying sense of wonder at how people seemed smaller once the life force had left them, as if the volume of space they occupied in life was just a self-protective illusion. She felt the place on the corpse's neck where the pulse should have been. Judging by the rigor mortis, she decided he had been dead for nearly ten hours. Suddenly Samorin turned around and asked the Ambassador, 'Were you the first to enter the room?'

'The second. The first was my Chief of Security over there.' He motioned to a tall quiet man in a beige suit, who nodded briefly.

'Did you notice anything odd?'

'What could be odder?' Tsiranana asked, pointing to the body.

'Was that all?'

'I only noticed it was very cold. I had to switch on the heaters.'

'A murderer who is economical with electricity! Hmmm, interesting,' Samorin muttered to himself.

Anna decided to call in the fingerprint men, and the Ambassador insisted that he and Samorin remain in the room. Samorin moved restlessly around, inspecting the windows and the walls. He had pulled on a pair of white latex gloves. The fingerprint men arrived and began dusting every available surface in the room. The police photographer had also arrived, and Anna asked him to wait outside until the fingerprinting was done. Anna saw Samorin pick up a magnifying glass from the dead man's table in one gloved hand and check the Samsung heaters on the walls.

'That could be evidence,' she said sharply, 'leave it alone.'

He ignored her, kneeling down beside the door of the dead man's private entrance and examining the keyhole for a long time. She walked across to him.

'Found anything, supersleuth?' There was mockery in her voice.

Samorin looked up and smiled.

'Nothing.'

'Obviously.'

'Yes. Exactly what one is supposed to find. Nothing.'

The murder angered Anna, its slyness and the subsequent melodrama, going against her policing instinct. India might not have the sophisticated laboratory equipment and police profilers Scotland Yard and the FBI used, but the police scientists were a dedicated bunch. She knew the murderer was someone from inside the mission. It was only a matter of time before they found a fingerprint or a torn piece of fabric, or something that linked that individual to the dead man. Or perhaps it would be an unexpected witness, someone who was not supposed to be there: a secretary working late, a janitor who needed the overtime. Investigation was all about patience and detail – one went through mountains of paperwork, listened over and over again to interrogation tapes, laid cunning traps inside the questions. Then there was of course forensic science, with its instruments and techniques which should be able to tell her who had been in that room and doing what in the last twenty-four hours.

There was an alternative, one that involved the use of violence and threat, which she knew could not be used here, at the embassy. She recalled policing in Kashmir, undercover agents revealing hiding places of terrorists who were then summarily shot without having been questioned. Interrogation was not merely about obtaining information on the enemy, it was also a process of self-discovery. A good interrogator discovered things about himself that he had not been aware of previously – his capacity to inflict pain and his passion for cruelty. A great interrogator invariably destroyed his suspect; his was an inquisition that went beyond the mundane matters concerning the crime and ended in the total deconstruction of his captive's soul. The real secrets were always there, and once the morale was broken, they spilled out faster than the blood of beatings.

Anna knew all about the destruction of morale, the demolition of trust, the cruelty needed to discover the truth: arrest a suspect, someone who had been fingered by Military Intelligence as likely to become a terrorist leader, and parade him in an open Jeep through the town, making sure that everyone could see him. Then keep him locked up for a week before they set him free. Raid some known hideouts and the man was as good as dead – they would find his body later in a gully, blindfolded with hands tied behind his back, shot in the head in the fashion of execution meant for traitors. These men would go down on their knees inside the interrogation chambers, begging to be killed rather than freed. They would confess to conspiracies and give out locations of safe houses in exchange for relocation for themselves and their families.

Kashmir was a war zone, and fear was the greatest weapon. In order to be a good cop, you had to be a practitioner of fear. In order to be a great cop, you had to be an artist of fear. And Anna had become a great cop: for Irfan's sake.

They had hated her in Kashmir. Informants had told her that the Hizbul Mujahedeen and other terrorist groups had put a price on her head. She didn't care, walking without cover along the centre of the main street, leading her men on patrol, machine gun at the ready. The militant coming around the corner, skidding to a halt, his gun trained on her, meeting her eyes, stopping. Anna tensing, her chest tightening in anticipation of the bullet's impact on Kevlar, and the man suddenly turning and running.

Fear.

They called her *Bhootni*: the demon cop. When the interrogators failed to get information from captured Afghan and Somalian guerrillas – those who had been trained by fascist mullahs in the *madarassas* along the Pakistani border, in the wombs of the Taliban and *jehad* – they went to her as a last resort. Her fellow officers hated her for being a woman with men's blood on her hands, they spoke of her as a demented

65

murderess. To seek help from her was anathema to them, but when the terrorists looked up at their captors with arrogant eyes and spat on them, calling them *kafirs*, proclaiming they were not afraid to die for Allah, it was Anna Khan who was able to extract their secrets.

Under armed escort the prisoners were brought to her interrogation chamber, in the basement of a heavily guarded building protected by machine guns. As the hardened men in chains stumbled down the stairs, the sight of this woman in khaki uniform waiting for them in the gloom took them by surprise. They were manacled to an iron chair bolted to the floor and suddenly the lights would come on. And they screamed at what they saw around them – splashes of blood, some brown and dried and some glistening red, to which shreds of pink flesh and wormy yellow strands of brain tissue were still stuck, smearing the dirty, stained surface of the basement walls. Dark pools of blood had collected on the floor, gelatinous and thick, drying between the tiles. In a corner, knots of intestines were piled up, buzzing with a dense cloud of fat flies. Occasional shards of bone glimmered, with little scraps of flesh. Then the lights were out and Anna's boots echoed in the dark basement chamber, as she walked about the room behind the prisoner. His ears would strain to catch what sounded like the noise of steel being sharpened. Chained to his metal chair, unable to see her but imagining her whetting the knives, the prisoner would begin to whimper softly. Anna knew the babbling, the talking would come later.

But what the terrorists did not know was that the gore came from the local butchers' shops. What mattered was not simply fear, but how to manipulate it. The fear of pain, that most ancient enemy of man. And the marriage of pain and time, the riddle of endurance.

One had to be an illusionist of fear.

But this was not Kashmir, Anna realized. Here was a crime committed in an embassy in New Delhi. A different sort of murder demanded different tactics.

She nodded to the police photographer as he was packing up his camera and tripods, and greeted the pathologist Dr Umre who had come in to inspect the body. He would tell her that death had been instantaneous, she knew, but what had killed the man? The Ambassador had returned to his office, and she saw that Samorin was no longer in the room either.

'Where did he go, the private detective?' she asked the photographer.

'He went downstairs.'

Anna followed the steps down to the basement, and found Samorin sitting at a small Formica kitchen counter, doodling on a sheet of paper. A sudden fluctuation in the electric current caused the freezer to give a loud shudder, making Anna start. Samorin laughed and Anna threw him a look of disgust.

'Cool job,' she said, unable to keep the sarcasm out of her voice, 'just sit here doodling, and bill the embassy later for a fat fee.'

'I don't take money for my work.'

'Oh?'

Momentarily thrown by Samorin's reply, she looked around the basement, at the shower room and the kitchenette, and the freezer in one corner. Samorin pointed at the shower.

'Check in there. See anything odd?'

67

She opened the sliding door and looked in, and found the bathroom immaculate. The inside was laid with grey tiles, the faucets ringed with brass. A pair of matching towels hung from shiny golden rods and the bathmat looked clean.

'I'm going to get forensics down here,' she said. 'I'm sure they will find blood, washed off while someone took a bath.'

'So you didn't spot it.' Samorin shrugged and went back to his doodles.

'Spot what?'

'There is no soap in the bathroom,' he said. 'Everything is in order, but there is no soap.'

'Maybe he used bath gel, and didn't like soap,' Anna said brusquely, 'maybe he had allergies.'

In the yellow light that came in through the narrow windows, Samorin looked like a dark hawk. Anna shivered.

'It's cold in here.'

Suddenly Samorin looked up at her, and the intensity in his gaze silenced her. It was like a great dark flower opening, a carnivorous understanding absorbing everything it touched. He began to draw with strong, bold strokes and Anna went over to look. He was drawing a coffin, with what seemed to be wires sticking out of it, plugged into a socket on the wall. Samorin turned to her, a strange, wild freedom in his eyes.

'Now I know how it was done,' he announced.

He pointed to a corner of the basement. Anna saw a rectangle of wall lighter than the rest, indicating a picture had once hung there.

'What, he was killed with a painting?' she sneered.

Samorin pointed to the deep freeze.

'Get someone in here to move that,' he said. His eyes were intense, feverish. His mouth was trembling in the beginnings of a cold smile. Anna called her constables down; it took four strong policemen to move the freezer. One of them let out an exclamation and picked up something from behind it.

A broken picture frame, from which the canvas had been sliced off.

The painting itself was stuffed further down, a small study of three apples on a plate on a wooden table.

Samorin asked for a light, and Anna gave him her torch. He slid the frosted glass cover off the deep freeze and scanned the insides slowly, shining the torch over the packets of frozen food. Anna looked over his shoulder. Samorin gave a low whistle. He bent down to peer closer, his breath pluming over the ice mist. From a pocket, he took out a magnifying glass.

'Look,' he said, straightening up and wiping the glass.

'At what?'

He shone the torch through the smoking ice, its beam a milky column of slender light. He held the glass above the spot that was illuminated. There, on the frosted surface of plastic film covering a package of zebu burgers, was preserved a perfect fingerprint. Anna gasped.

'Close the lid, or your evidence will melt away,' Samorin said. 'Just like the murderer did.'

CHAPTER FOUR

Samorin sat in a reverie in Charles Tsiranana's study, beside the French window. On his lap was a drawing pad, and the sketch pen was loosely held in his long, bony fingers. Anna noticed that his hands were well cared for, the nails trimmed and filed, and she found herself wondering what his touch would be like.

The thought surprised her, a bird that had suddenly flown in from nowhere and circled inside her with insistent wingbeats.

It would be like placing a fingertip against the surface of a strong-flowing river. The thought opened itself, a swift smoothness, which, if allowed to spread, could drown you.

She was suddenly angry. She had not thought of any man's hands after Irfan. Why should this strange man, his head sunk on his chest deep in contemplation, the white streak of hair a Saracen's crescent, suddenly enter rooms she had closed behind her a long time ago? Papers were scattered on the carpet around him, and one had fallen upon the *shatranj* board, upsetting some of the pieces.

'He says he knows how Mr Zafy was murdered, but doesn't tell us how,' her voice was harsher than necessary. 'Is he going to find out by drawing silly faces?'

Ambassador Tsiranana held a finger to his lips. He looked annoyed. Samorin did not seem to have heard her. An unseen aircraft hummed from a distant height. A dog howled from the brush and rock, its cry distorted in the wind like a cloth being tugged and torn. Anna called her office on her cellphone.

'Have forensics got anything more on that finger-print yet?' she asked her secretary.

They were still working on it. She had told them to run it through the Central Records Computer as soon as they were able to format it properly.

Fat chance we'll find anything, she thought to herself. The ghost who killed Radama Zafy and disappeared from a locked room would hardly show up on the police computers.

'We will need to fingerprint some of the embassy staff,' Anna told Tsiranana. The diplomat pursed his lips.

'Everyone? That would create a lot of hostility in the mission. And some of the senior diplomats are politically connected. They would certainly object to being treated like common criminals.'

Anna's cellphone rang. She listened without interruption, her expression acquiring a severity which, the Ambassador noticed, seemed to justify the unpleasant sobriquet she had picked up in Kashmir.

'Not everyone,' Anna said, turning to the Ambassador after she had finished speaking, 'Radama Zafy had some close friends in this mission.'

Tsiranana sighed and looked away. She noticed the bags beneath his eyes and the lines of weariness around his mouth. He looked exhausted.

'And not just in the mission, but also outside,' she said more gently. 'That call I got was from someone who knows a part of Delhi well. Dinners with tables topped with coke in the drawing room and condoms in the bathrooms. He is also a frequent guest at the farmhouse parties of some of Delhi's fashionable set.'

'What did Zafy have to do with them?'

'It seems he was part of Delhi's gay network, Mr Ambassador. An individual's sexual preferences do not concern me. But this is murder.'

'What else did your informer have to say?'

'That Zafy had many boyfriends, and some of them were young men from modelling agencies, and a couple of fashion designers.'

'So what are you going to do? Arrest the entire homosexual population of Delhi?'

'That won't be necessary. My source also mentioned another Malagasy who has been seen with Zafy twice. Someone who works for your embassy.'

The Ambassador's shoulders slumped. He ran his palm across his forehead and sighed.

'Well?' Anna asked.

Tsiranana sighed again, and reached for the phone.

'Ask Philibert Stansi to come here,' he said, pressing a button on the phone on his desk.

'Charles, wait.' Samorin's voice broke in. 'Not yet.'

Anna turned to him fiercely.

'Oh? Do you want him to escape? Mr Samorin, I

know you found a fingerprint in the freezer and there may be something in it, but it doesn't mean anything yet. Forensics haven't come up with a match. I ought to arrest you for withholding information, and I would have if I weren't so sure you were full of bullshit.'

'It was not difficult to understand how it was done. Only, you need a mind as twisted as the murderer's.' Samorin looked at Anna faintly amused. 'Think of everything as a gigantic picture. You need the patience to examine it within you. You have to enter deep inside the picture, go through its creation all over again, anticipating every stroke of the brush, every little cross-hatch, every generous sweep of colour until you are at the point where it is being drawn. No matter how long ago.'

'And what is it that you saw?' Her voice was derisive.

'Evil.' Samorin shrugged. 'I always examine the picture of evil.'

The unexpected answer silenced Anna. She opened her mouth for a rude retort, but bit it back.

'Well, it's a great, dark and complicated vision,' Samorin said. 'And everyone sees pictures differently. Some look at the colours, some at the technique, and some at the style. People look at pictures the way they are conditioned to.'

'Which is how?'

'To believe that ultimately, they are not real.'

'And what do you see?'

'I look at the picture itself and take it into myself. Then I close my eyes, and it comes alive in me. Every detail, every nuance births ghostly architecture within my head, until I discover that I am standing inside the picture.'

'But what does it tell you?'

'It tells me more than what it shows,' Samorin said. 'It tells me about the man who painted the picture.'

The policewoman frowned in frustration.

'Come here,' he continued, holding out his hand.

Anna looked at the Ambassador, then at Samorin, searching for signs of ridicule. But all she saw was a small smile deepening Samorin's mouth at the corners, and his eyes, open and calm. Inexplicably, she wondered how his mouth would taste; Irfan's had tasted of cardamom and cloves, with a faint presence of bitter young leaves. Again, she was furious with herself.

'Please,' Samorin said softly.

She walked over to him, holding herself straight, as if she was following an unfamiliar emotional path.

'Look at this dwarf,' Samorin said, caressing the bonsai on the window sill, 'doesn't it make you think of evil?'

'Does it?'

'Evil is a subtle art,' Samorin said. 'It is like this bonsai. Perfectly sculpted with a devious intelligence which snips a bit here, binds a bit there. It is inside all of us, on the mantelpieces and window sills of our lives.'

Tsiranana gave a small cough behind them.

'If the gardener will forgive me.' Samorin bowed.

'Evil, and so tiny?' Anna interrupted. 'I think you are wrong, Samorin.' It was the first time she had called him by his name, but he appeared not to notice.

Evil, a bonsai? A subtle life, nurtured with patience, cultivated with skill. No way, Anna thought through gritted teeth. Evil was a violent explosion, a screaming zamiel – the gardener of nightmares. Evil was gunfire in the night, something flung at the door while tyres screeched away into the dark, gears clashing. Evil was a bundle wrapped in a green flag, a beloved's head grimacing its final farewell, the hair matted with blood, muscle and tissue hanging down, bloody threads from under a severed neck. Irfan's head, his beautiful eyes swollen and shut, his penis and testicles stuffed inside his mouth.

'The enemy of Kashmir,' the writing on the bizarre packaging had read, 'the enemy of Allah . . .'

Anna's shoulders shook, and she bit her lip hard, drawing blood. Her eyes were clenched shut, tears shivering in them.

'You have to understand evil, not merely experience it,' Samorin said gently.

'I know it better than you,' Anna hissed at him, 'and it is not a small, pretty tree.'

'But it is, Commissioner,' Samorin contradicted. 'It depends on your perspective, what you are. To an insect, it is a giant tree. See its perfect limbs. The flawless miniature branches bear exquisite, delicate leaves. This bonsai flowers in spring, its leaves spiral down in the autumn wind. Evil lives like this inside all of us, in its mutant perfection, until suddenly, one fatal moment, it becomes a colossus. It shoots out through your breast, its tendrils digging into your skull, its roots sucking up the sap of your heart. Its boughs explode through your life, and the devils come from nowhere to nest on its branches. Then you become a puny insect beneath it.'

Samorin's chest was heaving, his fingers clenched. There was sweat on his brow. Anna was taken aback by the transformation.

'So what did you see, back in the basement of the

room where Radama Zafy was murdered?' Her voice was hushed.

'Flashes of intent, forming like ink falling on water, spreading and latticing into shapes and patterns.' Samorin's voice was low and hoarse. 'I saw a man becoming a murderer.'

A painting on the wall, a fluctuation in voltage calling attention to an icebox, fingers tearing down the canvas, rolling it up . . .

'What did he do? Tell me Samorin, and how did he do it?' she asked him.

Samorin shook his head as if he was surfacing after a long swim.

'You suspect Stansi, don't you?' he said.

'What about him?' Anna asked guardedly.

'I have a hunch,' Samorin said. 'It's still very vague . . . Can you get one of your fingerprint people up here?' He turned to Tsiranana. 'Charles, we need to go to Stansi's office.'

The Ambassador nodded.

They walked out of the room, crossing over to the eastern side of the embassy building where Philibert Stansi's office was. They looked around the diplomat's room, which was large and square with a picture of President Didier Ratsiraka on the wall. Stansi's desk was cluttered with press releases and newspaper clippings, and the Ambassador made a small moue of disgust at the untidiness. The wastepaper basket was brimming with crumpled papers. Anna picked it up and emptied it on the grey carpet.

'Bills, newspaper cuttings, memos . . . nothing obvious here,' she muttered.

At the entrance to the room was a small cubicle. A puzzled expression appeared for a moment on the

Ambassador's face. He picked up the phone on Stansi's desk.

'Stansi's secretary, where is he? Oh, reported sick has he?'

He put the phone down, and scratched his chin. Samorin noticed that Tsiranana was wearing the pocket watch he had given him for Christmas, its gold chain glittering thinly against the dark fabric of his suit.

'You like the Patek Philippe, I see.' Samorin chuckled.

The Ambassador looked up in momentary confusion, his hand still resting on the telephone, and then smiled wanly.

'Is this a time to talk about watches?'

'It is a token of friendship,' Samorin said, 'and nothing reassures us more in times of confusion than friendship.'

The Ambassador looked at Samorin quizzically. The phone rang.

'Your fingerprint men,' Tsiranana told Anna.

'Please have them sent up here,' Samorin said, smiling at the policewoman.

It took only about fifteen minutes for the two experts to find matches for the print Samorin had discovered inside the freezer. The clearest imprint was on the receiver of the red telephone on Philibert Stansi's secretary's desk, which was the extension to his private line.

'Quick,' Samorin said, 'we have no time to waste. Do you know where this man lives?'

Stansi looked so lost, sitting on the sofa with his face in his hands, his tie loosened and his collar open. His thin shoulders were shaking.

The murderer looked at his lover with tremendous tenderness. 'You need to be brave, Philibert,' he said gently, running his fingers through the other man's strong, wiry hair.

'They suspect me of the murder, Jean Paul,' he sobbed, 'I could see it in that woman's eyes.'

'You are safe.' The murderer knelt down beside the sofa, taking Stansi's face in his hands and kissing the salty lips. They had the phlegmy taste of fear.

'How?' Stansi sobbed, rocking gently. 'They knew that Zafy was my lover, my benefactor. The police will investigate and find out that Radama and I used to frequent all the gay hangouts in Delhi — brother-Saturdays at Soul Cove, Purohit Bala's farm orgies . . .'

'That was such a long time ago,' the murderer crooned softly, averting his face so that Stansi would not see the twinge of jealousy he could not suppress, 'but I wish you had told me.'

'I thought you knew. You were Radama's boy yourself.'

'Radama brought me out of poverty,' the murderer's voice was softly regretful, 'but he was a bad man. He used people, without caring for their hearts. Until I met you, I did not know what love was.'

'Now what do I do? Where do I go?' Stansi looked up with haunted eyes. The murderer smiled reassuringly.

'We are free,' he said, getting up and going across to the small escritoire near the bay window. 'Look!'

He took out the papers and diskettes he had stolen from Zafy's safe.

'There are millions in this,' he said, 'and we can escape to Greece. I know the brothers in Athens. They will keep us safe until the outcry is over. Maybe

78

they will send us to Cyprus, or Turkey. No-one can reach us there . . .'

He stopped mid-sentence; Stansi was standing up, pointing at him. His voice was shaky, and his eyes brilliant with fear and suspicion.

'Where did you get that from?' he croaked.

'From Radama Zafy's safe,' the murderer answered cheerfully. 'And now hurry. Let us get our passports and be gone.'

But Stansi seemed to be in a hypnotic trance.

'How did you get these?' he stammered.

'I took them after I killed Zafy, of course,' his lover smiled.

Stansi sank to the floor, and the murderer suddenly recognized the revulsion in his eyes. He stretched his hand out with a wry expression.

'Come now, Philibert, this is not a time for weakness. We have to go.'

'No, no, no . . .' the Counsellor for Public Affairs moaned. 'What have you done? Now it's all over. They will get you. They will hang you, and me with you.'

The murderer slapped Stansi hard twice on both cheeks.

'Here, drink some water and pull yourself together. We have to leave now. Pack our bags.'

'They'll get us,' Stansi's voice was trembling on the brink of hysteria. 'We are lost.'

'Get up, Philibert, and let me handle this. In no time we will be sipping daiquiris by the Mediterranean.'

'You fool, you moron!' Stansi was screaming. 'Do you think the politicians will rest? It is their money you are stealing. They will hunt us down.'

'You are behaving like a coward,' the murderer said contemptuously.

'Give yourself up now, before it is too late, they can't try you here. You have diplomatic immunity. Bargain with the politicians back home, I will talk to them, broker a deal. It will mean just a few years in prison. The embassy would not risk a scandal.'

The murderer shook his head gently, his voice dropping to a sad whisper.

'I always knew you were weak, but I thought you loved me,' he said, stepping over to his lover. Philibert Stansi recoiled from him, raising his hands to protect himself from a blow.

'No, I am not going to hit you,' the murderer said, 'I am going to leave now. With all this.' He held up Zafy's disks. 'I plan to lose myself somewhere on a Greek island, and outlast Interpol and Ratsiraka's men.'

He took a thin length of wire from his pocket, looping it around his fingers. Stansi's eyes were on it, wide with fear and disbelief.

'You are going to kill me, are you?' he asked in a pleading, childish voice.

'I grew up in the streets of Toamasina. It was a rough world Radama rescued me from,' the murderer continued to speak in a soft conversational tone, moving around until he stood behind the diplomat, 'and my father taught me many things. He grew up on those unforgiving streets too and had learned its rules early. I garrotted my first man when I was ten: a French Malagasy mongrel who wouldn't pay a gambling debt.'

Stansi was a frozen statue, leaning against the sofa. The air was rancid with the odour of sweat and fear, and the stench changed as Stansi's bowels emptied. The murderer clucked his tongue reprovingly, drawing the wire gently around his lover's throat.

'I was seeing a picture in my mind,' he sighed, tightening the wire, 'of you and me, and the ocean.'

Stansi began to gag.

'Diplomatic immunity, Philibert?' The murderer's low laugh was deep with sadness. 'Do you take me for a fool? How can I claim diplomatic immunity when I am just your secretary?'

That was when Anna Khan shot him.

'It was when the shower opened and the water began to fall on him that the idea struck him. How to murder Radama Zafy,' Samorin said, raising the crystal glass to his mouth. The air had the faint waft of malt.

They were sitting in the Ambassador's study, the dawn a faint pewter on the horizon. Anna never knew when dawn came to the city; there was too much light pollution in the night sky.

'You must try some Laphroaig,' Samorin said, getting up.

For the first time, Anna smiled at him. It softened something in her eyes. Samorin chose a glass from the sideboard and poured the whisky.

'I have never been much of a drinker,' she said apologetically, picking up the glass.

'Oh, there is still time,' Samorin reassured her.

'The shower,' Tsiranana interrupted.

'Yes, the shower,' Samorin said, taking a sip, sighing and sitting back, 'Where it began. I stood inside it when I went down to the basement and looked out through the glass. I noticed the white patch of paint-work, and I wondered what had happened to the picture which must have hung there. Going by the way Zafy's room was kept, he was a fastidious man. If he had wanted to remove a painting, he would have

81

replaced it with something and not have left a blank patch on the wall. So I started to look for it.'

'And when you found it . . .'

'Behind the deep freeze,' Samorin said with a short laugh, 'crumpled, but curved. Still damp. It was then I understood how the murderer killed Zafy.'

Anna abruptly looked up from her drink, the knowledge suddenly opening inside.

'He made a cone with a thick tip, filled it with water and waited for it to freeze.'

'Absolutely. A canvas, four feet by three feet, filled with water and placed inside a deep freeze vertically would harden into a solid spear of ice. All he had to do was to wait. My guess is he let it set the night before and used it on the old man the next day.'

'The heating was switched off so that the ice wouldn't melt when it was brought up? But that doesn't make sense.' Anna shook her head. 'He would want it to melt as quickly as possible.'

'A calculated risk,' Samorin said. 'And all murderers work on chance.'

'How would he get out? The only way out was to open the private door with its key,' Tsiranana interrupted, 'but Zafy always kept the key in his pocket.'

'Don't you see?' Samorin leaned forward. 'The soap. It was missing. That is something that got me thinking. In a bathroom as finickily kept as Zafy's, where did the soap go? Then the solution struck me. He must have extracted the key on a previous day and made an impression on the soap. He was out of the embassy through Zafy's private exit, leaving no trace behind.'

'But the guards? And their records?'

'He must have let himself in through the side

gate when the guard's shift changed. There is a three-minute gap, which is plenty of time to punch an entry code, cross the small corridor and enter Zafy's rooms.'

'And I turned the heating up full.' The Ambassador sounded rueful.

'Oh he was clever, a true artist.' Samorin laughed without mirth. 'He upset the carafe of water to disguise the melted weapon. An artist all right.'

The room was getting lighter, a red stain spreading across the sky in the distance. The birds were waking up in the trees. Ambassador Tsiranana got up.

'I am grateful for this, Samorin,' he said. 'If there is any way we can repay you, please say so.'

Anna saw Samorin's eyes twinkle in the grey light.

'As a matter of fact, Charles, there is something,' he said. 'I have always liked cats.'

The Ambassador looked incredulous. His voice dropped to a whisper.

'You can't seriously mean . . .'

Samorin smiled.

'I do.'

'Another fosa?'

Samorin nodded and turned to Anna.

'*Cryptoproxa ferox*, found only in Madagascar. The most uncomplicated of feline hunters among cats, great speed, powerful feet. Goes straight for the head, then opens the body with a slash of its front paws. And after its kill, you wouldn't guess it has just fed. Keeps itself impeccably clean. I have one and she needs a mate. They'll make a pretty picture together.'

Ambassador Tsiranana sighed.

'I will have to speak to President Ratsiraka,' he muttered. Anna smiled.

'Speaking of pictures, I saw one by Dhiren Das in the reception area,' she said.

'Dhiren,' Samorin said ruminatively, and Anna noticed his eyes were suddenly secretive.

'Do you know him?'

'I did, once.'

CHAPTER FIVE

A week later, when Samorin walked into the sunlit atrium of the Malagasy embassy where Dhiren Das's latest exhibition was being held, he caught sight of Anna standing in a far corner, gazing at a painting and oblivious to the crowd milling around her. The afternoon sun coming in through the glass ceiling illuminated her profile, as if an aura surrounded her.

Cigarette smoke curled upwards in disembodied wisps, and the murmur of conversation was a broad, grainy hum. Samorin nodded to Ambassador Tsiranana, who held an unlit cigar and was being buttonholed by a small goat-like man. Samorin smiled sympathetically and the Ambassador responded, with a pained expression. His interlocutor glanced across and met Samorin's eyes. The detective recognized the man, who ran a website for one of the media corporations. He looked annoyed as Samorin made his way towards them. Tsiranana, on the other hand, looked relieved.

'. . . will put his paintings on our website.' Samorin heard the tail end of the sentence, which was cut off abruptly.

'Sorry to barge in,' Samorin said pleasantly, turning to the journalist, 'but it's such a surprise finding you here. I didn't know you knew anything about art.'

The man shifted on his toes, pulling at the sparse goatee that grew like a dirty shrub from his weak chin. He had round eyes magnified by owl-like glasses, and a small pot belly.

'These days editors have to know everything,' he said stiffly, 'or, at least, that is what I learnt at Columbia.'

He had a small squeaky voice, ambushed in places by an American accent. Easy to have picked it up in six months at Columbia, Samorin thought. Free fellowships from the American government were not the only perquisites of being a friendly Third World journalist; a flaky accent was part of the deal.

'Everything?' Samorin raised his eyebrows. 'Oh, unless you know everything, you cannot be a newspaper editor, right?'

The small, pimply face darkened at Samorin's sarcasm. Even the Ambassador looked slightly uncomfortable.

'I see you know each other.' He cleared his throat.

The editor inclined his head reluctantly, as if loath to admit it. Samorin winked and said that he would see them around and hailed a passing waiter for a drink.

The atrium was huge and airy, with pastel walls and a small dais at one end. The ceiling was all glass, enormous rectangles held in place by squares of concrete casings, and the supporting columns were of thin black marble veined with white. It was where the embassy held its cultural activities: seminars, the occasional movie and art shows. Ambassador Tsiranana, unlike his predecessors, had changed the social profile of his mission in a subtle way, and a small country like Madagascar with its closed government and a lifetime dictator was now written about in many of the national dailies in glowing terms.

But then that was Delhi. A city of politicians and diplomats. Their parties were all about power and cloistered agreements, with a smattering of celebrities – mainly dancers, artists, editors and fashion designers. The Page Three sections of the Delhi papers were full of the antics of these habitual party-goers: identical guests at identical parties.

Today's was no different, Samorin saw. There was the socialite with the large white teeth who looked as if she lived for such gatherings, her camera-hungry eyes seeking out wandering photographers. With a loud baying laugh, she spotted one and waved at him. She immediately threw her arm around a fat politician who was clutching a tumbler of Scotch to his sagging chest and happened to be close at hand, and both broke into a grimace as the photographer turned to aim his camera at them. The flashbulb was an intense blue star; the photographer turned away as they turned away from each other too, as if they had suddenly remembered something most important to do.

A bald journalist in his trademark ill-fitting kurta was talking to a retired policeman, who looked as if he had been drinking since morning. '. . . the koschun I was asking the PM was . . .' The cop was squirming in

87

the journalist's grasp, and Samorin noticed that nobody looked at anybody's face while they talked, always searching across shoulders for the next celebrity or passing photographer. Samorin looked for Anna across the heads of the crowd, and spotted her talking to a young writer, the author of a critically acclaimed book that had earned him a huge advance but not many readers. She appeared faintly bored as she listened to his stuttering voice, as if eager to return to Dhiren Das's landscapes, while he brushed his curly unkempt hair away with one dark, pudgy hand, making intense little gestures as he spoke. She was suddenly aware of Samorin looking at her and she turned to meet his glance, her eyes opening wide for an instant. The writer followed her gaze, and seeing Samorin his porcine face wrinkled in a displeased and insincere smile.

Samorin raised his wine glass to them. Anna returned the salute, and he walked over to her, deftly avoiding the air-kissing guests and other arrivistes, circling around a group that was listening in a drunken stupor to '. . . the koschun is . . .'

Anna held out a cool hand, which Samorin briefly pressed between his palms. Her skin was soft and smooth.

'You know each other?' she asked.

The writer nodded, and Samorin smiled.

'The retired cartoonist,' the writer said. 'Who doesn't know Jay Samorin?'

'Oh, he is part of my past,' Samorin riposted lightly, 'all those newsrooms and editorial meetings, trying to find an exalted human angle to tribal massacres or political sleaze. While this chap is still attached to the exalted positions, I quit.'

'Throwing a dead pigeon at the editor while walking out of the job, I was told,' the writer said maliciously. 'Only a cartoonist would find symbolism in it, I suppose.'

'A dead pigeon?' Anna raised an eyebrow.

Samorin smiled.

'It's a long story,' he said. 'I'll tell you about it sometime.'

They were joined by the writer's wife, a pale, slightly hunched woman who watched dotingly over her husband's every move; her large black eyes habitually anxious, her pink tongue licking thin lips periodically.

'I was saying to the celebrated author here that these days one reads about writers more than one reads their books.' Anna gestured towards the couple.

'Isn't that a blessing sometimes?' Samorin asked. 'It is usually better than reading what they write.'

The author's frown deepened — he fingered his designer tie and dragged on a Dunhill. His wife simpered while smoothing the collar of his black shirt. He sighed, gratefully accepting comfort.

'Boss, incest won't go away,' he stuttered. 'This is a sick country. Everyone is fucking everyone, the poor are tortured and exploited by the rich, who want to bleed them for the sake of DVD players. Conscience, boss, we are a nation without conscience. I told Salman that.'

'I know Salman Khan is a very popular film star,' Samorin said, deadpan, 'but what does he have to do with literature? I thought he was too busy poaching and beating up girlfriends.'

The author looked at him pityingly.

'Salman Rushdie, Jay,' he said.

'Oh,' said Samorin, 'Salman Rushdie!'

A society photographer zeroed in on them, and the author turned his back and hid behind his wife.

'I hate photographers,' he whimpered like a spoiled child. The cameraman shrugged and moved away.

Leaving the novelist and his wife behind, Samorin and Anna strolled along the walls, absorbing the colours and themes of Dhiren Das's paintings. The artist seemed to prefer large-scale canvases, and his works were full of ruthless force. The backdrops of his landscapes looked as if they had been hacked out of rock, while the foregrounds surprised with delicate detail, enhancing the impact of the paintings. Subtle colours and careful brushcraft brought out details of faces and posture: chocolate-skinned people of Madagascar were drawn with startling clarity, pelts of aye-ayes glistened as though alive, each leaf or stem of bushplant seemed to grow on the canvas. At the far end of the hall, one wall was completely bare, and a column of sunlight slanted to fall on a gigantic pedestal that stood empty. It was made of green marble and mounted on mahogany.

Anna stopped at a painting, unconsciously placing her hand on Samorin's sleeve. Dragonflies were depicted filling a blue sky over an endless savannah. A lemur swung down from a baobab that grew upside down, its magnificent roots seemingly clawing at the white puffy clouds above, while around the leg of the beast was coiled a blind snake. The landscape was sunlit and bright, but in the taut curve of the tree trunk and the chaos of its branches lay a tight, condensed terror: the lemur's face was sorrowful as it contemplated the snake, which bangled its ankle, the tail of the serpent a lethal black whip. Anna shivered.

'It is beautiful and frightening,' she said.

'I am glad, then,' a soft voice said behind them, and Samorin turned to see a face he hadn't encountered for many years.

The eyes were the same, cold and amused, with light green pupils and dark lashes. Only the face had subtly changed: Dhiren Das now cultivated a beard, kept closely trimmed, with the vanity of a white patch under his lower lip that was carefully groomed. The smile was mocking and flattering at the same time. Anna felt flustered.

'I am glad you find it frightening,' the famous painter said, 'because there is so much terror in beauty. It is the other side of the morning.'

Das followed the direction of Anna's eyes.

'Oh, that empty space!' Dhiren Das exclaimed. 'That will always be present at every exhibition of mine — the unmounted pedestal.'

'A neat trick,' Samorin interrupted, 'the press will love it, the critics will be intrigued.'

Dhiren Das's face twitched with contempt.

'It is no trick, that is the space I leave for my masterpiece. When I have finished it, my purpose as an artist will be over. Then I will hold my final exhibition, the unveiling of a one-piece show.'

He looked challengingly at Samorin, but there was no hint of recognition in his eyes.

Jay Samorin remembered that look in the thin mist of a faraway childhood morning under the sheltering deodar in the school grounds. The boy had lain trapped in Samorin's grasp.

'I am not afraid of you,' Dhiren's look said. 'I know what you can do.'

Samorin's hand was raised to strike, the flat hard edge poised to deliver a death blow to the throat. Yet the eyes that regarded him were curious rather than frightened. Samorin stood up and pulled on the other boy's lapels.

'Get up, Dhiren, don't let me catch you again, spying on me. I've told you that once before.'

'Afraid that I will tell the housemasters about your alfresco drill and you will get punishment from the Head?' The drawl was mildly contemptuous. 'If you want to play at being Bruce Lee at dawn, what is it to me?'

Samorin took a step forward again, anger tightening the muscles of his thighs, wanting to lash out at the cool, collected face.

'Go,' he snarled. 'If I catch you again, I will kill you.'

Dhiren rose with a little laugh and started towards the school building.

'Dhiren,' Samorin called after him, 'what did my father do?'

The other boy stopped and turned, a scornful gleam in his eyes.

'Why don't you ask your aunt?' he said.

Jay Samorin woke up the next morning with a start, facing a little doll dangling by a wire from his bedpost – head broken and tilted to one side. It was like a splash of ice water on his face. Puzzled, he grabbed the doll and examined it. School vacation had started two days ago, and the dormitory was empty. Aunt was going to be a week late collecting him, and there were only two boys left behind at school: Dhiren and him. As far as he knew, Dhiren never went home for the holidays.

The doll was made of an old sock stuffed with

cotton, shaped by wire wound tightly around the mid-section and extended to suggest the beginning of limbs. The head was a peeled onion fastened with pins, and with grimacing features sketched on with red paint. The face was a crude impression of a hanged man: eyes wide open, red tongue protruding from twisted lips. Dying juices oozed from the onion head, smearing the red ink like a wound. A dead doll. Something stirred inside Samorin, memories of a drive at dawn with Aunt, ghostly secrets whispered in the dusk. The blank walls of a house at the foot of a mountain, shadows in the lamplight, hushed voices behind closed doors – a faint collage of memories, brightening and then dimming in a dark dawn peopled by silent children, their hands caressing Aunt, the shadows eating away at her face.

A flicker by the door caught the corner of his eye, and Samorin ran outside clutching the doll. Dhiren was walking away and Samorin angrily called after him. 'You did this, didn't you? What does it mean?'

The boy turned and stood with a hand on his waist, one eyebrow raised in mocking interrogation.

'Aren't you a bit too old to play with dolls?' he sneered.

That was when Samorin hit him, the flat of his palm connecting with the side of Dhiren's face, and suddenly a terrible pain shot through his forearm and he found himself falling. The doll was flung up and away from him towards the blue sky through the arches of the school's veranda. Its head waggled as it rose, and Samorin checked his own fall by turning on his waist as he had been taught. With a sudden shock, he realized that Dhiren had fallen back into a *kalari* crouch, the right leg resting on one curled toe after delivering an outward lash. His arm throbbed where Dhiren had kicked him.

'Why, do you think you are the only one who knows *kalaripayattu*?' Dhiren asked. His eyes shone with a mad light and a thin trickle of blood flowed down his chin from the corner of his mouth.

'Who taught you?' Samorin asked, his voice unable to hide his astonishment.

'You.' The other boy gave a high, wild laugh. 'I watched you and learned. My master.' And he bowed mockingly.

'Who are you? Why are you always following me about?'

'You should ask your aunt,' Dhiren said with a mirthless giggle, 'she might know.'

Samorin was taken aback and he looked at Dhiren warily. What could his aunt have to do with the boy?

The doll lay on the grass on its back, its broken face gasping at the sky. Samorin went to pick it up. When he turned around, Dhiren was gone.

Later, walking along the small path that led downhill through the conifers and the nettles, which were golden with fallen pine needles, Samorin saw Dhiren crouching by a copse of trees. Samorin went up to him, meaning to ask him about Aunt and how he knew her, and a hundred other questions jostled in his mind. His adversary glared up defiantly.

'What are you doing here?' he barked.

Samorin saw a large wooden cage with a trapdoor that was pulled back by a wire attached to a smaller door. The cage had another partition at the back, and inside was a terrified mouse clawing frantically to get out. It scratched at the mesh while making tiny squeaking noises.

'What kind of a mousetrap is that?' he asked.

Dhiren laughed.

'I don't catch mice, dodo. I catch cats with this cage. The mice are the bait.'

'But why do you want to catch cats?'

'It's a game, you see. Cats catch mice and kill them,' Dhiren explained patiently. 'Nature is murder for the sake of existence, but the murderer has to pay for it. So I catch the killers and sit in judgement over them. And then I hang them.'

The boy's green eyes were cold and hard, and the wind that moved through the clearings of the trees made Samorin shiver.

'I am somewhat like a Caesar at the Coliseum,' Dhiren went on, concealing the cage cleverly behind some bushes, adjusting the open door carefully, an invitation to death.

Indeed, the masters at school had found cats hanged in the woods and presumed a gang of schoolboys must have been involved in some gruesome sport, typical of childhood. When stray dogs discovered the gardener's lame old tabby hanging by a school tie inside the disused cistern that once held the school's bathwater, the headmaster had instituted an inquiry. He had formed small squads of schoolboys to catch the culprits, each headed by one senior. Dhiren was in charge of one of the groups meant to catch the cat-killers.

'You are . . .' Samorin searched for the right word to describe Dhiren.

'Evil?' the other boy suggested politely, helpfully.

'You'd better confess to the headmaster, Dhiren. Otherwise, I will have to report you.'

'That is priceless, coming from you. Reporting me for killing cats while your father was hanged for murdering your mother.' The boy's voice dripped with sarcasm.

Samorin's mind reeled and a pit yawned in his stomach at the horror and malevolence of those words, spoken so calmly on that golden afternoon. Suddenly the kaleidoscope of broken images and words made sense – the stranger in the study, the life of imposed exile, Aunt's controlled quarantine that banished all contact with the outside world.

'No, no, it isn't true,' Samorin whispered, steadying himself against the trunk of a pine, hearing the wind swell and subside around him like a merciless, taunting sea.

'Oh, but it is, Jay.' Dhiren's voice sounded in his ear, his breath upon his cheek. Samorin cringed away from him.

'And if you tell on me and the cats, Jay, I will tell everyone in school about you. That your daddy was hanged for murdering your mummy.'

'Who are you?' Samorin asked, as his eyes met Dhiren's, and the gaze enfolded him like dark, suffocating cloth. Another night descended on him, ridden with smoke and mist, in which shadows swam with velvet stealth.

'I am someone you have met before, Jay, but never recognized,' Dhiren's whisper was a mantra in his ear, 'just ask Aunt.'

Samorin stumbled away into the sunlit spaces that lay beyond the woods, seeing dimly through tears the old red brick of the school building. Aunt was waiting for him on the veranda, a small valise beside her on the yellow tiled floor. Her long dark hair was gathered behind her, the widow's white sari fluttering in the mountain breeze, her fawn-coloured mantilla drawn around her slender shoulders. Samorin saw her smile at him, and it seemed to him like a light brighter than the afternoon sun. Blinded by tears and pain, he ran towards her. Her eyes clouded as they took in his wounded state and she knelt down and opened her arms out to him, a fragrant, familiar sanctuary.

'So did you ever ask your aunt?' Dhiren Das asked Samorin, tossing the question lightly across his shoulder as he turned to walk away. Samorin's eyes opened in shock. He blinked once, twice, clearing his vision, and met the familiar sardonic glance from across the room where the painter now stood talking to a group of admiring journalists. The planes of his face were lit up by occasional flashbulbs. Ambassador Tsiranana was saying something. Dhiren Das was bending down, listening with courtesy and attention, but occasionally his eyes threw small, dark questions at Samorin. Samorin started towards Das, his fists clenched, and stopped. Anna's hand was on his arm, restraining him.

'Wait, throwing a dead pigeon at your boss?' she laughed, but her eyes were worried. 'Where did you get the dead pigeon from?'

'Oh, it came my way,' he said, joining in her laugh, but his eyes were still on Das. 'I was in the process of getting rid of many things. And once you begin, it is surprising how easily one's attic can be cleaned out.'

Anna drew him away from the party, her hand a gentle pressure on his elbow. They walked out of the building, towards the lawns, and sat on one of the green benches under a flowering laburnum.

'What were you cleaning out of your attic, besides dead pigeons?'

Samorin lit a cigarette, sighed. He remembered driving to work, three years ago, with the sour taste of

97

too much wine drunk the night before, the stale smell from Maya's mouth as she distractedly kissed him goodbye. Maya, his lover, a successful corporate lawyer who was beginning to appear more and more alien with her talk of MNC mergers and chairmen's dinners, and evenings spent in rooftop restaurants with Japanese clients who drank glasses of whisky as if it were water. His fellow editors at work also seemed alien, with their grand plans to save Indian society and restore its politics, quoting from articles they had written about how they predicted the fall of this minister and the rise of that. He viewed with contempt editorial meetings where everyone tried to come up with cynical one-liners, smart enough to cover up insecurities and lack of substance. Journalism was becoming more and more managerial, and bosses talked about HRD and accountability while recycling old story ideas and how they needed to liaise better with marketing.

'We are in the business of selling a product,' a young colleague had told him with all the pride of a revelation, 'and if I am able to deliver an advertising-driven editorial product, I am sure of upgrading my company car this year.'

Samorin was beginning to feel jaded. Exhaustion had enveloped him like an invisible shroud, and he was unable to respond to Maya's enthusiasm or the stratagems of his colleagues. He remembered how as a child he would sleep in the armchair in the portico of his house in the valley, secure with the familiar sounds breaking through his slumber: Aunt calling him to come to lunch, birds quarrelling in the trees, a dragonfly burring its rough wings in front of his closed eyelids.

He had not been prepared for the pigeon, which suddenly hit his windscreen as he was driving to work. It was a grey pigeon, flying across a grey road on a grey morning, under a grey sky. There was a thud, and he braked hard. An old man behind him, driving a beat-up old Fiat, hit his rear fender, and Samorin heard his tyres squealing a long while behind before feeling the impact.

The pigeon had left a small splash of red on the glass, and some feathers and dirt stuck on it. It remained there for many days afterwards and when he was driving Maya to the airport, she asked why there was a blob on the windscreen.

'It was the pigeon who did it, not me,' Samorin said defensively.

'What pigeon?' she asked in a terse little voice

'The one which ran into my car the day I quit my job,' he said.

'You *quit* your job?' Maya squealed in shock. 'And you never told me! I thought you were lounging around the house the last two days because you were too lazy to go to work.'

'I forgot to tell you, and you were too busy with your mergers and acquisitions, remember?'

'But your job was a glamorous one,' she protested, 'working for such a publication is not a joke. You should have asked me first.'

'Oh well. The pigeon was what started it, in a way. An old man then ran into me from behind because the pigeon ran into me first.'

'How can a pigeon run into you first when an old man is running into you from the back?' Maya's tone was quite hostile by now. 'I think you are making all this up.'

Samorin stopped the car. He opened the palm of his right hand in front of her face and thumped his left fist into it.

'Whack! Bam!'

Then he opened the fist and slammed the knuckles of his right hand into it.

'BAM!'

Maya narrowed her eyes, and Samorin could see her mouth clamp and stretch like a pained fish. She always looked like that when she was angry.

'The first one was the pigeon, the second the old man,' he said.

'Do you mind driving on, you are scaring me! And I will miss my plane,' she said. 'I have a job to do, unlike you.'

He shrugged.

'I'm sorry I said that, Jay,' she said, suddenly placing a hand on Samorin's thigh. 'That was mean.'

He smiled magnanimously. To forgive her insults was the one way he could feel superior to her.

'Want me to drive fast?' he asked, and suddenly gunned the engine. The Jeep left the side of the road and plunged into the morning traffic going towards the airport and Gurgaon. He heard brakes and horns behind them and Maya screamed.

'Why do you want to kill me, you bastard?'

He shrugged.

'I don't particularly want to kill anyone. I just want to get you on that plane.'

He felt her glaring, and noticed fleetingly how ugly she looked. When you begin to stop loving someone, they always begin to look ugly or slightly ridiculous. Her hair was tied back in a bun, and she wore a red turtleneck pullover under a denim jacket. Maya always liked to wear tight clothes, to make her breasts stand out. Her breasts looked better when she was wearing clothes, they were very boring when she was naked. He remembered she hadn't been naked with him for a long time.

'We need to talk when I get back,' she said.

'About pigeons? I am sorry I didn't tell you about it, I simply forgot.'

It seemed to him afterwards that he always forgot to tell Maya about the things which were important to him. The pigeon was one in a long series of unsaid, forgotten things. He did not tell her about Aunt and the birds that flew across the misty mornings over the paddy fields of his childhood. Or about the blue-barrelled gun Aunt lifted to her shoulder and aimed into the mist, through which the white cranes flew like linen loose in the wind.

'It was just a pigeon,' he told Maya.

'What are you talking about?' she said. 'Jay, I think you are increasingly losing the plot. You just sit there and mumble.'

'An epitaph for a pigeon,' he told her, feeling he had said something clever and sad.

It was a small grey hump of feathers and blood and lay on the side of the road, flung there by the force of the impact. Samorin had jumped out of the Jeep, dimly aware of the old man who was shouting at him from behind. He went up to the dead bird and squatted beside it. It lay near a dried pod of cow dung, where the grass was scraggy and brown. There was an old newspaper bag with a picture of the Prime Minister smiling on it. He reached out and touched the pigeon. Its eyes were open and round, small opaque stones of disbelief. The old man had come up to Samorin and was standing beside him, screaming now. Bespectacled, he had a long thin face and a grey moustache. Below his grey pullover he wore a white shirt and cravat.

'Pay me, pay me mister,' he shouted.

Samorin looked back at him and told him to shut up. The pigeon was not completely dead, he noticed. One of its legs moved slightly, as if an elastic band holding it to its stomach was loosening up slowly.

The old man caught the back of Samorin's blazer but he shook the frail, insistent hand off. He picked up the pigeon and stood. He raised it to his face and smelled it. Dust and feathers.

'They smell of the sky,' Aunt says, 'all birds do.'

A vermilion road runs down to the green rice paddies. The black palm trees scent the air, heavy with purple fruit. Aunt has pulled the free end of her white sari around her shoulders, tucking it in at the waist to give her gun arm free movement. She holds the gun that had once belonged to Grandfather in one hand and his small hand in the other.

Samorin took the pigeon with him to the Jeep, cradling it against his chest. Warming it under his jacket, he was dimly aware of the old man walking beside him, still gesticulating and shouting. A small crowd had gathered near the accident, and a policeman had parked his motorcycle nearby. Seeing him, the old man scuttled up and started shouting at him.

'Why are you just standing here? Arrest this man, he wrecked my car.'

The policeman walked up to Samorin. He was unshaven. His khaki collar was dirty but the holster on his belt was shiny and brown. Samorin held out the dead pigeon to him.

'Sorry. It flew into my windscreen,' he said matter-of-factly.

The policeman looked at it, and an expression of mild worry creased his forehead.

'Is it dead?' he asked.

The old man, whose car was still entangled with the Jeep's rear fender, caught hold of the policeman's sleeve.

'Do you know who I am? I will get you fired.'

'Get lost, Grandpa,' the policeman said wearily. 'I don't care if you are the President's chief rat-catcher. Just go away.'

'I think it is dead,' Samorin said, showing him the pigeon. The policeman touched its chest gingerly. The side of its smashed neck was dusty and damp with blood.

'We used to keep pigeons when I was small. My father used to,' the policeman said. 'He loved pigeons. I used to go with him carrying *bajra* seeds for them in a small gunny sack.'

'What happened to them? Do you still keep pigeons?' Samorin asked with the mild interest of coincidence. He opened the car door and placed the dead bird on the passenger's seat.

'Oh, Father died and there was no-one to look after the birds, some flew away, some the cats ate,' the policeman said. He laughed gruffly. 'What are you planning to do with it?' he asked. Samorin shrugged.

'I haven't thought about it. Do you think I should bury it?'

The old man was standing quietly beside them, listening in disbelief.

'What do you want?' Samorin asked him.

'You ruin my car,' he flared up, 'and then ask me

103

what I want. I want to be paid for the damage. Pay me now, mister.'

'Run away, old man, or I'll beat the hell out of you,' Samorin said.

The old man opened and shut his mouth twice, showing large yellow teeth. He turned to the policeman. 'Did you hear that?'

The policeman smiled at Samorin, a small ugly smile.

'You can take it home and cook it,' he said, climbing onto the seat of his yellow Royal Enfield, 'it's good for arthritis. But pigeons taste tough and the meat is stringy.'

The policeman kicked the starter of his motorcycle and Samorin noticed that his shoelace had come loose. The vehicle coughed as the engine caught, and the officer turned it around and spluttered away.

Samorin nodded and quickly leapt into the Jeep and started it. The old man was trying to open the Jeep's door. Samorin pressed on the accelerator, causing the Jeep to jump forward, and from the back came the sound of something tearing. The fender of the car behind came off and dragged on the road with the screechy sound of metal on asphalt, and then it fell away with a loud clang. In the rear-view mirror, he saw the old man standing beside the fender and looking down at it. Samorin could not read his expression, but saw that the traffic behind had slowed down, the vehicles making a loop around the old man.

The dead pigeon bumped around on the seat beside him, the inside of the Jeep suddenly filled with a dry, feathery smell. The air conditioning was on, and the engine made a clanking noise.

'Maya will disapprove of you riding in the car with

me,' Samorin told the pigeon, 'but then she disapproves of almost everything now.'

The dead bird nodded its wrecked neck as the wheels went over an unmarked speed breaker.

'But Aunt had a different way with birds.'

The mist is a separate, translucent substance. To the boy, the white cranes seem to fly lazily towards their death, their wings rowing in the air.

Aunt smiles at him. 'You need to be able to judge the distance, and then adapt to the change in direction.'

She sees the little crease on his forehead.

'You are thinking. What are you thinking?'

'What does direction mean?'

The morning is turning lighter, and the wind swims down the western hills tossing and turning across the green, wet breadth of paddy.

Aunt squats down beside him, and leans the gun against her shoulder. A fruit fly buzzes around the barrel, which has a diamond glint at its tip where the sun nicks the metal. She draws him into her lap, and he comes up to her forehead as he stands leaning against her. She smells of jasmine. She points an arm, long and straight into the mist, and asks him to lay his cheek against her palm.

'Squint along my finger,' she says.

He can still remember her finger, its alabaster length, with its pink nail gleaming.

'What do you see?'

'Everything,' he replies.

'Look again,' she urges gently.

Samorin sees the green fields and the palms, the clusters of coconut trees and hedges. The sky arches above the ash green of the trees and the thinning mist and the bamboo thickets.

'Keep looking, and you will understand,' she says.

Aunt's hand doesn't waver, and it hurts his cheek to squint along its length. After a while, her finger grows longer; it seems to have acquired a lean movement of its own, until it almost touches the bamboo leaves. Slowly, everything around the tip of the finger has begun to dissolve, and all the boy can see is a round spot of green as if at the end of a toy telescope. Then he sees a crane fly into it, and for an instant it is suspended at the end of Aunt's finger, as though affixed to that little circle into which the world has shrunk. He makes a grab for the bird, it is so near, loses his balance and sits down on the ground.

Aunt laughs, standing up in a quick fluid movement. She brings the gun to her shoulder. Suddenly the distance has grown back to normal, and he hears the flat slap of the gun coughing into the air and sees the crane float down into the wet rice paddy. A puff of white smoke is dragged away by a small wind.

'There,' she says.

She sends him into the fields where the bird has fallen. It is a glorious trophy, its musky smell not yet erased by the odour of death. He is allowed to carry it back home. Climbing up the veranda steps, he sees the cook Janakiyamma come out to take it away from him.

'Can't I keep it for a while?' he asks Aunt.

'Lunch will be late,' she says, taking the dead bird from him and handing it to the cook.

'It doesn't look dead, only asleep,' he says. 'Will I be able to shoot like you, so that what I've killed doesn't look dead?'

Aunt laughs her low silvery laugh.

'Aunt, who taught you to shoot?'

The muslin of a shadow passes over her in spite of

the sunlight of that bright morning. Her eyes are closed and her fists clasped against her sides.

'Aunt . . .'

'Your father,' *she says.* 'Your father taught me to shoot.'

Perhaps it was this knowledge that impelled Samorin to carry the dead pigeon up to his office, to place it on his desk and to contemplate. When Father swung in the air and birds flew past, did his last breaths mingle with the windspumes of their feathers? Did the dying heat from his gasping mouth under the black cloth steam the air, making the birds pause in flight? Father again . . .

He placed the dead bird on his desk, leaning it against his computer, adjusting its head so that it looked at him with round, dead eyes. He lit a cigarette and blew the smoke at its face.

'Even passive smoking can cause cancer,' he warned the pigeon.

Suddenly, the door opened and the room was full of people. His editor, a short man with a small paunch in tight jeans, followed closely by the supplement editor and a handful of assistant editors.

'I was told you . . .' his editor started and stopped, gaping at the dead bird.

'Lunch?' suggested Samorin hopefully.

Suddenly he felt tired. The faces around him, familiar yet remote, became gross caricatures. They looked like fat toads in the sun, gorged on flies and insects, and unconsciously he had started doodling on a piece of paper. Samorin saw his editor's eyes bulge as he saw the bespectacled frog taking shape under Samorin's felt pen.

Samorin got up and placed the pigeon in the man's

hands. He let out a startled squeak and dropped the dead bird on the floor. The others stepped back.

'Soon, my friends, soon nobody will be able to tell the difference between you and this dead bird,' Samorin said, and strode out of the room.

'And you never went back to your work?' Anna asked.

'No,' Samorin said, 'I went home instead, back to the hills and Aunt.'

CHAPTER SIX

Later, rising from his meditation in the *kalari*, Samorin felt lighter; the malignant shadow of Dhiren Das had retreated into the past. He remembered his return home, waking up through a shoal of shadows and breaking surface through a noose of ripples, rising up to the dim silver tides of a somnolent moon, calling out for Aunt in a voice that belonged to his childhood ... The sound of a car outside, its engine surging and stilling, returning from its journey in the chill of the mountain dawn.

Aunt ...

Samorin woke with a start. Rising, he went across to his bedroom window and looked out into the familiar courtyard; the old Studebaker gleamed among the quilted shadows of the great mango tree. The gabled roof of the east wing rose against the weak platinum of a morning sky, the plains below still sleepy with mist.

When he returned home after he had walked away from his job and his career, Aunt had met him on the veranda without any questions on her face. He had been struck by how her hair was climbed with white, a silver sickle curving away from her forehead to descend down to her back, a little like Indira Gandhi's. Samorin clasped her in his arms and was filled with wonder at how small she felt. During the growing years of his childhood she was the sheltering angel of his life, tall and strong, with her quick walk and decisive eyes. But now she seemed fragile in his embrace, her head barely reaching his chin. As he rested his face on the parting of her hair, he noticed a small smudge of red. He dabbed at it, but Aunt drew away and seized his hand, peering at the faint vermilion stain on his fingertip. Her eyes were agitated.

'What! You got married without telling me?' Samorin teased.

Only married Hindu women wore vermilion in the parting of their hair. The widow frowned, covering her head with the loose end of her sari.

'Don't talk rubbish!' but her voice faltered. 'Must be the brickdust. The labourers were relaying the pavement of the kiln at the back.'

'You are still young,' Samorin bantered, 'and beautiful.'

Aunt frowned, but her mouth held back a smile. Samorin stepped up and drew her to him.

'I have come home, to be with you for a while,' he said.

She entwined her fingers in his, and he noticed how his broad, large hand made hers appear smaller than ever before. She smelled of clean crisp cotton and jasmine. There was a fragility to her that he had never observed before. She could not have been older than forty-five, but there was a timelessness in her dark eyes that puzzled Samorin. It was neither sorrow nor loss but their shadows, as if a mystery, both painful and happy, had settled there. Aunt moved with the lightness of a dancer. As he walked beside her through the large lanai that ran in arches along the house towards the wing that housed her quarters, he suddenly wanted to sit on the shaded portico under the awning and drink tea in dainty porcelain cups with her, the way they used to when he was a child. It was an old ritual of theirs. Whenever he came home on vacation, he would take tea with her on the balcony outside her bedroom in the evenings. The silver tea service would be placed on a lacquered Chinese tray covered by a white lacy cloth, the tiny spoon tinkling in the china as Aunt mixed the fragrant tea leaves with hot water. There would be plates heaped with *masala vadas* and *bondas*, and a side dish of *kozhakattas* – sweet dumplings filled with brown sugar and coconut.

'Taking me to tea, Aunt?' Samorin asked.

Aunt laughed, as if something had suddenly been let free within her. Her pace quickened. Samorin lifted her in his arms and her sari fell away from her head, hair uncoiling and falling loose over her shoulders, the surprise sparking across her eyes like a falling star – she drew a sudden breath and her breasts heaved. Samorin noticed the black *rudraksha* against her pale throat, slim and marked with faint wrinkles. A small pearl shone in her delicate pink ear lobe; Aunt gasped, cardamom edging her breath.

'Put me down, you silly boy!' she laughed, but her hand was across his shoulders.

'Oh no, you used to carry me when I was little,' he said, 'all the way from the steps to your room. It's my turn now.'

Smiling, she snuggled her cheek against his chest, her eyes closed. Samorin carried her through the shadows of the pillars that pulled away over them as they passed. His footsteps clapped on the tiled floor. Aunt hummed under her breath an old song, an ode to Krishna: '*Kani kanum neram Kamalanetrante . . .*'

The tune brought him back to a shore he had sailed away from a long time ago.

It is thus that we realize how far we have travelled, Samorin thought as he carried his graceful, beloved matriarch in his arms to the old ceremonial sanctuary. A small snatch of song, a phrase spoken by a stranger, a flash of light falling on a passing face can throw us back in time. There is no going back, but those are the signs of our lives. In them we recognize love, danger and death.

He set her down gently on the marbled floor of the portico, and Aunt looked up at him with wet cheeks and shining eyes.

'My son,' she whispered, drawing his head to her breast. 'You will always be home to me.'

They sat quietly side by side as the afternoon lengthened into the evening, watching the shadows of the *asoka* trees on the edge of the lawn travel across the darkening grass, where a few butterflies hovered. The sky was pale, with bolts of pink and purple as if a haberdasher had unfurled his wares in a hurry. The mountain wind that wandered down from the green hedges of the tea plantations, through the clusters of pine and rhododendron, carried· dragonflies whose wings glittered like crushed glass. The last of the tea had long gone cold, the *unniyappams* and *bajjis* consumed. Samorin lit a cigarette.

'I don't want to go back,' he said.

In the fading light, Aunt's smile was the smile of a seraph.

'We will see,' she said gently.

' "Pure-eyed Faith," ' Samorin quoted, ' "thou hovering angel girt with golden wings . . ." '

They heard a car grinding up through the drive and stopping in the gravelled courtyard. The engine grumbled, a door slammed, and the voices of servants could be heard.

'Must be Warden Madhavan Nair, I can recognize the rattle of his Landmaster car anywhere,' Aunt said with a slight frown. 'But he hadn't phoned he was coming.'

'Warden Madhavan Nair? Warden of what?'

'The jail, but he is retired now,' Aunt said hastily, 'he is an old family friend.'

Samorin saw a tall, thin man hurrying along the veranda towards them, accompanied by one of the servants. Aunt rose and gestured for the attendant to leave. Samorin drew up a white rattan chair for the visitor. The man looked at Samorin with a smile and suddenly froze; his eyes opened wide, his mouth parted slightly. Then he laughed.

'Jay?' he said, extending his hand, 'I am Madhavan. You look so much like your father. For a moment I thought Shekhar was here.'

'You knew my father?' Samorin asked quickly.

Aunt cleared her throat. With an uncharacteristically gay laugh, she asked Nair what the reason was for his pleasant but unexpected visit.

'I tried to phone, but couldn't get through,' he apologized. 'It's about Savita.'

'What about Savita?'

Nair's face crinkled in concern. 'Her baby arrived dead, strangled by the umbilical cord. Savita is in Emergency Care. We're going to have a lot of trouble over this.'

'I'm coming with you to the hospital,' Aunt said, turning to Samorin. 'Jay, please ask the driver to bring the car around.'

Madhavan Nair insisted they take his car instead.

'I'm coming, too,' Samorin said, 'if I may. Who is Savita?'

In the car, Aunt told him Savita's story. She had been widowed at twenty, her husband bitten by a cobra when he was out diverting irrigation to his rice paddy. She refused to sleep with her brother-in-law, who accused her of being a whore and threw her out of the house. Aunt had found her sleeping under the banyan tree of the Widow's Village, and had asked the women to take her in. There had been no room in any of the houses, except one – Kamala's.

'That was my first mistake,' Aunt said softly, 'letting her stay with Kamala. Then I hadn't known. That was my second mistake.'

Samorin was puzzled.

'Kamala?' he asked, feeling rather stupid. 'Who is she? What did she do?'

He saw that Aunt was upset. He took her small hand in his; it felt hot.

'Do you remember the mornings when you used to come with me to the Village of the Widows?' she asked.

He suddenly understood. The eyes in the gloom, a small gold band gleaming on one slim finger as the door closed . . .

114

'The last house!' Samorin exclaimed. 'Is that who she was, Kamala?'

'An old regret,' Aunt said.

'You are a strange one, Savitri,' Madhavan Nair's voice broke in, 'taking a child to the village.'

Aunt turned fiercely on him.

'It was my atonement, Warden,' she said sharply.

'Atonement for what?' Samorin asked.

'For my own life, my son,' she said in a gentle voice as her fingers brushed his cheek, transient and full of remorse. Samorin did not understand; he felt as though he had been thrust into the middle of a strange play, its characters enigmatic and faceless, their roles esoteric. He dimly sensed he had a role in it, too, but wasn't sure what that was to be or what his lines were. Suddenly he felt overcome by the mystery of the evening, and he turned towards the woman who was his greatest strength and ally, one who had sealed a bargain unbeknownst to him and for a price he would never know.

'I am a widow, but I was fortunate. First, to have a father like mine, and then to know someone like yours,' Aunt explained. 'But there were the other widows. I had to do something for them. They had no money, they were pariahs. Many of them were selling their bodies to feed their children. In the beginning, I used to take them food and clothes. Afterwards we became more organized. There were donations from friends, grants from the Government. But for some, like Kamala, it was charity and she hated that.'

'Tell me about Kamala,' Samorin said quietly.

It was Madhavan Nair who spoke. 'The first time I saw her was when I was still the jail warden. She was so young, and beautiful, but her beauty had a ferocity

115

to it that scared me. She walked around her cell, sniffing the air. At first I thought she was touched in the head.'

Kamala was pale-skinned with dark eyes, sharp white teeth glinting in her wide red mouth. Her hair was long and braided down to her hip and she wore a soiled white sari. The dirty imprint of a palm marked her blouse and when the warden looked at it, she laughed.

'The policemen,' she sneered, 'they think every woman is public property. But now they know better, one of them has no testicles left.'

Her left eye was bruised, the cheek below swollen.

The police had raided Kamala's house in the Village of the Widows and she was brought to court and charged with prostitution.

'You like me?' she had asked Warden Madhavan Nair, while peeling the *pallu* of her sari from her chest. He looked away.

'When my husband disappeared, I went to the police,' she said, 'and they only laughed at me. "What a piece of goods," they sneered, poking my breasts with their polished canes and pinching my bottom. "Don't worry. We shall all be your husbands one by one." And after we learned that my husband wasn't coming back, and his father had thrown me out of the house with my four-year-old son, the first one to visit me was the Circle Inspector . . .'

'But why did you go and live there? Couldn't you have gone to stay with your parents?' Nair had asked.

'They are dead,' she said stonily. 'Fortunately, I had a little money my husband had given me before he disappeared. I used it to buy a house so that I didn't have to live on the charity of the Samorins. Where else could I go except to the village of my sisters? How else could I have brought up my son?'

Kamala did not see herself as a whore, but as an avenging angel who wielded power over men who sought to buy her favours. She exploited the misfortune of the widows, selling their loneliness to strangers from the neighbouring cities of Coimbatore and Trichur: politicians, policemen, owners of factories and private businesses. Aunt had tried to stop it, which had earned her the wrath of the prostitute and some of her powerful friends.

'Kamala kept sniffing the air inside the jail,' Madhavan Nair remembered. 'She said she could smell her husband there.'

Aunt shivered, and squeezed Samorin's hand.

'I would always visit her and her son first,' Aunt said, 'and she would receive me so haughtily. But her boy would cling to my fingers the way you would, and when she was put in jail I took on the responsibility of caring for him.'

'But why?' Samorin asked. 'What was she to you?'

Aunt looked out of the window at the landscape speeding past the car.

'She was special,' she said with finality in her voice.

Much later, Samorin was to learn why, from the old newspaper archives that were housed in the dusty municipal library of the town, with its statue of Mahatma Gandhi upon a pedestal protected by scarlet gladioli in the middle of the courtyard. Truth Will Prevail, the plaque at his feet read. The high vault of the library ceiling was pierced by beams of sunlight coming in through the skylights. Motes of dust peppered the beams, ceiling fans hung down from long stems and whirled like antique propellers. There were rows of dark wooden benches and tables like church pews, with old files of the *Mathrubhumi* newspaper spread out in front . . .

The trial. His father . . .

Higher and higher, leaping into the smoky, sunlit heights of the library's ochre vault, lashing out at the cobwebs ribbing the sooty corners, scattering the pigeons gurgling on the cupola; soaring away through the shattering glass of the Gothic windows and passing the porcelain face of the clock on the tower; becoming a mere speck in the sky, riding the air with the hawks, until the figure swinging at the end of a rope inside the jail enclosure dwindled to invisibility . . . Higher and higher . . .

The trial . . .

Black and white photographs on fading yellow newsprint. He sees Kamala. Her dark eyes confront the photographer, lips tight and firm. Standing beside her is a tall dark man in a striped shirt.

'The alleged lover of the murdered Shyamala with his wife in court.' Samorin reads the caption.

Shyamala Samorin, his mother. And this man is her alleged lover!

He turns the pages, his gaze falling on the photograph of a tall man accompanied by policemen: Samorin sees his father, a bandage around his head, eyes bright, smile subtle. He touches the precious, unfamiliar face, feeling a phantom shock to his fingertip, spreading through his hand and arm, making his hair stand as if the wind had breathed into the grass.

Father of goodbyes, father of a trail of blood, father of a sorrow without a grail to drink from.

Father. Murderer.

Father looks out calmly from the grey of another

page and another time: he has Samorin's eyes. He holds his head like his son, chin tilted up as if he bore a famous title, a small smile unconsciously curled at the corners of his mouth under a chevalier's moustache. He is wearing a pilot's uniform, and Samorin idly wonders where the reporter had got hold of that particular picture. Next to him is a photograph of his mother, curly-eyed and full-lipped, with a small mole gracing her chin. Her resemblance to Aunt is very strong.

He feels nothing as he encounters his parents for the first time. He knows that he will, later, in his sleep, when his mind releases itself from the warrior's will and swims the dark river of dreams: the river that carries the corpses of the day, of the years, full of the detritus of that which constitutes the wasteland of any man's experience. He now understands why his aunt had insisted on the discipline of the *kalaripayattu*; being a warrior was in the mind first, and life was a battlefield. For him, especially, with his hidden legacy of death and shame, she had realized that a day would come when he would have to open old, closed doors.

'Squadron Leader Shekhar Samorin arrested for the murder of his wife Shyamala.' Samorin read the report. 'Found unconscious on the floor with his rifle beside him . . . it is clear that he shot his wife first and then turned the gun on himself. But the bullet only grazed his temple, rendering him senseless . . .'

The report was in florid Malayalam, in the dramatic style crime reporters of the time preferred. And the case had all the signs of local notoriety: the accused was an aristocrat and young. He was also a native, with many privileged friends. Besides that he was a

119

war hero – a fighter pilot who had fought in the 1974 India–Pakistan war, taken part in the famous battle in the Western Sector where Indian planes had turned the churning sands of Rajasthan into a graveyard for Pakistani tanks. He had married his childhood sweetheart, Shyamala. His own estates bordered those of his wife's, rich in cardamom and cloves, with row upon row of teak and coconut trees flourishing along the border of Spicewater Lake. He had taken early retirement after his father-in-law, the barrister, had died, and now lived with his wife and son, and his widowed sister-in-law. He had returned from his club early after a game of bridge, in which he was beginning to win modestly, was interrupted when his partner was suddenly called away. He had plucked a rose from a hedge on the way home and entered his bedroom from the outer door to surprise his wife with his early return. She normally read or listened to Vividh Bharati on the radio while waiting for him, but this time, when he tried the door, he found it locked.

In his deposition, he said that he had called out for his wife and knocked on the door, but she hadn't responded. He finally used his spare key to open the door, only to find his wife on the bed, a sheet pulled up to her chin, naked and terrified. A man had been hiding by the window behind the curtains, and was trying to climb out. The pilot had yelled at him, and the intruder had turned, grabbed a rifle on the wall and fired. After that, Samorin's father said he remembered nothing.

The prosecution had turned it into a case of murder for greed, alleging that there was no lover, that he had murdered his wife for money, for her estates.

It was then that the defence sprang a surprise.

They produced as their star witness the victim's sister, the widowed Savitri. She testified that she had seen a man fleeing the grounds the night of the murder. The sound of shots had awoken her, and on her way down she had to pass the great staircase window, which looked out into the grounds. She saw the figure of a man running, disappearing into the trees. A half-moon lit up the night, bright enough to identify him as Sivadas, a man who used to visit her sister often. Once she had caught them embracing in the park, and her sister had pleaded with her to keep it a secret from her husband, pledging that she would never do it again. Sivadas was produced in court, but his wife, Kamala, swore under oath that he was with her that night.

'My husband is loyal to me and loves our son,' Kamala was quoted as saying in a newspaper article. A journalist had asked her if she believed her husband had had an affair with the murdered woman. But in the photograph that accompanied the article, Sivadas was looking away from the camera.

The defence offered a plea, saying the accused had acted in a fit of jealousy, and the killing was a crime of passion. His war record was produced, his university degrees, his varsity cricket trophies, the fact that he had a young child who would grow up an orphan.

But the verdict was murder. The sentence: Shekhar Samorin was to be hanged by the neck until dead for the wilful murder of his wife.

They had appealed to the Kerala High Court but had been turned down.

In the top left of another front page was a photograph of his father. 'Squadron Leader Shekhar Samorin was hanged yesterday at 5.30 a.m. The body was turned over to his closest relatives by the jail warden, Madhavan Nair. The cremation will be private, held within the grounds of the family estates.'

The Hindustan Landmaster had slowed down, and was turning through the yellow gates of the Government Hospital. Giant fans of tamarind trees hooded the facade of the building. A single neon light illuminated the front entrance. Samorin followed Aunt and Madhavan Nair into the reception and asked for the doctor.

'Oh, the good Samaritans are here,' a sarcastic voice rasped from the shadows. What Samorin glimpsed at first was a gigantic mound, wrapped in white. He had never seen anyone so utterly gross: a huge woman sat on a bench in the shadow of the stairs. She resembled a gargantuan toad, her neck disappearing into folds of glistening, sweaty flesh, her arms bloated and dappled, her great bosom wrapped in a white silk sari. Malevolent eyes stared out of a face that had lost all its shape. She caught his glance, and frowned. Then she started shaking, her entire body heaving and quivering silently. Samorin realized she was laughing.

'The murderer's son,' she giggled, pointing a swollen, beringed finger at him. 'So you have brought him out at last, Savitri.'

Aunt put out a restraining hand, but Samorin stood immobile, dumb with shock.

'Go,' the woman said, in a wheezing, gulping voice. 'Get out of my sight. Leave my poor girl alone.'

'Kamala, leave my nephew out of this,' Aunt spoke

firmly. 'Savita needs help, her baby is dead. She herself . . .'

'I am all the help she needs,' the gross shape hissed. 'We whores stick together. Ask the duty nurse for her admission papers. You will find that I am her guardian.'

'I am going to court first thing in the morning,' Aunt said grimly. 'I can't leave her to you. How many more abortions, miscarriages? The child will be dead.'

A whip of a noise lashed out from the gloom, a laugh so full of contempt that it made Samorin cringe.

'The courts! Bah! Haven't we met in court before, and weren't you satisfied enough? And you, Warden Madhavan, being such a do-gooder after lording it over the unfortunate wretches for years; wasn't it you who hanged the boy's father? And now, look at you toadying up to the Samorins!'

Samorin turned and walked swiftly out into a night of chirruping crickets. The wind was harsh in the trees, and a pale moon bled into the dark. Aunt's footsteps followed him, and he heard her cry out his name as he passed the tattooed light into the shadows. His pace quickened as he passed the gates and entered the shade of a great banyan tree. Suddenly he jumped aside to avoid a car that came screeching around the bend in the road on its way to the hospital. The headlights blinded him and he threw up one arm to cover his eyes. As the vehicle passed he lowered his hand, and saw the brief, fleeting silhouette of the man behind the wheel.

The driver looked familiar.

Only much later, returning home after hours of

wandering through the night, hunting his ever-changing shadow until weariness made his muscles scream, did he pause on the smooth, moonlit steps of the house and realize that the man driving the car was his old schoolmate Dhiren Das.

CHAPTER SEVEN

The next evening, Samorin played chess with Tsiranana and lost all three games.

'You are losing your touch, maestro,' the Malagasy said. 'Is there something on your mind?'

'Have you known Dhiren Das for a long time?' Samorin asked.

The diplomat's face tightened imperceptibly. Then he smiled.

'A great painter,' he said. 'But I gather you don't like him.'

'Why do you say that?'

'Ah, we chess players know things. I saw you together at the exhibition yesterday and your body language gave you away.' Tsiranana looked at his watch. 'The charming policewoman is meeting me at six, she wants some papers concerning Radama's unfortunate death. Wrapping it up, she said.'

Samorin got up to leave. Tsiranana waved him down.

'Please stay. I think you and she get along well together.'

Anna was on time, and gave Samorin a brief hug. She refused the diplomat's offer of a drink. Samorin sensed a nervous agitation in her; her fingers were restless, playing with her clothes and hair, and her brow was furrowed. When Tsiranana excused himself and left the room to get the papers, she turned to Samorin and said, 'I want to speak to you about something.'

They left together, and Samorin asked her to drive with him. The Jeep swung out of the parking lot and on to Shantipath, its fat tyres screeching. A dilapidated bus, coughing black soot, was rumbling along ahead in the fast lane. Its rear had been mangled in an accident, one of its panels ripped open and clattering against the tin sides. The rear windows were cracked and held together with adhesive tape. Delhi's urban sculpture, Anna thought, as Samorin honked and swung sharply to the left. She grabbed the dashboard to steady herself, glancing in the passenger-door mirror at her white official Ambassador car following behind. The faces of passengers turned as Samorin overtook them: dark blurs framed within grimy windows. The bus driver was a middle-aged Sikh who was hunched over the wheel, a figure in khaki wearing a spangled green turban.

'That was a bit of a savage exit,' she said softly, 'and I'm sorry about yesterday. And glad, too.'

'About what?'

'Sorry that you were upset about something. And glad that we talked.'

Samorin shifted uneasily in his seat and did not say

anything. He knew Dhiren Das, Anna was certain, and she guessed that it was not an acquaintance that gave him pleasure. Yet her policewoman's instinct told her it was not a good time to ask, even though what she felt was much more than the curiosity of the habitual enquirer. The recollection of Samorin's expression when Dhiren had spoken to him made her feel uneasy. That a man who styled himself as an unflappable virtuoso of the dark could be so unsettled by the painter.

'Where would you like to go?' Samorin asked.

She looked at him, studying the sharp profile against the speeding rectangle of the Jeep's window. Black hair with a single white streak swept back from his smooth forehead. A small scar on one of his high cheekbones, just under the left eye, gave him the appearance of a warrior, while the light of the early evening lent his skin a golden lustre. She noticed that his nose was beaked like that of a predatory bird and his fine nostrils flared slightly. His lips curved slightly down at the corners, giving his mouth a stern expression above the strong lines of a clean-shaven jaw. His long fingers rested lightly on the steering wheel. Sensing her scrutiny, Samorin turned towards Anna and smiled.

The sky was plumed with the colours of the evening, blue and puce, interrupted by flocks of home-flying birds. New Delhi was green and manicured around them. Butterflies fluttered on the grass like fragments of torn letters. The traffic islands at the junctions of roads were laden with chrysanthemum and gladioli, the purple bougainvillea hedges darkening with early shadows. She imagined the air around the rose gardens sweet and heady, a perfumed sunlight softened with the breath of leaves and petals. She could see lovers lingering there in the drunken air, tarrying in a parting intoxicated with flowers. Anna felt faintly embarrassed. She cleared her throat.

'I had wanted to speak to you about something,' she said, 'but I wonder if I should.'

'Murder or art, Commissioner?' Samorin's voice was woody and low, holding a cautious laugh that put Anna at ease.

'Aren't both the same at times?' she asked.

She liked the sound of his laugh. A little like Irfan's, low and controlled. Suddenly she missed Irfan, his scent, the way his fingers clasped her waist, the taste of his mouth.

'You are suddenly quiet, Anna,' Samorin said.

It was the first time she had heard him speak her name, and it made her feel uncomfortable. As if she welcomed the strange intimacy of its sound shaped by his voice, her name arising from deep inside him, sculpted by the muscles in his neck and baptized in the hum of his blood, wet with his saliva as it winged through his throat, ascending from the lifebreath of his lungs. It was like a spell that knocked on her heart, making her breathless and drunk. She suddenly wanted to ask him to stop the car; she needed to get out and run.

'Am I?' she asked, her voice unnecessarily sharp. 'I was puzzled about something. But I don't see what you have to do with it.'

'You are the one who asked, remember?'

'I'm sorry, I shouldn't have. Stop the car, I would like to go home now.'

Samorin reached across the gearshift and covered her hand with his. Instead of angering her, his touch calmed her suddenly. This surprised her. His palm was dry and firm.

'Whatever it is, Anna, happiness is not always planned. Mostly it comes by accident, like good friendships.'

Anna laughed, surprising herself with the bitterness of the sound.

'Happiness is not very important to me,' she said.

'What is, then?'

You are, she wanted to say, the epiphany of it startling her like a sudden rush of river water. You are important, with your severe mouth and restless fingers, with your oblique mind and strange obsession. We are both travellers of evil, templars who fight best alone, and win because we are lonely and do not guard any vulnerable treasure. I saw your eyes when Dhiren Das spoke to you, and what flew across the calm glass of your face was a dark and malignant hawk, its reflection traducing your heart. I have also felt thus, and I have cried unwitnessed and silent, my imagination a mausoleum and my will, steel without a heart.

'Happiness may not be important, Anna, but the lack of it often is.'

Anna slumped against the back of the seat, and watched the dusk being erased by the city's lights.

'I live far away from Delhi,' he said. 'But if you like, you could come home and have dinner with me. We could open a bottle of Château Margaux and eat some curried shrimp and *aviyal*. And you could talk to me about what is puzzling you.'

Anna's fists clenched, aware of the grip of her gun pressing against her breast. Then she let out her breath.

They had reached the outskirts of Gurgaon, where

129

one periphery of lights ended and another began. Samorin reduced speed while groves of eucalyptus and jamun trees hauled their nets of shadows across their route, the humpbacked clusters of bush on either side outlining the uneven, stony countryside. Delhi had spread its wings into Gurgaon: they passed a tiny Italian restaurant displaying a huge, illuminated cut-out of Marilyn Monroe on its roof, her red dress blowing against long legs in the hot suburban wind. Her crimson lips were parted into the night. Elsewhere baroque cherubs on white marble pilasters gleamed in windows advertising garden furniture, Reebok and Nike shops offered factory discounts.

'Never seen anything so bastardized,' Anna said. 'Delhi's suburbs!'

Samorin chuckled under his breath.

'I grew up in the mountains,' Anna continued, 'in Landour. When they left India, the British sold their mountain homes cheaply to Indians. We had a lovely Welsh cottage called St Asaph's. From there, on a clear day, you could see as far as China. The snow on the Himalayas shimmered like satin in the sun.'

'Do you still have family there now?'

Anna nodded. 'Dad potters about the garden a lot in summer. Mum is buried close by.'

Samorin only had a vague memory of Landour, the sister town of Mussoorie, in the Himalayan foothills. But he knew the Landour cemetery where the dead slept along ancient terraces cut into the hillside. Samorin remembered the Tibetan mastiff he had once seen prowling among graves which dated back to the 1800s: stone angels on crypts, cracked marble sepulchres, lids askew on baby tombs. The Mussoorie wind climbed up the valley, whistling through the

130

pine forests, wet with the ghost spray of the dead Doon river whose phantom route still escorted the road, a whitened track of sand and stone. The earth wore a deep cassock of shade, and pine cones lay among those graves like desultory memories.

When a British officer, who had set out on a hunt two centuries ago, became homesick in Mussoorie, he decided to build a cottage there and call it Mallingar after his home in Scotland. The village was called Mansoori, after the tiny *mansoor* flower that grew on hillsides thick with fir and rhododendron. Iris bloomed on the slopes and white daisies floated on invisible stems above the grass. It grew to become a favourite retreat for the denizens of the Empire who ruled India at that time and were escaping the terrible heat of the summer in the plains. They liked to promenade along its mall and hold gala balls at the sprawling Savoy Hotel. A brewery was built for the soldiers who had set up the barracks in Mussoorie, and later a picture palace for entertainment and a church to save their summer-weary souls.

After Independence, the hill station of Mussoorie became an inexpensive tourist haven. Its haughty sister Landour turned away those noisy would-be visitors with their blaring Hindi film music from their car stereos, who littered the slopes with empty wafer packets and *parantha* wrappings. Samorin remembered strolling with Maya down the meandering road that hugged Landour's hills; it seemed that sleep itself slept there, among the dark, grassy slopes on which pines stood guard.

'I grew up in the mountains, too,' Samorin said, 'with Aunt.'

'Did your parents die early?' Anna asked.

131

Samorin did not reply immediately, and Anna realized that he had suddenly withdrawn into himself.

'Yes. They did.' His voice was curt, discouraging.

'Did you go looking for pine cones in the hills?' she asked with a sudden cheerfulness, changing the topic. 'Irfan and I used to . . .'

She stopped suddenly, the dead name falling from her lips as if from an ambush. She felt a locust swarm in her eyes and mouth, memories of fierce joys, sharp pain and anger, always anger.

'Irfan?'

Anna lit a cigarette.

'A loss.' Samorin said, 'Irfan?'

'He was my husband,' Anna said softly. 'We'd known each other for ever, we even went to school together.'

The night was thinning with a sourceless light, and the purple shadows of overhead trees danced by like harlequins on the waxed bonnet of the Jeep. They had left behind the little clusters of wayside shops and restaurants, and were now climbing up into the rangy, open land the army used for night marches and mock patrols. The road was now empty, apart from Anna's white Ambassador faithfully following behind.

'No,' said Samorin.

'No what?'

'There were no pine cones where I grew up,' he said, thinking of the large and venerable trees in the foothills of the Western Ghats. The walks were narrow and soft with fallen leaves, and the bramble fences bright with spicy scented flowers. The tea gardens scented the wind with a subtle flavour that was both young and heady.

'If you drove up from my ancestral home to Ooty

132

and Wellington, you could find pine or cypress, though not as easily as you would find in Mussoorie,' Samorin said. 'Aunt had a summer cottage there. We'd usually stay for a couple of weeks when it got too hot in the valley. The place is very much like Landour, a colonial relic . . . ah, we're almost home.'

'You are really far away from Delhi,' Anna said.

'One can never live too far away from Delhi,' Samorin laughed, 'the third most polluted city in the world.'

They turned onto the small track that curved into the darkness between two gigantic banyan trees. The Jeep's headlamps lit up their gnarled, entwined roots hanging down from the darkness above. Like brown snakes mating, Anna thought with a shudder, remembering the clean tall conifers of her childhood. For an instant, the headlights reflected on golden eyes shining from among the darkness of the leaves above, a copper daub gleaming along black, curved branches, a Cheshire cat's shimmering grin that was extinguished as the car passed. Anna craned her neck back, upward into the night that crouched among the leaves, and thought she saw a shape moving swiftly through the trees. A panther? A big cat?

Samorin parked in the quadrangle, and Anna got out. The huge glass facade of the house greeted her like the illusion of a galaxy, and she gasped, seeing reflected the distant lights of Delhi and the stars in the night sky. Servants came out discreetly to greet them and Samorin instructed them to look after Anna's driver, who had just pulled in behind them. He led her through the hall that was lit with immense crystal chandeliers; a Hussain horse hung on the black granite wall that stood opposite the transparency of the glass facade. A door opened into a smaller room over-looking the countryside. The room had been built around a massive oak tree, creating an illusion of touching the sky, the foliage blending with the stars. The ceiling, too, was made of glass. A cushioned swing-chair was suspended from one of the great oak's branches. Shelves had been carved into the trunk and were stocked with liquor. Samorin took a bottle of Talisker and offered Anna a drink. She smiled and accepted the glass, and settled down on the swing-chair.

'I haven't had a drink in a long time,' she said softly.

Something moved in the shadows outside. As the white linen curtains billowed through the open glass door, a long form padded in from the darkness. Anna gasped, her hand going for the gun at her left breast. Samorin raised his hand.

'It's only Sasha,' he whispered as the big cat came in. It looked around the room, golden eyes widening in the sudden light, and growled softly at Anna. Samorin put his arms around its dark fur and scratched its chin, but it gazed unwaveringly at Anna.

'What is it? A panther?' she asked uneasily.

She took in the maroon fur streamed with sable highlights and the creamy blaze of its underbelly. As Samorin quietened the great cat, it winked its whisky-coloured eyes, lynx-like in their intensity. Its forehead was flatter than that of a panther or a leopard, its body low-slung like a giant mongoose's. Its paws were as big as paddles and its powerful-looking tail was dis-proportionately long.

'Sasha is a fosa, or a *Cryptoprocta ferox* if you prefer the Latin name,' Samorin said. 'The deadliest carnivore in the world. She weighs only fifteen pounds and measures just fifty-six inches from head to tail; capable of explosive speed, with no delicacy reserved during attacks launched face first, front claws slashing the stomach and eviscerating her victim like a feline Jack the Ripper, puncturing the cranium and crushing the jawline in one go. A great pet to have.'

'That thing is a . . . pet?'

'My pet,' said Samorin with a laugh, 'though a fosa being anyone's pet is unheard of. In fact, fosas themselves are rarely heard of.'

He caressed the cat's furry spine, causing her to roll over and expose a white belly.

'Where did you get her from?' Anna asked, her voice hushed.

'A gift from Ambassador Tsiranana,' Samorin answered. 'The Ambassador is an old friend. He and I met at Oxford where we both were reading History. A few years ago we were on safari together in Madagascar. In the Ampijoroa forest we came upon a fosa in a losing battle with lemurs, outnumbered twenty to one, which is rare because usually lemurs are no match for this cat. We shot a few and the rest ran, but by the time the wardens arrived and we could get her medical help, the fosa was dead. But she'd left her cub behind. Sasha was nothing but a small, snarling, spitting bundle of fur, but when I took it in my arms, it quietened suddenly.'

Anna looked at Samorin's hand stroking the cat's fur: the hand of a warrior. The elegant fingers were so different from Irfan's, which were short, stubby, dexterous, but there was similarity in the way they moved, as if barely touching surfaces they passed, yet sure and strong. The cat began to purr softly. Anna looked at this strange man with his outlandish pet, kneeling on a rug in the middle of a pagan room where a tree grew through a roof into a bejewelled sky, with city lights glimmering through the thin, restless night mist.

'What are you, Samorin?' she asked, curious, in spite of herself.

Samorin looked up and his eyes were those of a kestrel, guarded, hooded.

'A man interested in evil, who calls himself a student of murder, a dilettante of crime,' Anna continued, her voice low, edgily amused. 'What did you do for Tsiranana for him to give such a rare creature to you?'

'Oh, it was a small favour for his government. Nothing as mundane or ugly as Zafy's murder.'

'It was abnormal, the way you saw the murder in your mind. Almost as if you had done it yourself.'

'Read Chesterton's *Adventures of Father Brown*. That gentle Catholic priest becomes a murderer in his own mind each time evil is committed.'

'Do you, too, then become the murderer?' Anna asked.

'Worse, I become death's darkest angel,' Samorin said, his voice twisted with a sudden, fierce pain. 'I empathize with evil. I become its dark landscape, its bloody rivers flow through me, feeding the carnivorous vegetation. And, within myself, I set a trap for the serpent.'

'I do not know anyone who talks like you,' Anna said, 'it's very melodramatic.'

Samorin laughed and got up. He walked over to the bar and downed his drink in one gulp.

'Evil is melodramatic. And life, evil's camouflage, is so mundane.'

'Life, or death?'

'Oh, death is just a means to an end where evil is concerned.'

'And what is the end?'

'The human soul, Anna. Evil wants to fashion the human soul after its own form. And the irony is, of course, that it has no form of its own. That is why evil is so difficult to recognize.'

Anna clenched her eyes shut, remembering Irfan's violated face, the sightless eyes. The beloved lips a grimace of caked blood and dust and unbearable pain.

'I have seen it. Once.'

'Then what did you do?'

'I spread its seed,' she said harshly. 'The look that I saw on my husband's mutilated face, I wanted to repeat it, to paint it everywhere. On the faces of children, old men and women. And I did, as much as I could. But I could never get it quite right.'

Anna's shoulders shook as she remembered. Patrolling the deserted streets of Srinagar, Baramullah, Sopore, picking up men running from her armoured vehicle bristling with machine guns. Sometimes she shot them without thought – a simple reflex, trying to exorcize the memory of Irfan's dead face. She needed to be able to see him again as lay sleeping beside her, the white moonlight streaming through the winter-frosted window of their bedroom. She would kick wailing mothers aside while storming into hideouts and dragging out surly men, executing them with a pistol-shot to the temple. She would walk down the empty, narrow *galis* of the town, always keeping to the middle of the road so that her men could draw courage from her, even though they kept to the shadowy sides of verandas in the anticipation of an ambush or a burst from a terrorist's sub-machine gun. Oh yes, she tempted death bitterly, she mocked it.

'You know, sometimes they shot a cop and left him for us to find, having booby-trapped the body,' Anna said, 'and whoever went to it would get blown up, killed or maimed. But I was never afraid, I just didn't care. I would lift the corpse and drag it away from a crossroad or a street corner so that traffic could resume.'

'Evil is not interested in death, it is just a by-product,' Samorin said. 'It is life that evil feeds on.'

Anna's forehead was lined in thought, and then she gave a small crooked smile.

'Perhaps you are right,' she said, 'and if so, then you are just the person I need to consult.'

'About what?'

'Death,' she said.

The fosa lifted its head and stared at Anna, its amber gaze steady. She fancied she saw primordial instincts trapped inside those eyes, like prehistoric insects humming around ancient corpses millions of years ago.

'I want to talk to you about someone named Salma. I'm worried about her.'

'Who is this Salma?'

'She is both a friend and the sister of my dead husband, Irfan. She is convinced that her doctor is murdering her mother. By making her sick with leukaemia. And that she will be next.'

A quiet knock on the door interrupted her, and a servant came in to announce dinner. At first they ate in silence. Samorin noticed that Anna seemed distracted, merely picking at her food.

'Look, I can't prove anything,' she said, laying her

fork down beside the unfinished remains of *pilaf* and *aviyal*. 'Salma's mother fell ill last week. Her doctor is a Dr Dubey and the old lady is fanatically attached to him. She was widowed when she was young, and her son Irfan was her most prized jewel. After he died, she became a ghost, aimless, vacant and lost. At least I had a purpose.' Her mouth shivered in a small grimace.

Samorin nodded.

'She met Dr Dubey at a party in Dhiren Das's house. The doctor runs a shelter for widows in Brindaban, and is the head of a voluntary organization called Aasha. Das also has his studio retreat in Brindaban; perhaps he finds inspiration there as it is the birthplace of the god Krishna.'

Samorin remembered Das's Krishna paintings – a succession of canvases with the blue god dancing in the company of his *gopis*, his beloved cowgirls who were all clad in white. In the tradition of widows the women's heads were shaved, and they wore no ornaments. Critics had hailed them as masterpieces of absolute compassion – a vision of a god who never abandoned the women who loved him, those who were abandoned by their own.

'Dhiren Das again,' Samorin said softly. 'My thumbs prick. But what does he have to do with the doctor?'

'Nothing, except that the doctor is his neighbour and a patron. He must be one of Das's biggest buyers. Both his house and practice are full of Das's sculpture and paintings. Dr Dubey specializes in leukaemia. And a lot of his patients die of it.'

Samorin lit a cigarette and poured himself some more Cabernet Sauvignon. Anna refused.

'The brides of Krishna,' he said, leaning back in his chair.

'Yes, the brides of Krishna. And the good doctor also runs a huge shelter for widows, which is funded by Western agencies. A shelter where Irfan's mother spends most of her time working, with the widows. Salma fears that her mother is going to leave all her money to Aasha, after she dies.'

'It bothers her . . .'

'Of course it does, especially when she is convinced that her mother is being slowly murdered. But how can a doctor give someone cancer? It's not that he is feeding her radioactive *dhoklas* or something.'

'Sounds a bit far-fetched. But wasn't there a prostitution scandal recently involving the widow shelters in Brindaban?' Samorin asked.

Anna gave a curt laugh.

'Nothing new about it, widows have always been vulnerable to organized prostitution in this country,' she said. 'God knows, we've busted enough rackets. Certainly in Kashmir, they were easy pickings for the Afghan and Pakistani mercenaries. Your husband gets shot by the army or the police, and you get raped by the guerrillas and . . .' Anna spoke bitterly, shrugging.

'Kashmir is a war zone. But even in the rest of the country there have been enough scandals.'

'True. The Government gives funding to such widow shelters. Local politicians and the home wardens appropriate most of the money and then pimp the women to town officials and police chiefs for favours. And of course the widows cannot go back home because they are considered pariahs and are believed to bring bad luck!' Anna laughed derisively. 'Bad luck, indeed! It goes without saying that their property has already been taken over by relatives. It's just part of the Great Indian Middle-Class Saga. Newspapers write about it for a week, there is lots of editorial outrage, and then another scandal somewhere — someone bribes someone and is caught on a spycam, Pakistan fires a few shells across the border, Parliament gets engrossed, and it's back to business as usual.'

'Rather cynical for someone of your age,' Samorin said. Anna looked up, quick to take offence, but lapsed into a bleak smile when she saw the compassion in his eyes.

'I have been to Brindaban,' Samorin said. 'It's a place that reeks of both myth and misery. Those narrow, dark streets and the temple courtyards with their crumbling wooden balconies, from where Krishna is brought out on a palanquin in all his smiling finery for everyone to see. And then there are the widows allowed to shelter in the shop verandas in return for sex with the shopkeeper or with the beat constable or even with the local thug.'

The brides of God, the damned wives of divinity, Samorin thought.

And the Hare Krishna Temple, rising up like a flaw-less alabaster edifice of faith, with its cluster of Western devotees bearing burlesque names like Paramapadmananda and Neelalohitananada, whose smiles were gentle and eyes fierce. They came in search of a blue-skinned god with a playful smile and a canary-yellow sarong, who played his flute in pastoral serenity, in a garden fed by a river so mythical and powerful that serpents as tall as heaven lived in its waters, and beautiful doe-eyed damsels smelling of herbs and butter danced amorously to the summoning will of his lute. The tragic idyll of Brindaban, a paradise of perpetual green leaves and fragrant pastures beside the humming flow of the great river

Yamuna, where Krishna's true love, Radha, died forsaken after he became a warrior in the violent, complex art of battling evil. But for those with the shaved heads and lilted accents, who came in search of Krishna from as far away as Wisconsin and Stuttgart, the holy life derived its meaning from white linen and wooden sandals. They chanted the *Gita* in mid-Western accents or guttural syllables, and rode rickshaws pulled by sweaty, dark men who slept in the slum clusters by dirty *nullahs*. Brindaban, the Eden of complexity.

'Salma is having a lunch for her mother at the Imperial Hotel this weekend,' Anna said, 'and the doctor is always a favoured guest. Dhiren Das may well be there, too.'

She paused and glanced at Samorin. His face gave away nothing.

'I can arrange an invitation for you,' she continued. 'Would you come?'

The policewoman left a short time later. As the tail lights of her car diminished into distant red fireflies in the endless carbon of the night, Samorin thought about her moment of departure. She had leaned out of the car window, touched his hand briefly, and asked in that by now familiar voice that reminded him of freshly opened red wine in the summer sun, 'What was it that Dhiren Das wanted you to ask your aunt about?'

CHAPTER EIGHT

Anna phoned Samorin at home to ask whether the invitation to Salma's lunch had reached him. It had.

'Maybe we could go together,' she said, 'if it would make you more comfortable.'

Anna lived in a government apartment in Moti Bagh, and the armed guard in his green wooden sentry box at the gate made Samorin wait until he had phoned inside. Jay Samorin parked his Jeep and walked in, along a small gravel path that skirted a thick bank of lawn. Rows of roses, marigolds and daisies were planted along the edges of the compound, skirting the wall, separated from the lawn by a border of bricks, their teeth set diagonally in the ground. The air was mild and fragrant.

Anna met Samorin at the entrance, a thin golden bangle gleaming on her arm as she held the door open for him to come in. Her wrist was slim, and Samorin noticed the faint blue of a vein beneath the skin. The thought came to him that Dhiren Das would have loved to paint her hand. It was perfectly shaped, with slender fingers, the mounds full and well formed, nails pink and cared for. He felt a small stab of jealousy and frowned it away.

He imagined her hands on his chest, running up against the hair and muscle, her fingers drawing tiny, tight circles on his skin.

As he passed her and she stepped aside to let him in, her hand moved away from the door in a floral gesture like a dancer's, the wrist swaying away, the bangle sliding down – the nearness of her momentarily intoxicated him. Then he remembered all the blood on that one slim hand, the blood of reprisals and executions. He felt her breath on his face as she stepped back, a hint of cloves, and her black, fragrant hair brushed his arm like a passing shower. He was inside a cool drawing room with heavy curtains drawn and lamps turned on low inside their huge shades. She closed the door behind them and Samorin lightly touched her shoulders and kissed her on the cheek. Anna smiled up at him.

She wore a white linen sari with a gold border and a Poonam Bhagat brocade vest in an attempt to hide her shoulder holster. She caught Samorin's look and shrugged.

'I'm not going to be caught unarmed ever,' she said defensively, 'like Irfan was. He had been out on a jog when his killers caught him.'

It was the first time she had talked to him about her dead husband, and Samorin did not respond. He walked over to the black leather beanbag beside a silk Kashmiri carpet. He was wearing black jeans, boots and an ivory-coloured short-sleeved shirt with a Chinese collar.

'Learnt the trick from Sasha,' he said, sitting down. 'Make yourself comfortable wherever you are.'

Anna laughed, the narrowing of her eyes indicating she didn't quite believe him.

'Will you have a drink?'

Samorin chose a vodka Martini, and Anna poured herself a Heineken.The lamplight shone on the gold *zari* of her sari border and on the length of her bare arm. Samorin noticed the faint down on her skin, a copper sheen, and wondered idly how it would feel to touch it.

'This is the first time someone's come over in years,' she said.

Samorin bowed down from where he sat. Upon a walnut table lit by the arc of the lamp beneath its shade, he could see a framed snapshot of Anna with a handsome man in a turtleneck sweater. The man's arms were encircling her, holding her from behind, chin on her shoulder, eyes laughing. It was a black and white shot which seemed to have been taken in the dappled shade of trees, the trellis of shadows blurring the background. The man had very black, very curly hair and a well-trimmed moustache. Anna looked strangely shy in his embrace, but her smiling eyes were proud and content.

'You photograph well,' Samorin said.

'Kashmir,' Anna said with a sudden sharpness. 'Taken a few days before Irfan died. The paradise of deception. Idyllic, calm and beautiful, but hiding so much horror!'

Above, to the left of the photograph, upon the wall hung a painting of Krishna in blue jeans and a yellow scarf, playing the lute into a night where the golden coin of a full moon hung over a sleeping city, its verge smoking with cloud. The crown on the god's head was slightly askew, revealing stray locks blowing in the wind, and the peacock feather on it glowed with iridescent colours. A river flowed between him and the city, a river with the face of a serpent, yet a river. Samorin recognized Dhiren Das's signature style.

'You like Mr Das a lot, I see,' Samorin observed, changing the topic.

'But you don't. Can I ask why?' Anna said softly.

Samorin's eyes were hooded against her interrogation. He sensed her curiosity about him and the underlying attraction he held for her. At the same time he was aware of her slyness, the cunning of an habitual examiner who knew the tortuous back alleys of the mind. He finished his drink and stood up.

'Perhaps we should go,' he said.

'Without giving me an answer?'

Anna was also standing up, and Samorin went over to her. Her eyes looked suddenly witchlike, black and deep, spangled with golden dust. Samorin noticed one stray silver hair above her temple. As he reached out to smooth it, she took an involuntary step back and her lower lip quivered.

'How many answers do you want, Anna?'

The spell was broken. She laughed, almost a girl's giggle. 'Isn't that what the police always need – answers?'

Samorin took Anna's hand and led her to the door. He could feel the slight tension in her, resisting his touch.

'Let's drive,' he said. 'I'll tell you on the way.'

The October air was sharp and cool, and wings of

flower beds brimmed over the edges of the little traffic islands that connected intersections. Fountains changed shape in the wind, swells of water rose up against a pale Delhi sky, and the trimmed green hedges along the road were patch-coloured with bougainvillea. The sidewalks were carpeted with violet blossoms. A man in a Nike sweatshirt jogged along in the company of a golden retriever, which stopped periodically to investigate interesting nooks and crevices. In the grassy quadrangles of housing blocks, children played badminton and cricket. A cluster of dishevelled crows bathed in the careless, swinging spray of a garden sprinkler. A roadside barber had set his chair under a tree and nailed a mirror onto the trunk. He sat leaning back against it, reading a newspaper and smoking a *beedi*. A red striped towel was slung over one shoulder. Samorin glimpsed their Scorpio passing in the barber's mirror, and a snatch of a Hindi song hung briefly in the air.

Kabhi tho nazar milaa lo, kabhi tho kareeb aao,
Jo nahin kahaaa tha, kabhi tho samajh jaao . . .

When will you meet my gaze or come near? Why don't you understand what the unspoken means?

'He was much younger then. And he didn't have a beard.'

'Who?' Anna asked, unnecessarily checking her lipstick in the sunshade mirror of the Scorpio.

'Dhiren. Weren't you asking me about him?'

'Oh, Dhiren Das,' she said with a self-conscious laugh. 'I didn't think you were going to tell me anything.'

'He was much younger,' Samorin repeated.

'Tell me from the beginning,' Anna said, laying her hand on the dark denim of his thigh. Samorin covered

147

her hand with his, and this time she did not remove it.

'The beginning was such a long time ago, Anna. The beginning was in the mist and sleep-heavy hours, full of shadows and whispers, something primeval. But let us start from when I found his cat traps in school, and he taunted me about my father.'

'Pull over, Jay,' Anna said, 'and talk to me.'

Samorin parked under a huge *gulmohur* tree, its shadow covering him like a memory interwoven with sun and shadow. As he talked, the *gulmohur*'s heavy flowers occasionally fell on the roof of the car. A crow cried, and for a long time afterwards he would always associate the sound of falling flowers with the beginning of his relationship with Anna.

Through the striped sunlight on the lawn, with the mountain wind hoarse in the valleys behind, the boy ran towards his aunt. She was waiting for him in the school veranda. As she stooped to greet him, he put his arms around her waist and buried his face in her breast. She noticed that he was shivering.

'What happened, my little warrior?' she murmured, stroking his hair.

Clothed in her embrace, enveloped by her familiar, reassuring scent of jasmine and Chanel, he looked out behind him for his tormentor. But the courtyard was empty, and the wind that nodded in the furry branches of the great cypresses was gentle. He could see the red roof of the chapel rising into a blue sky threaded with flimsy clouds, the weathercock on its tip looking like an inksplat. From one horizontal bar of the weather-vane was suspended a small huddled shape, swinging in the breeze. He gasped. Aunt followed his eyes, her hand flying up to her mouth.

By the time the caretaker had cut the dead cat down, Samorin had told Aunt about Dhiren Das. Fury darkened her face, deepening her eyes, but alongside the anger and hurt Samorin sensed the presence of a distant, inexplicable sorrow. Samorin sat on the wooden bench in the corridor outside the principal's office while Aunt was inside, talking to him. The principal was an ageing Irishman called O'Heary, who had started at the school as a young English teacher when India was still a part of the British Empire. He had stayed on – the last of the great white gurus – and he was to generations of students a stern but benevolent Mr Chips. His white hair fell across his forehead and his eyes were blue. Rumour had it that the red spots on his cheeks were the result of brandy rather than of pigmentation. The buzzer sounded and the school *chowkidar*, Ram Singh, was summoned into the principal's room and promptly sent out again. He returned with Dhiren, and the boy cast a dark look at Samorin.

'Squealed on me, did you?' Dhiren hissed at him as he passed. 'You'll suffer for this. I swear.'

After a while, Aunt came out and led him by the hand into the waiting taxi cab. As the car rumbled down the twisting hill road, she told him not to worry.

'Everything will be all right.' She ruffled his hair. 'I've sorted out the matter with the principal. That boy won't bother you any more.'

He looked at her beloved, familiar face, and sighed. A few grey hairs he hadn't seen before had appeared near her temples, and there was a hint of soot under her eyes. The question he wanted to ask hurt his throat, lodged like trapped poison.

'Yes, my darling?' Aunt asked, taking his small hand

in hers. Her hand was warm and soft, and even if it was but for a moment, it stilled his furious heart.

'Did my father kill my mother?' he asked.

The question froze time. The young Samorin felt that he was caught in an unreal cusp, the sounds of their journey the only reassurance of reality: the rumble of the car's engine from under its shivering bonnet, the creaking doors, the protest of the seat springs. The wind raced uphill alongside and around them, scattering pine needles and cones as it came, whipping Aunt's sari around her face. She wound the window up and turned to lift his chin with her finger.

'No. He didn't,' she said.

The boy felt as if he had passed into another climate that while soothing him, was full of distant shadows. He placed his head in his aunt's lap, breathing in the crisp cotton, feeling the soft rise of her stomach against his forehead. Her fingers played with his hair.

'Sleep, my little prince. We have a long drive ahead.'

The sun had reached its calescent meridian, warming Samorin's hands on the steering wheel. Occasional trucks roared past, overloaded with grain and cement bound in tarpaulin, making the parked Jeep shake. Anna lowered the window and lit up a cigarette with a slim Cartier lighter. India Kings, Samorin noticed.

'So,' she said, flutes of blue cigarette smoke escaping through her nostrils, 'did you find out the truth about your father?'

Samorin reached for her cigarette. He took a drag on it before placing it back between her lips.

'What I found was a story,' he said, almost speaking to himself. 'Reaching home, spending the first night of my return from school in Aunt's bed, lying in her arms again as I used to when I was very small, and listening to her voice in the night . . .'

The moon came in through the window, bringing the shadows of the night with it. They played on the walls like a forest pantomime and lay across the silver-washed floor like fallen puppets. He snuggled up to Aunt, his leg flung over her hip, and her arms encircled his chest.

'Little one, your father was a wonderful man. A very brave man.'

Her voice was crossrun with depths. Samorin yielded to it, his eyes open to her treasured face in which her dark, bright eyes had taken flight to another sky. It was the first time he had heard her talk about his father.

'Was he handsome, Aunt?'

'Oh yes. And tall and slim, and he always looked you straight in the eye.'

'Tell me about his eyes, did he smile a lot?'

'His eyes were clear and honest and when he smiled, they would crinkle.'

'Then why did Dhiren say he killed my mother? Did Father not love her?'

'Oh yes, he did,' and the boy detected a small tremor of sadness in her answer, 'perhaps too much. He did not kill her.'

'Was my mother beautiful too, like you?'

Aunt's laugh was strained.

'She was beautiful. And both of them loved you very much.'

She told him his father had been a pilot in the Indian Air Force, that he was an ace with sixteen kills in the dogfights of the Indo–Pak war. He had many

151

friends even in the place of his birth: both Madhavan Nair, who was his flight lieutenant and a schoolmate from childhood, and his batman Venu Kurup were from Manali. All of them had joined the Air Force together, and when Father was given command of his squadron, Nair had flown with him.

'During some afternoons, when you were a small baby sleeping in your little crib, your mother and I would be sitting on the big bed in her bedroom playing gin rummy,' Aunt remembered, 'and suddenly the sky outside would fill with the roar of jet engines. We would throw the cards down on the bed and rush out. A shame it was sometimes, because so often when your father flew over in his silver MiG, I would be holding a winning hand . . .'

Aunt laughed, remembering running outside, looking up at the flat plate of a china blue sky. The silver bird that had flown from the Madras airbase would be looping a sign in the firmament. The plane flashed down the gleam of the midday sun, curving and pirouetting, writing her sister's name in the sky with its jetstream, drawing a huge white smoking heart, the universe a palette of the pilot's romance. Even after the plane had left, roaring away into the distance, the heart would linger in the sky for a while like a gigantic smoky kiss.

'One day your mother was away in town with your grandfather and your father appeared like a silver arrow,' Aunt said, a small sad smile playing on her face, 'and I ran out. I waved to him as he curved through the sky, the silver smoke arching in its pursuit, and I cried out that Shyamala wasn't here. And he wrote my name on the sky, as if from that great distance and speed he could see that it was me below, waving to him. To me, he became a silver hawk.'

The eagle of memory, the lover in the sky, the calligrapher of aerial flirtation, when did you become damned?

'Your father was a special man, and I want you to know that he was not a murderer.'

'But then Dhiren Das said he was. And that he was hanged.'

Aunt's face was pinched with a sudden bitterness, and she murmured something about gratitude under her breath. Samorin did not understand.

'You don't have to believe everything you hear, Jay.'

'Then why was he hanged?'

Aunt placed her fingers on his mouth, hushing him. The moonlight was brimming in her eyes, and the dark, thick lashes were tipped with quicksilver. Against him, her small breasts trembled.

'One day you will know the truth, I promise,' she whispered, 'until then trust me.'

The school vacation passed slowly and languidly, and Jay practised his *kalaripayattu*, getting up at dawn as usual. The *gurukkal* told Aunt with pride that if only the times had been medieval instead of the 1970s, the boy would have become a warrior in the mould of the fabled Aaromal Cheykor or Thacholi Othenan. Samorin played in the grounds of the estates with Chami and spent the afternoons exploring the hill paths with the ageing German shepherd, Kaiser, by his side. One evening, returning home, someone stepped out from behind a banyan tree to block his path. Kaiser growled, the fur at the nape of his neck standing up. It was Dhiren. Samorin stepped back, dropping unconsciously into a fighting stance. His antagonist laughed loudly.

'So we meet again!'

'What are you doing here?' Samorin asked sharply.

'Perhaps following you?' Dhiren's voice held innocent mockery. 'Nah, you overestimate your own importance to me. That's a nice dog you got there. Aren't you glad it's not a cat?'

Samorin took a step forward, and the German shepherd barked.

'You touch my Kaiser, Dhiren, and you are dead.'

'Kaiser, Kaiser . . .' Dhiren called out softly, loosely circling the dog. The animal was barking furiously, and Samorin tried to quieten it.

'C'mere Kaiser,' Dhiren said, gazing into the dog's face, holding its eyes with a steady stare. The dog stopped barking and began to whimper. Samorin called out to it sternly, but Kaiser suddenly turned and ran down the path towards the house. Samorin turned to Dhiren.

'You are a monster!' he yelled.

'It's not over yet, Jay.' His enemy came closer and stood a few feet away from him, just out of arm's reach. 'You ratted on me at school. No-one punishes Dhiren Das. There will be payback.'

Samorin turned on his heels and walked away without a word. Dhiren called out after him, 'Payback! Remember Samorin, payback!'

As he ran up the stone steps to the gate of his house, crossing the tiled roof of the *kavalpura* into the courtyard, a woman leaving the house stepped in his way. She was dressed in white, like Aunt, and her thick black hair was tied in a plait. Her hips had a voluptuous sway to them as she walked. She looked at Samorin with dark, cold eyes and gave him a malicious smile, her mouth red with betel.

'Oh, the little master returns, huh?'

'Leave him alone, Kamala!' Aunt's voice cut across the courtyard like a whiplash. The woman turned to look at Aunt, who had come out on the veranda. She gave a high, shrill laugh and stroked Samorin's cheek. Her touch felt so cold.

'You should send him to me, one day. I could teach him a few things he would love.'

She laughed again, coarsely.

'Another day, then,' she said and walked down the steps.

Later, lying in bed, with the last lamp out and the night suddenly opening its doors and releasing its myriad noises – the chirruping of crickets, the call of the nightbirds, the rustle of the western wind in the rough palm leaves – Jay Samorin remembered the last house on Widow's Street. The gaze came to him again, a dark hibiscus opening in the mind, and he recognized the woman in the courtyard.

In the morning, Kaiser was missing.

CHAPTER NINE

The Imperial Hotel is Delhi's best-preserved hotel from colonial times, built as part of the English drive to create the city of New Delhi. Myth says Delhi is an amalgam of seven cities, each built upon the ruins of the previous one. Recently renovated, the Imperial's long driveway is fringed with palm trees and its white facade and perfect green lawns lend it an atmosphere of elegance borrowed from another time. The British had chosen their favourite contractors for the job, giving them prime real estate in the middle of the new city, and the result did not disappoint. They built Luytens's Delhi, with its wide, tree-lined avenues, nursing whitewashed bungalows with snowy, gleaming exteriors that were visible through foliage of *neem* and *jamun*. The Viceregal palace dominated the landscape from its perch on Raisina Hill, like a gigantic, benevolent guardian. Now the houses look asleep among the green and are inhabited by India's politicians and bureaucrats, while a largely ceremonial President occupies the Viceroy's erstwhile lodgings.

Jay Samorin and Anna drove in from Curzon Road, now renamed Kasturba Gandhi Marg, into the circular amphitheatre of Connaught Place. Renaming roads was a post-colonial gesture of freedom, replacing the names of pathways with those of Indian personalities, throwing out memories of conquests and viceroys. So Queensway became Jan Path, the Road of the People. For a brief period, after the 1977 Emergency was over, a motley crowd of politicians who had never tasted power before ruled India. It was a crumbling coalition led by an austere prime minister, who came to be remembered more for his recommendations on drinking piss than for good government. Meanwhile a bandanna-wearing politician called Raj Narain, whose only claim to fame was to have defeated Indira Gandhi in the elections, took it upon himself to rechristen New Delhi. The heart of New Delhi became Ground Zero for new names; Lady Hardinge Hospital became Lok Nayak Jayaprakash Narain Hospital, a mouthful for any impoverished patient whose misfortune it was to find succour among the bedlam of the capital's over-crowded public hospitals. Soon enough, the mania caught on.

The elegant Connaught Place, with its slim white columns supporting graceful colonial arches and louvred windows, was next. A Congress politician, who was a sycophant of Rajiv Gandhi, brought a motion in Parliament to rename the hub of Delhi after India's ruling dynasty. So the outer circle of Connaught Place became known as Indira Chowk and the inner circle as Rajiv Chowk. The maternal embrace of nomenclatures did not help the pedigree come back to power, but the legacy of obsequiousness remained. The great ghosts of history set to rest by small men.

So Jay and Anna drove into Jan Path, past the Tibetan curio shops selling beads, brasswork and mirrorwork skirts. Migrant women, colourfully dressed, hawked dhurries and faux handpainted miniature paintings at outrageous prices to foreigners. The uniformed guard at the gate searched under the chassis of the car with a mirror attached to a stick.

'The gift of Kashmir,' Anna muttered, 'a bomb for every Indian.'

Terrorists had brought their violent signature to Delhi, exploding car bombs in crowded markets and shopping centres. Occasionally, parking lots or cinemas were evacuated following bomb scares.

Samorin handed the Scorpio over to valet parking, and a tall, paunchy doorman wearing a bright red turban and a filigreed cummerbund saluted them smartly. Inside, the foyer was whisperingly cool, and the tourists were mostly foreigners. They had a bemused look about them as they sat on the deep Chesterfields and imitation Hepplewhite chairs – it was home reincarnated, but somehow subtly made exotic. Tall potted palms shivered in the air conditioning, telephones rang discreetly, and a fountain gurgled quietly. The hotel was all high ceilings and long corridors, with framed prints depicting British life in India. There were photographs of colonials with dead tigers and turbanned natives, the tiny-waisted memsahibs in whalebone corsets and billowing skirts holding pretty little umbrellas against the tropical sun. A restaurant serving colonial food was named after the Danielle brothers, who travelled through the Empire's subcontinent making wonderful sketches of the period. There were three floors with balconies overlooking a gigantic atrium, and the decorators had used the theme of the three centuries of British rule in India for each floor. Anna's heels clapped on the polished marble as they walked along the corridor.

'I miss the old bar though,' she said. 'Irfan and I came here once, for a drink before catching a flight to Srinagar.'

Samorin remembered the huge ballroom with its wooden dance floor at one end, offering entertainment by a talented but lazy orchestra clad in ill-fitting suits. At the other end was a large, sprawling bar with a gleaming brass counter. Lord Mountbatten, the last Viceroy of India, is said to have given his farewell speech to a room packed with His Majesty's subjects in that bar, clambering onto the brass counter to gain their attention – the hall had been so crowded that there was no standing room. The renovation of history also claims its victims: Mountbatten's pedestal now lay in some back-room store in the hotel.

They walked through the coffee shop into the little foyer that was the entrance to the lawn, with its undulating slopes and bright garden umbrellas shading white wrought-iron chairs. The buffet was laid out under a striped canopy, and staff hurried among the guests with trays laden with cocktails and canapés. Samorin lifted a vodka and tonic from a passing waiter's upheld tray and Anna raised an eyebrow, smiling.

There were quite a number of people on the lawn. Samorin recognized a couple of politicians who were regulars in the society pages of the city newspapers.

An ageing disc jockey was paying attention to a very young, tall model on his arm – his chin came up to her cleavage. She had bored eyes, heavily protected by mascara, and her fat, pouty mouth sipped what looked like a margarita. A group of middle-aged women in chiffon saris gossiped around a table under a blue and green striped umbrella, their voices carrying across to where Samorin stood.

'Oh, but Sheela's new Merc costs only thirty-six lakhs, it's not the top model . . .'

'But her husband bought it for her as a guilt present. You know about him and that young television presenter . . .'

Their faces were rouged and threaded, some revealing the expensive tautness of facelifts. Chalky midriffs bulged out of their blouses, and fingers flashed with diamonds and rubies as they gesticulated or raised their cocktails to their painted mouths.

'Anna, oh I'm so glad you are here,' a young, high voice called out, and Samorin saw a tall woman in a tan silk sari walk across the lawn towards them. She had left a cluster of people who sat underneath a *gulmohur*; the group parted a little and Samorin's eyes met a familiar, cold gaze. The afternoon temperature seemed to drop. Samorin's skin crawled, and he looked away from Dhiren Das who stood talking to some people in one corner of the lawn. But then Anna's sister-in-law Salma, as she was introduced by Anna to Samorin, was with them, her thick mass of hair with its coppery nimbus shining in the afternoon sun and her wide grey eyes filled with delight at seeing her friend. Her chin was small, but resolute, and it had a little black mole on its tip. She wore a diamond nose ring.

'So where is your mother?' Anna asked.

'Over there,' Salma said, gesturing behind her, 'with those nice people.'

'Doesn't sound like nice people, the way you say it,' Samorin ventured. Salma shot him a suspicious look.

Anna patted her arm. 'He is a friend.' she said.

Salma gave a little shiver.

'Friends!' she said, 'I don't know about anyone any more. Oh Anna, I'm so worried about Mama.'

'I'm here, I'll take care of it now,' Anna said, 'we'll take care of it now. Samorin and I.'

Salma suddenly looked away, and Samorin saw that her eyes were wet. Her shoulders trembled.

'Oh how I wish Irfan was here, with us now, protecting us,' she said in a small voice that concealed a sob. Samorin noticed Anna's mouth tighten as she took her sister-in-law's arm.

'There, you'll ruin your make-up. Let's go and sort it out.'

Samorin watched them walk away across the lawn towards the hotel foyer, Anna's arm around her friend's shoulders.

'Charming, isn't it? Ah, women!' a voice said at his elbow, familiar and well-remembered. Dhiren Das stood behind him, his head thrown back, the black mane of hair tied in a gleaming ponytail behind him, the well-trimmed beard glistening in the sun. He held a glass of pink champagne in one strong hand, the little clusters of bubbles chasing each other to break on the surface. The man's presence was palpable, Samorin felt it like a great slab of living ice next to him. The painter's voice was low and pleasant, but in its baritone were occasional fluctuations of urgency. He thrust a hand out.

161

'Haven't met, haven't been introduced. I am Dhiren Das.'

So Dhiren was going to play the polite stranger, Samorin thought as he clasped the outstretched hand, hardening the sides of his palms involuntarily. He felt the fierce voltage of his adversary's grip. The man and his games, he said in his mind, I'll play along for now.

'Jay Samorin.'

'Oh, the cartoonist!' Dhiren Das said, bowing with a flourish. 'Delighted! I've been a great admirer of yours. I'm glad we have met at last.'

'At last? We must have met before, surely,' Samorin said.

Das spread out his arms in an exaggerated gesture.

'Delhi is such a large city, and I meet so many people. In fact I spend most of my time trying not to remember people I've met.'

'Is that good for an artist?'

'Ah, but I am a painter, not a cartoonist like you, whose life depends on remembering faces. You chaps are of savage persuasions, exorcizing your souls onto paper, warts and all. Especially the warts. Wartists, rather.'

Das laughed and sipped from his champagne.

'But some faces you always remember,' Samorin said softly.

The sun dropped in the painter's eyes, and for a fleeting second dark dreams swam in them.

'Maybe. But not as the same face.'

The women returned. Dhiren threw a muscled arm around Salma's shoulders. She seemed to have suddenly become light-boned and tentative, as if the presence of the artist dimmed her. Samorin saw that

Anna, in whose eyes there was now a cold look, had also noticed the change.

'Come along, Salma, let us find Mama,' Anna said. 'I haven't seen her for a long time. So much to talk about.'

Dhiren Das did not release the girl. She stood motionless, strands of her hair blowing back into his face in the breeze. Dhiren raised one eyebrow mockingly.

'Why don't you run along dear? You'll find Mrs Hassan with Dr Dubey. No doubt discussing her excellent health.'

Salma looked at Anna with a plea in her eyes. Samorin stepped forward. The afternoon seemed to have shrunk into a series of tableaux, and the murmur of conversations, snatches of laughter and the swish of silk receded into an infinite distance. The grass seemed endless, stretching away into the clustering shadows of the trees; the buzz of traffic reached them from outside the garden's high white walls garnished with flowering vines. Sunlight fell on them, golden and dreamy, but it felt cold. Samorin's eyes locked with the painter's, met the challenge of his mocking smile.

'Come, Salma,' Samorin said.

'You go,' Salma whispered, 'I'll come soon.'

Samorin did not realize that his hand had found Anna's. She released it suddenly and walked away. Samorin followed her.

'Jay,' Dhiren called out from behind him and Samorin turned.

'Jay, stay in touch.'

They found Salma's mother talking to a fair-skinned balding man in an Indonesian shirt and black trousers,

163

who was bending solicitously over her. He held a glass with a wedge of lemon stuck in it in one hand and a cigarette in the other. Anna ran the last few steps to the old lady, who looked up at her with a worried smile.

'Dr Dubey, my physician,' Mrs Hassan said in a weak, low voice, 'this is my daughter-in-law, Anna.'

The doctor smiled at them, showing snowy, capped teeth.

'A pleasure to meet you. Salma has told me so much about you. You are with the police, aren't you? Isn't it an unsuitable job for a woman?'

'You read too much of P. D. James, doctor,' Anna said, going over to Mrs Hassan and putting her arm around her.

'Oh, the life I lead leaves me little time for books. But, I must admit, James is a favourite. I love the denouements.'

'Meet Samorin, doctor. A friend.'

'Not the Jay Samorin? The cartoonist? Even we villagers who live in remote places have heard of such a famous name.'

Samorin took in the perfectly tailored shirt, the sharp crease of his trousers, the gold Armani spectacle frames.

'A villager, is that right?' Samorin raised his eyebrows. The doctor laughed, producing a high-pitched noise like a tame hyena.

'Well, Brindaban is a village. And my hospital is in Brindaban. I also run a shelter for widows.'

'Do you care for widows a lot, doctor?'

The doctor shrugged and shook his head sadly.

'I try and do my bit for those poor women. We are the only voluntary organization in the area carrying out medical work. Free hepatitis vaccinations, free polio drops, and a free clinic. And we have nearly a hundred widows of all ages, from all over the country, in our shelter. Many have been abandoned by their families, many cheated of their land.'

'He is a very compassionate man, our doctor,' Mrs Hassan broke in, 'he never rests.'

'Mrs Hassan has been to Aasha,' the doctor said, 'many times. She sees the work we do there.'

The old woman nodded.

'But it's a lonely life, isn't it, doctor?' They heard Dhiren Das behind them. He had come up to them, Salma beside him, his arm still around her.

The doctor laughed and shrugged.

'I have you for a neighbour, Dhiren. Can't get lonely with you around.'

'Oh, I drop in for a drink now and then, and sometimes the good doctor comes over for dinner. My studio is practically next door, ten acres of my own world. When I'm tired of painting or doing a sculpture, I love the doctor's company. We sit on the lawns and discuss the human body. Both of us are specialists, in our own ways.'

'You flatter me, Dhiren,' Dubey said.

'What do you specialize in, doctor?' Samorin asked casually.

'Cancer. Leukaemia, especially. It's a tricky disease.'

Samorin nodded. 'And I gather you have spent time in America.'

The doctor's eyes clouded. Then he smiled.

'You mean the accent still remains?'

Samorin smiled back.

'You must visit Brindaban, Jay,' Dhiren Das said, 'it is a special place. Full of shadows, an abode of living ghosts. Krishna, the god of widows, rules it, and

165

sometimes, when I walk along its narrow, sleeping streets, I can hear his lute call.'

'And what does it bring, his lute?'

'Phantoms, Jay, phantoms of dead men who dance in the dreams of their living wives. I have been trying to find the soul of Krishna. It haunts Brindaban, the apparition of love and all that is lost in romance, all that is doomed and beautiful.'

'And if you find it?' Anna asked.

Dhiren spoke as if in a trance. 'Then I will create my masterpiece, my final work. I will invoke the soul of Krishna and consecrate him in my art. It will be my *pièce de résistance*!'

Samorin saw the intensity in the artist's eyes, the manic obsession.

'The soul of Krishna, Dhiren?' Samorin said. 'I wonder. It was Radha, his eternal lover.'

The damsel of antiquity, doomed to pine forever for her departed god, abandoned by him as he left his garden by the river. Radha, wandering distraught along the banks of Yamuna that also mourned for Krishna, lost in the memories that filled the sensuous twilights and rich crimson dawns. Laughter in the gardens of Brindaban, moonlit couplings in marble gazebos – hers was the unfulfilled story of an abandonment. Dhiren Das's eyes gleamed.

'Ah, Radha, oh Radha,' he muttered, drawing Salma closer to him, 'Yes. You have a point, my dear cartoonist.'

He released Salma, threw back his head and laughed. He laughed at Delhi's grey October sky, tears running down his face as convulsion after convulsion of some inexplicable, perverse mirth gripped him. Choking on the champagne he had drunk, he flung the glass away, watching it shatter on the grass. A worried-looking waiter in a shabby white tunic hurried to pick up the pieces.

'What's so funny, Das?' Dr Dubey asked nervously. To Samorin it seemed for a moment that the doctor was afraid of Dhiren Das.

'The truth, the answer,' the painter replied, wiping his eyes, and a short giggle escaped from his lips. 'Sometimes what the eye of genius doesn't perceive, the mind of the satirist does. Many thanks, dear Jay Samorin.'

He bowed. Samorin did not rise to the bait.

'I have been working on a great piece,' Dhiren said, his voice dropping to a conspiratorial whisper, 'and I have been unsure about it, trying to explore its form. The great dance, the great final cosmic dance. But this is not the *tandava* of Shiva, but the love dance of Krishna. And now I have found its soul. I must hurry.'

'You are a painter of the universe, aren't you?' observed Samorin drily, 'but I am its critic. I do not believe in shades of colour, only in the definitiveness of black and white.'

'Isn't that simply rather boring?'

'No. It's good and evil, Dhiren, the simplicity of the universe.'

'How droll,' Dhiren Das said, walking away towards the bar. 'So like a comedian to want to have the last word!'

Salma had been standing, as if bewitched, and now she slumped down on the chair next to her mother. Her eyes were far away. Anna placed a hand on her shoulder, but she didn't appear to notice. The doctor cleared his throat.

'I have to leave I'm afraid, the good Swede who

167

funds me is in town and I have an appointment with him.' He turned to Mrs Hassan.

'I will come over to the house tomorrow. We will do some tests then, but you will be fine.'

'What tests?' Anna asked suspiciously.

'She has been complaining of tiredness and dizziness,' Dubey said. 'I think the last time she visited Brindaban, she worked too hard. Your mother-in-law has a kind heart, my dear. She gets really upset when she sees the plight of all those widows. But I try to look after them the best way I can.'

'Mother, I don't think you should take any more tests,' Salma said, her voice sounding hollow and tired.

'Nonsense, my dear, Dr Dubey is an angel. I'm just tired, that's all. A couple of vitamin shots, I'll be OK.'

The doctor grinned and nodded.

'She is in safe hands, Salma. Your mother is precious to us.'

'I bet she is,' Samorin caught Anna muttering under her breath. He noticed that she seemed to have taken a dislike to Dr Dubey.

'I want to go now,' Salma said, 'and take Mother home.'

'Do you want me to come with you?' Anna asked.

Samorin saw Salma's gaze searching the crowd and come to rest on Dhiren Das, who now stood talking to a woman dressed in a sequinned Rina Dhaka outfit. The painter's hand was on her shoulder, and he leaned forward to speak in her ear, but his eyes were on Salma. Salma shivered like a small bird and then drew her shoulders back.

'No, Anna. You stay. I'll take Mother home.'

Anna didn't move, and stood by Salma, one hand on

her shoulder. Salma looked up at her with a wan smile.

'I mean it. I'll call you in the evening. Maybe we can meet at Rick's for a drink. Will seven thirty suit you?'

Samorin's eyes were drawn back to Dhiren Das. The woman in the sequinned dress suddenly leaned forward and licked the side of the artist's face. He slapped her. She stepped back with a cry, her hand to her cheek. But she was smiling. Samorin took Anna's hand and led her away. As they passed him, the painter, who was now being hugged by the woman he had slapped, called out to Samorin.

'Hey Jay, how is your dog?'

Samorin stopped and turned.

'Did you ever find Kaiser?' Dhiren Das asked, his tone scornful, teasing. His eyes met Samorin's, cold and sardonic. Anna grasped Samorin's arm, restraining him. Samorin shook her hand off and smiled.

'I have a cat now,' he said softly, but there was infinite menace in his voice. 'Maybe you'll meet her some day.'

'Oh, I love cats,' the painter laughed, 'much more interesting.'

'Well, at last, you may meet your kind of a cat.'

Dhiren Das's laughter escorted them out of the garden.

CHAPTER TEN

The Polish singer who played the piano at Rick's had a pale Modigliani face, wispy, brandy-coloured hair piled up in a small chignon, and a soft pink mouth always parted for the next song.

'Killing me softly with his song . . .' she lamented, the sound of the piano fluttering in the dimness of the bar. Her head was tilted to one side, as if she were expecting someone in a tuxedo to materialize behind her and offer her an orchid. Samorin had always hated the song, it reminded him of a loser with an unhealable heart. The singer's large, inky-blue eyes scanned him, as he sat sipping Scotch on a bar stool. He nodded and raised his glass to her, a gesture she answered with a smile of such bright sweetness that he was startled. He saw it fade as her eyes moved away, and Samorin followed her gaze to see Anna stepping through the crowd towards him. It was his turn to smile. He stood as Anna put her arm around his shoulder and kissed him lightly on the cheek. She smelt good.

'Drink?'

'A vodka, please. With a dash of lime and a splash of soda. Where's Salma?'

Samorin shrugged. Anna had taken the stool next to him. He noticed the way she sat, liking it – her body turned towards him, her elbow on the bar counter, the other hand on her lap, fingers idly drumming on her black leather bag. Prada, he noticed. One leg was crossed over the other, the cuff of her black denim jeans riding up to show the glimmer of a thin gold anklet. She wore open-toed sandals with high heels, which she had hooked over the steel railing around the bar, and a black silk shirt with a thin leather waist-coat meant to conceal her shoulder holster. A small diamond was held by a narrow gold band around her neck. Samorin wanted to pour a thimbleful of cognac in the hollow of her throat and lick it. Anna caught something in his eyes and smiled, not really divining his thought, but recognizing the promise in it. The pianist was now singing 'Strangers in the Night'.

Rick's was full, its deep sofas with retro steel frames packed with drinkers and their dates. A young man sat with his arm around the waist of a girl in a tight lilac dress and Preity Zinta curls. He held a beer bottle by the neck in his other hand, and bent low to breathe something in the girl's ear. She giggled. People leaned forward with their elbows on the round tables, frothy with spilled beer; cigarette smoke turned the air blue.

Samorin felt like saying something trite, like tossing a cheap coin in a disused wishing well. The air was tightly strung with the energies of people, shot with laughs and sharp sentences, the slap of hands high-fiving, the cackle of lips mwah-mwahing. A young man with gelled hair, still a boy really, slinked past, his hand brushing against Anna's back. He yelped as she caught his wrist and swung him towards her.

'Hey, what's your problem?' he squealed. 'Let go, you're hurting me.'

Anna shrugged. 'Sorry, just reflex. I don't like being touched.'

Samorin placed his hand on hers. She smiled, her eyes wary.

'It's Salma, isn't it?' he asked.

Looking at her watch, Anna nodded. But Salma was suddenly beside them, materializing in the smoky light, her hair dishevelled and her eyes sooty, her lower lip heavy and red as if recently kissed. She stood out among Rick's black-clothed clientele in her white sari and rose-coloured blouse, her skeletal fingers shimmering with stones. Anna took her hand in hers. Salma sighed.

'Traffic?' Anna asked conversationally, almost as if offering her an excuse, knowing full well that Delhi at that time was easy to drive through.

'Took a cab,' Salma tossed her head, 'didn't feel like driving.'

Samorin asked her what she would like to drink. Salma giggled suddenly.

'Should I?' she asked archly, turning to Anna.

'Of course, if you want to.'

'Isn't he a handsome man?' Salma gestured towards Samorin. 'Your new lover?'

Samorin cleared his throat and beside him Anna stiffened. She took a sip of her vodka. Salma turned towards Samorin.

'You like my sister-in-law, don't you?'

'Salma, cut it out.' Anna spoke sharply. 'He is not my lover. He is here to help you.'

Salma leaned against Samorin and clicked her fingers at the barman. Samorin felt her breast against him, soft and full, smelt the shampoo in her hair, the perfume on her neck, and leaned away from her to see Anna looking troubled. Salma ordered a Bacardi and Coke for herself.

'With a lemon wedge stuck on the rim of the glass, please,' she instructed the bartender. He was a dark young man wearing the regulation blue tunic with a black collar; his eyes were yellow with cigarette smoke, but looking amused.

'So,' she purred, letting the word hang in the thick air of the bar, leaning her back against the stuffed leather edge of the counter. Samorin smiled.

'So, what is it, sister?' Anna asked gently.

'What is it that the two of you don't like about Dhiren?'

'Who said we don't?'

'Oh, I know,' Salma said. 'He told me. That Samorin is envious of him.'

Samorin let out an incredulous laugh.

'The envy of artists, he said, of the imitator towards the original,' Salma continued. 'He says you covet his genius.'

To Samorin, it seemed as if the painter was with them suddenly, a malevolent intelligence insinuating hints of its ill will.

'The one genius he possesses for sure is evil genius,' Samorin said before he could stop himself. Salma looked at him with mild amusement.

'That sounded so bitter,' she said. 'Is it because you

173

have only a talent for caricature, while he is the original?'

Anna laid a restraining arm on her shoulder. Salma laced her fingers through her sister-in-law's, raising her hand against her cheek.

'Samorin is a big boy. I'm sure he can look after himself,' she said.

He read the challenge in her eyes, the pretence of a mockery she believed was real. It was as if Dhiren stood behind the troubled curtain of her gaze, and he leaned forward to meet his enemy's eyes in hers. This is a strange seance, Samorin thought to himself, forced to be the ally of a woman he barely knew because someone whom he cared for had requested it. He met Salma's eyes. He was vaguely aware of Anna's palm on his thigh, a soft, worried pressure of reassurance, and then he immediately felt the scalding touch of her sister-in-law's. He smiled at Salma, taking her hand in his.

'You are worried about your mother, aren't you?' he asked gently.

Salma glanced at him fiercely and gulped her drink down, asking the waiter for a refill.

'What do you know about it?'

'Very little. Only what Anna has told me,' he replied. 'That you believe someone is trying to murder her by making her fall sick and that, somehow, Dr Dubey is involved with it.'

'Stop patronizing me, Samorin. I know you don't believe me, I know you are thinking that this woman is crazy, that you cannot just give someone cancer.'

'The Americans did, in Hiroshima. Anything is possible.'

'How comforting,' Salma's tone was harsh, but Samorin felt it concealed the trembling of a sob, 'a history lesson.'

'Listen, get serious, Salma,' Anna said, 'you know something we don't. Or at least you suspect something. What is it?'

'I told Dhiren about my suspicions,' she looked at Samorin defiantly, 'and he said Prakash Dubey couldn't even give a cough to someone, let alone cancer. Besides there is no way you can give someone, I mean literally *give* someone leukaemia. But I'm sure that villain Dubey has found a way.'

'Why did you have to tell Dhiren about Mama?' Anna asked.

Salma whirled around, spilling some of her drink on Samorin. She placed her glass roughly on the bar counter and gripped her sister-in-law's shoulders.

'Mama is dying, don't you see that?' she said fiercely, 'and I don't know what to do, who to turn to for help. You had Irfan. I never had anyone, except Mama.'

Salma's eyes took on a faraway look, as if she were seeing a private vision that was both sunlit and sad. 'Dhiren is painting me these days,' she said, her voice slightly slurred. 'You had Irfan and now you have this man, Anna. I have nobody but Mama.'

She was leaning loosely against Samorin, her arm thrown over his shoulder. He could feel her alongside him, see the fuzz on her cheekline, copper in the light.

'And you would love to draw me too, wouldn't you?' she purred, her mood changing for a moment and becoming flirtatious.

Samorin disengaged himself from her, getting up from his seat. Anna was looking anxiously at him, and he could see that she was becoming irritated with Salma. He smiled.

'Relax, Salma, and sit down.' His voice was hushed, reassuring. 'How did you meet Dhiren Das?'

Salma frowned and drew a deep breath.

'I met Dhiren for the first time when I went to see an exhibition of his paintings at the Madagascar embassy. They sponsor him a lot.'

Samorin made a mental note to check up with Ambassador Tsiranana on this.

'I loved the paintings, and I found Dhiren very attractive . . .'

A small smile lingered on her lips, a delicious little memory reliving an anticipation.

'Very elemental, if you know what I mean. Those hands of his are so strong, those long, blunt fingers. I wanted so badly to become a painting of his.'

'You are, aren't you. He is painting you,' Anna said, unable to hide the tremor of irritation in her voice. Salma grabbed her arm.

'You don't understand, I don't want to be merely painted by him. I want to be the painting itself.'

Samorin shivered, revolted by her need. It was like a terrible, carnivorous heart devouring itself, a vampire of desire that was turning upon itself. Suddenly he saw Salma as a little girl lost in a land of succubi, an abandoned Gretel for whom the road led only to perdition. Somewhere in that haunted forest, Dhiren Das waited with the patience of a powerful satyr, a Pan of tortured but powerful imagery. It was that power of his to breathe life into the most bizarre of fantasies that trapped Salma in a poisonous addiction. It was Dhiren Das's world, and he populated it only with those he wanted, changing them irrevocably. Salma was just feed on the way, just another trapped cat.

Every man has one ancient enemy, Samorin thought, whom he will fight in the end. There was no victory or defeat, only survival. It was then he decided that he would try to save Salma from the painter's spell, and not just because of what he felt for Anna, but because he knew he owed himself that.

Salma sensed something was suddenly different in Samorin, and she moved imperceptibly closer to him.

'I want to talk to Samorin alone,' she said, turning to Anna, 'can he have a drink with me and drop me home?'

Anna got up and pushed her chair away. She reached across to Samorin and touched his arm briefly, and without a look at her sister-in-law turned on her heel and walked away. Samorin got up to follow her. Salma laughed, slipping her arm through his, holding him back.

'Afraid of me now, are you, you big bad wolf? She can find her way, our little Anna with her gun, who is always sure of herself.'

Samorin wanted to leave the bar, to abandon Salma to the smoke and babble, to look for Anna, reach her, take her long fingers in his palm and stroke them softly. But he thought of her departure a moment ago, slim back held straight, hair moving like a halo around her face. She had turned back to glance at him briefly before disappearing into the lobby.

'Help her,' Anna's look had said, 'I love her.'

So Samorin took Salma by the elbow and gently steered her towards the door. Salma arched her neck to look back into his face, her sharp white lower teeth biting her wet red lip in a smile. She slid her arm

177

through his, and as they walked together he could feel the heat of her skin through her clothes.

'You driving me home?' Her voice was husky.

'Where do you live?'

Samorin drove and Salma lay back in the passenger seat, giving him directions, her head tilted towards him, watching him with burning eyes. Her smile never faded. The streetlights of Delhi flashed upon her as they passed, the mercury and sodium swirling their pigments on her skin. Salma's sari had slipped away from her breasts. She shone golden and silver by turns.

They took the lift to her top-floor apartment. The drawing room was large with high ceilings, and a wall of plate glass looked out into the jewelled landscape of night-time Delhi. An early moon rubbed its light against the dome of the Mughal tomb in the middle of Lodhi Gardens, burnishing the ancient trees that had been planted around the death of one of its long-dead emperors. Beyond the twisting wall, shaded by *neem* and laburnum trees and the scattered luminosity of the sleeping city, the river Yamuna glimmered like a broken scimitar.

Salma came up behind him and put her arms around his waist, pressing herself against him. Samorin gently disengaged himself and led her to an ottoman by the window. She stretched out her arm and drew him down beside her. With a small sigh, she placed her head against his shoulder. Her breath smelt of liquor.

'You are so different from Dhiren,' Salma said softly. 'You are like a river, while he is a waterfall. No wonder Anna is falling in love with you.'

Samorin looked at her through narrowed eyes.

'Don't pretend. As if you don't know. But you don't

love her, do you? You can love only yourself.' Her voice was bitter.

Samorin did not answer.

'Just like Dhiren. In fact you could be twins,' Salma said. 'You are a giver, and you will give so long as it makes you happy. Dhiren is a taker. And you know, sometimes, being taken can be more pleasurable than being given to. Oh, and when Dhiren takes, he takes everything you have, and leaves you as empty as eternity. He leaves me so depleted and breathless that I need to be reborn again after each time.'

She took his hand and placed it on her breast. Her nipple felt hard and long through the fabric of her blouse. He moved his hand away and stood. Salma pouted.

'Don't you desire me?'

'You are very desirable,' Samorin said, 'but I gave my word to Anna that I would help you. Please tell me what it is that you are afraid of.'

Salma stared at him with brightening eyes, the fringe of her eyelashes glittering with tears. Then she shivered, put her face in her hands and began to cry. Samorin sat down beside her, his arm around her shoulders, and she leaned into him like a sail collapsing. He stroked her hair gently.

'I'm so afraid,' she whimpered. 'I'm so afraid that Mama is dying.'

'Tell me about it.'

In the momentary silence that followed, Samorin went across to the bar and filled glasses with ice, pouring a Bacardi for her and a Scotch for himself. Salma gratefully took a gulp of her drink and asked Samorin to light a cigarette for her.

'I'm sorry, I'm not myself these days.'

He smiled encouragingly.

'Mama was widowed very young and did not remarry. Papa belonged to the Rajapur royal family and was a diplomat. Old money, and lots of it. As children, Irfan and I travelled all over the world, living in Vienna, London and Paris. Those were the happiest days of my life. Papa died when I was twelve and we moved back to our house in Delhi. We had to be put into schools, and Mama was more comfortable living here than she would have been living in one of our houses in Rajapur. She had grown up in Delhi, studied here. When they came back from postings abroad she always looked forward to polishing the furniture, taking off the sofa covers and laying out the carpets. We used to have parties every week. The chandeliers would be lit, and music would be playing, and when we were children Irfan and I would peek through the banisters at the guests in their sharp suits and glittering jewellery, and wished we were grown-up, too . . .'

Salma smiled, remembering.

'In Rajapur, all Mama would have been able to do was to play bridge with the wives of army officers and attend Sunday lunches with old friends,' she continued. 'She wanted to do things for people, and Papa had always been a great inspiration for her. She told me once about driving with him on a weekend to Rajapur and passing through Brindaban on the way. An old widow crossing the road had almost fallen under the wheels of their car. Mama had got out to help her and Papa was standing behind her. "The hatred in her eyes when she looked at Papa and me was like a curse, Salma," Mama said, "there was so much painful loss inside her that it had turned into hate." From that moment on Mama believed that she was doomed. When Papa died, she knew she had to go to Brindaban.'

'What was she doing there?'

'Working with the widows. She took me with her once, when I was grown-up. The shelters were horrible, especially the government-run ones. Often there would be no electricity, and the food was very basic. It was as if these women had died along with their husbands, and existed now as living corpses. The younger ones were being used for sex by the officials of the shelters, peddled to local politicians and police-men. Mama moved petitions in court, met ministers and MPs she had known through Papa. It made her very unpopular in Brindaban. She received death threats, obscene phone calls, and one night her car was vandalized.'

'Was she afraid? Were you?'

'I was afraid for her, but she didn't care. Then one day she heard about a shelter that was being demolished by the municipality to build a guest house. One old woman was refusing to leave, and she was clinging to the pillars of the veranda, insisting that the building be torn down with her in it. Mama went to see her, and they recognized each other immediately. "I knew you would come, my daughter," the old woman told Mama. "I wish you had killed me that day, instead of braking. My life has been a tomb all this while, and now they are tearing down the tomb too."

'Mama brought her to our home in Delhi. I was at Stanford then and only came home for holidays. It was then that I met her. She was rude and fat, and seemed to have the constitution of a horse. But Mama wouldn't allow me to say a word against her.'

'Why?'

'Mama's guilt. She hoped that by keeping the widow with her she could expiate her curse. It was while I was in New York, copywriting for Saatchi, that she died. Mama wanted me to pack up and come home. It was as if she had been widowed all over again.'

'Where does Dr Dubey come in?'

'Mama has always been an admirer of Dhiren Das.' Salma's eyes flickered up at Samorin. 'She loved his paintings, and once she sat for him. He painted her as a resplendent bride against a lush landscape full of peacocks and parrots, a picture that still hangs in her bedroom. She said it reminded her of the way she was with Papa; each time she looked at herself in the painting, it felt to her as if Papa was still alive.'

Dhiren Das, the painter from hell, the conjurer of a magic so dark that it had a melody even sweeter than the souls of angels.

'Dhiren was a frequent visitor to our house. He spent a lot of time with Mama, and they spoke of things that were both cosmopolitan and esoteric. He knew about astronomy and alchemy, he could regale Mama with tales of his travels in the Pyrenees. Mama, whose world had shrunk after Papa's death, was suddenly a traveller again with all his stories.'

'And you?'

'I did not know him well, then. I was engaged to Nayan, a software engineer. His father and mine had been friends. One day I was walking down the driveway after Nayan had dropped me off home after dinner. Dhiren was coming out of the house, going towards his car. He saw me and stopped. "I want to paint you," he said. He grabbed me by the waist and pulled me to him and kissed me. No, he actually bit my lips, chewed them as if he were eating them. I came then and there, standing in the driveway of my house, glued to him, and it was the most violent orgasm I've ever had. Just kissing him. And then I knew that I would have to fight this man all my life, or never be free. And I wondered, did I want to be free?' Her voice sounded small and lost.

A ragged cloud dragged itself over the moon and the lamps in the room seemed to glow brighter.

'You will be free when you want to be,' Samorin said gently, stroking her hair. 'Tell me about Dr Dubey.'

'Dr Dubey and Mama met at Dhiren's house. By then we were lovers, but Mama did not know it. I have a suspicion that Dr Dubey already knew, because of the way he smiled at me whenever Dhiren was around, as if he shared a secret with me about his friend. And the doctor invited Mama to spend time at his shelter, to see the hospice and work with those who were dying of cancer. Mama would spend days with the dying men, comforting their wives, being there for them after they became widowed. And my first confrontation with Mama came when I knew that she was spending huge amounts of money on the widows' project.'

'Why should it bother you?'

'It was Papa's money, and Irfan's. I never liked Dr Dubey. There is something too smooth about him, like a lizard on a glass pane. I told Mama that Papa wouldn't want his money to be squandered on a crook like Dubey. The next day, Dhiren asked me to stay out of it.'

'Dhiren?'

'I was hurt that Mama confided in Dhiren about what I had told her. It was as if she had no secrets from him. She had taken to spending most of her time at

Aasha, sometimes several weeks at a stretch. Working with the poor women, she said. Late last week I got a call from Brindaban saying she had collapsed and been admitted to the hospital. Dr Dubey said it must have been fatigue, and that he had been giving her regular vitamin injections. I took her away from there, though she didn't want to come, and checked her into Max Healthcare. The consultant there, a friend of mine, told me her symptoms could mean leukaemia. He is running tests on her. Meanwhile she has gone off to Brindaban again, insisting that she be treated by Dr Dubey.'

Salma looked up abruptly at Samorin, her eyes burning. Then her mouth twisted into a small, ugly smile.

'Do you think I'm crazy?'

Samorin got up and took Salma's hand in his.

'Of course not. Let me find out more about the good doctor. Meanwhile say nothing to Dhiren.'

Salma threw her head back and laughed. 'Afraid of him?'

Samorin placed his empty glass on the little cocktail table near the sofa.

'Don't go, yet,' Salma said, her voice soft and low. She raised her arms towards Samorin with a moan. 'Help me, please. Kiss me. Make love to me. I am so alone.'

Samorin kissed the tips of her fingers.

'I have to go,' he said.

CHAPTER ELEVEN

The pixels of Samorin's dream were being broken by the incessant ring of telephones amidst the crashing of the sea. He was in a city he knew but could not name, strolling along the beach. He and Anna had walked into the water, and he was returning to fetch the blue denim jacket he had hung on the railings that ran along the beach. The wind bit. He had noticed that Anna was suddenly missing, and it was as if she had never been there. The dusk was turning into the cobalt blue of a deep night. His cellphone began to ring and he grasped for it in his pocket – it felt different – it was a different phone. This disoriented him, and Samorin looked around, to find another lying at his feet. As soon as he stooped to pick it up it started to ring, playing an old Hindi film theme. He pressed the answer button and heard laughter he recognized as Dhiren's. He bit his lip, and realized that Dhiren was talking to someone else and laughing: by some arcane magic of dreaming the phone had allowed him access to the painter. He heard a woman's voice answer, rainy with laughter: it sounded like Anna's. He felt sudden black rage grip his chest and hurled the phone into the sea. Suddenly phones were ringing all around him, teasing him with deceitful promises of familiar voices. Samorin opened his eyes to escape from their clamour, and caught the handset by his bedside on its last ring.

'You sound really gruff,' Anna said.

'Sorry, weird dream. What time is it?'

'Three. I couldn't sleep.'

Samorin took a drink of cool water from the carafe beside his bed.

'Did you sleep with her?' Anna's voice was tight.

'No. Was that what was keeping you awake?'

'Partly. I saw the way she was touching you, looking at you.' She sounded remote, yet hesitant, as if she was subdued with effort. 'You are an attractive man, have I told you that? That wild cat of yours goes with you pretty well.'

'Thank you. But you know, I wouldn't have slept with her, Anna.'

'I was worried more about Salma than you. She wanted you, and even more so because she thought you were mine.'

'Am I?'

Anna did not say anything for a while, and Samorin held the receiver to his ear, listening to her breathe. He pictured the vast night sky, turning with the slow Ferris wheels of galaxies and powdered with the pollen of uncountable stars. He imagined Anna's mind swimming among them, absently and unconcerned, just to be free of her immediate realities; he smiled.

'You are smiling,' Anna said. 'I can feel you smiling.'

'You are a good cop.'

'I left you at the bar and went to the shooting range,' Anna said wearily, as if she was remembering a past anger, 'and now my palms are aching. I haven't been using the gun as frequently as I did when I was in Kashmir.'

'Scored well?'

'Two misses, sixty-seven hits, out of which fifty-five were head shots. Right through the brain, between the eyes. Want to have a drink?'

The watch upon Samorin's wrist glowed three fifteen.

'I have some Talisker left over from the other night. And Sasha is awake anyway.'

The fosa looked up from the chaise longue, its small ears quivering at the mention of its name, the sound of its master's voice. Its eyes were like witches' amber, and the long, immaculate tail that curved gracefully onto the cool marble floor trembled briefly.

It was nearly four in the morning when Anna pulled up in front of the house. Samorin opened the door to her, feeling a brief flutter of the night breeze as she walked in. The moon was whitening the trees, and he noticed that the eyes of his visitor were burning very bright, lit with some inner fever, banishing sleep.

Samorin seated her on the low couch by the French window. He drew the curtains back, allowing the moonlight to mix with the lamplight in the room. He poured whisky into crystal tumblers, filling Anna's with ice and adding water for himself.

'It's a lovely night, or dawn if you prefer it,' she said, sipping from her glass, throwing her neck back to let the whisky trickle down her throat. He looked at her as she placed the glass upon the small round table beside her, observing her long, slim fingers return to rest on her lap. Her hair was loose, embroidered with an aura of moonfire, and when she turned her face to look at him, he noticed a dimple form and vanish on her smooth cheek.

'I was jealous tonight.' she said abruptly. 'I had thought the woman in me was dead, killed the day Irfan died. I discovered I was wrong.'

'Salma,' Samorin said.

'Yes, Salma. My greatest weapon is my intent, and Salma's is her sexuality.'

Samorin thought she sounded bitter, and Anna, guessing his thought, gave a fleeting smile and continued.

'I've known her since she was a kid, from the time Irfan and I became friends in our little hillside Mussoorie. She was very jealous of me, and when Irfan fell in love with me, she hated me for having taken him away from her. I tried to explain to her that she was his sister, and important to him in a way I would never be. "Love can be different, Salma," I told her, but she just stared at me in anger. She was seventeen then, and already gorgeous, with straight black hair and a narrow waist. Two days later, Irfan came to me, shaken. I was reading in bed at home – Rimbaud, I think – and I still recall a bird singing somewhere in the trees and the din the monkeys were making on the roof. I will never forget the look on his face. Dazed, as if God had slapped him or something. He sank down beside me on the bed, and put his head on my chest. He was shivering. I stroked his hair, holding him to me, and he started to cry.'

'Salma tried to seduce him,' Samorin said.

'Yes, isn't that scary? She took her clothes off in front of him and lay on his bed asking him to fuck her. "Am I not better-looking than that Anna of yours?" she asked him.'

'She was his sister and wanted him for herself, the way you were going to have him,' Samorin said. 'Classic amorality combined with low self-esteem. Pop Freud.'

Anna hugged herself.

'Salma loves me, I know that, but she also wants to possess what is mine,' she said. 'When she got married and moved to New York and found a job in advertising, she told me that she was going to be happier than I was with Irfan. Poor child.'

'She came back . . .'

'Yes, her marriage broke up. She said she was being beaten up by her husband and came to live with Mama in Delhi. Mama was by then working with widows.'

'Salma tells me your mother-in-law has gone back to Brindaban, to the hospital run by Dr Dubey,' Samorin said. 'Apparently a cursory check-up by Salma's doctor has got her worried. He is running the usual blood tests for leukaemia, but the results aren't known yet.'

Anna stifled a gasp. Her eyes were sharp and bright.

'All those cancer widows at Aasha, and Mama in hospital among them, we have to get to Dubey's dirty secret!' she said.

'If he has one,' Samorin ventured.

'Jay, my palms are suddenly cold,' she said.

'Why?'

'When I was in Kashmir, and after Irfan was killed, my palms would always turn cold in the presence of danger. Maybe I had killed so many men that death had granted me the gift of premonition. Danger is death's calling card, you know, and I learnt to recognize that bloody pasteboard long before anyone else.'

'Did it bother you?'

'That I killed? No. In the beginning, it was hate and vengeance that led me. Some of the terrorists I shot were mere boys, the hair on their chins barely showing. And it would fill me with both bitterness and wonder that children so young could have done such terrible things to the man I loved. "Look at them sleep," I would tell myself, "look at them, Anna." I would be crouching beside them, in my khakis, laying my gun close to their skin so that the bullet-warm barrel would impart its vanishing heat to their deaths. In my mind, I would reach out and stroke their soft, dead hair. I created their deaths, and their ghosts would belong always to me. Just as they had bonded Irfan to themselves, wrenching him away from me. Each time I killed a terrorist, I was liberating myself.'

She turned to look at him, her eyes full of the challenge of an interrogation. 'Do you find me a monster?'

'No. Everyone is a monster, you just need the right password.'

Anna laughed a short, mirthless laugh.

'What's yours?'

Samorin shrugged. The fosa had come down from its perch to squat beside him, as he sat leaning against the deep Bandhini silk cushions thrown upon the Moroccan rug. He rubbed the beast's nose with the tip of his forefinger. It tossed its head and winked with pleasure.

'Jay, could your password be D-h-i-r-e-n?'

Samorin was startled, suddenly wary of the woman

near him. He realized that here was another hunter of evil, who had read maps that were far bloodier than he ever would see. She sat with the easy grace of a lioness, familiar with blood and cruelty – it gave her poise an effortlessness that did not seem entirely human.

'Dhiren? Why do you say that?'

'The key to your secrets is in Dhiren,' Anna said with the assurance of a clairvoyant, 'secrets even you did not know existed.'

The early light of dawn infiltrated the night, clearing the shapes of trees and hedges with stealthy patience. The faraway Aravalli hills began to emerge dimly, and Samorin felt that he was caught between the parentheses of awakening and stupor. The whisky had warmed him, the encounter with Salma had troubled him, and now here was this strange warrior woman for whom he felt a strong need, throwing him a gauntlet he did not want to pick up. In that changeling hour, memories were like moths flustered by the coming of the day: murmurs came to him from behind the locked door of Aunt's room, the Prince of Children whistled to him from a distant wilderness, the Vampire of Cardamom Hill combed her hair with her back turned to him, and dead cats swung from the weathercocks of another climate. A bird swooped down and was caught for an instant against the square glass of the window that was being washed by the morning light, and he thought he glimpsed a form suspended in the air, against the sky, dancing at the end of a thin black rope. His fist clenched.

'The universe is a deliberate interlock of circuits,' Anna said calmly, her hands folded in her lap, spine straight, looking at Samorin, her oval face framed by

191

falling hair. 'In the pursuit of its secrets, you stumble upon many of your own.'

Samorin knew she was baiting him, that here was a master manipulator of minds whose passion was the secrets of others.

'Aren't you interested in secrets, Jay?' she asked gently. She was looking at him with eyes that mocked him, spangled with memories and the shadows of souls and their perfidies. Samorin gazed up at the lightening air, the earthless womb of his secret that challenged him.

'The warrior is taught to shirk nothing,' he thought to himself, 'and he searches for his way through the patterns of his moves. The *adavus** determine the fighter's destiny, and in the fluidity of their purpose is the release of his karma.'

He opened the door and stepped out onto the lawn, his bare toes curling instinctively to read the contours of the terrain. He felt the dew-wet grass and the earth hard underneath, his calf muscles flexing into a *garuda*† pose as he stretched. He clenched his shoulder tendons and tightened the small of his back as he felt himself elongate and expand, becoming one with the air. He flowed sideways towards the wall in a rapid movement, the earth leaving him as his right foot lashed out against the rough stucco, springing up and thrusting him towards a sky turning bloody with dawn's sweep. As he rose high and then higher, to a height greater than any gibbet's, his arm lashed out in reflex as something flashed at the corner of his eyes – a swift, time-challenging blur – and his rigid and

* *adavu*: kalari move.
† *garuda*: eagle.

192

powerful fingers closed on a hurtling shape. His mind multiplied into infinity, seeing the shimmer in the grass below, a golden snake, and the panic in the amber, black-rimmed eyes of the kestrel interrupted in its swoop for prey.

As Samorin floated down, his fingers opening to release the bird, he saw Anna rise in the air to meet him, her hair spread like a dark fan behind her, eyes locked into his as they came face to face. He saw the sweat drops gleaming above her upper lip, and saw her hand shoot out to seize the bird he had just released. He landed on his front foot, leaning back automatically to turn around upon the ball of his heel to confront the adversary who would be descending in a moment. His hands, held at an angle to his chest to deliver the death blow, were restrained as Anna landed beside him, her hand held out to stay him. Her hair was in disarray, covering her neck and face, her breasts heaved. The diamond in the hollow of her throat gleamed in the young sun of the day. The hawk lay dead in her hands, its neck broken. Anna shrugged with a brief expression of regret, and threw it away. It landed in a clump of bushes, and Samorin saw Sasha cross to them in a blur from the house, heading towards breakfast.

'You . . .' he said.

'They taught me this Jackie Chan stuff when I was on assignment in America,' Anna said, wiping the sweat from her forehead. 'There was a young Chinaman with the NYPD who had grown up in the Bronx with his grandfather. It was like something out of *Karate Kid*. But where did you learn to leap like that?'

'*Kalaripayattu*,' Samorin's eyes were still on her,

193

aware of the power she exuded, 'an old family sport.'

Anna stepped up suddenly, gathered the collar of his shirt in her fist and pulled his face down. She kissed him roughly, licking his mouth, biting his lower lip. She tasted of whisky and salt. As Samorïn reached for her she pulled away.

'You have to earn me, baby,' she whispered in a mock Michelle Yeoh accent, 'I have belonged to only one man before.'

Samorin raised his eyebrows, suppressing the breathlessness he felt. Anna smiled and stroked his cheek gently.

'Now we sleep,' she said, linking her arm through his as the morning opened up around them, breezy and fragrant, 'and when we wake up, we go to Brindaban.'

CHAPTER TWELVE

In myth, Brindaban was the garden of the blue god. The blue god Krishna was the lord of its arbours that were nourished by the river Yamuna, sister of the great Ganges, whose source was the knotted hair of the sleeping destroyer, Siva. The gardens of Brindaban were always in bloom. The perfumed air would be redolent with *chameli*, *gulaab* and *raat ki rani*, borne down to the water in the wind's drift, blessing the women who bathed in the river with skins that smelt of flowers. The playful god Krishna cavorted in the glades of Brindaban with his women – the *gopis* – summoning them from their homes with his enchanted lute. He made music standing with one leg crossed at the ankle, yellow *angavastra* revealing a blue, boyish chest, the peacock feather stuck in a jewelled headband jauntily waving in the breeze. His music was always irresistible to the women; it woke them with the ardour of an unseen lover, beckoning them to play among the scented secrets of Brindaban's bowers. The lute led them into a passionate dance among the moonlit spaces, while Krishna's doomed lover Radha lay entwined in his arms, her soft white thighs grasping his dark waist, her scarlet mouth upon his nipple.

The nights of Brindaban were nights of abandon. The music turned the dancing *gopis* into Krishna's wives, and Radha was his queen. Brindaban was also the grove of valediction, in which a disconsolate Radha, abandoned by Krishna, spent her life waiting for him to return from the great wars of the *Mahabharata*. It became a doomed garden of faith, whose gardeners were love and loss, and whose earth was watered by the tears of forsaken women.

As Samorin drove Anna through the narrow streets of Brindaban, he thought that desolate tears of abandoned women were about the only thing that had not changed in the town today. No gardens were visible except for the ragged clumps of green in-differently maintained by the Department of Public Works. The Yamuna river was dirty and sluggish; washermen rinsed the clothes of their unsuspecting customers in its waters. The roads were narrow and broken, noisy with overloaded tri-scooters and trucks. Tinny, smoke-belching buses with passengers stoically packed in like sardines groaned along, adding to the din with the squawking of flustered, indignant chickens in mesh baskets tied to the top. Samorin and Anna passed clusters of cows that dozed in the middle of roads, holy traffic islands around which drivers had to navigate. The International Society for Krishna Consciousness had a big ashram and temple in

Brindaban; cycle rickshaws ferried Hare Rama Hare Krishna pilgrims about, their yellow garb and shaved blond tufts looking whimsically out of place. The Hare Krishna sanyasins are regarded as a local curiosity in a country which had once been ruled by the white-skinned.

'Krishna duty-free,' Samorin laughed as he manoeuvred the black Jeep through the crowded, rain-eroded roads, nodding towards the Hare Krishna temple as they passed. 'Do you think we can find anything here?'

Sasha gave a low whimper from the back seat as if answering her master. Anna laughed.

'Unlikely,' she said. 'Can't see Dhiren Das coming here. He doesn't like competition, even from a god.'

'Got to find Aasha,' Samorin said. 'The earlier we find it the better. What's the pretext? Dr Dubey would hardly be expecting a courtesy call from us, especially if he has something to hide.'

'Do we need a pretext, Samorin? Mrs Hassan is a patient there.'

Samorin pulled over to the side and stopped behind a pickup truck full of tethered livestock. A buffalo reached out with its velvety snout towards the vehicle's windscreen, and a couple of goats craned their necks and rolled their eyes. Sasha gave a low, throaty growl, and the animals suddenly sensed the presence of a predator. The buffalo strained against the rope, groaning loudly, and the truck began to heave. The goats started bleating and falling over each other in a bid to escape. Samorin reversed the Jeep and pulled out, searching for parking space ahead. An adolescent tree threw its sparse shadow dispiritedly over a bunch of bicycles leaning against railings. A gigantic cardboard cut-out advertising a Hindi film loomed against the pale, metallic sky; Madhuri Dixit's mouth was parted like a huge red flower.

'Who do we ask for directions to the widows' home? The goats?' Anna made a silly joke.

'The streets are too narrow for the Jeep,' Samorin replied, waving a cycle rickshaw over. Its owner paused upright on the pedals in imitation of a street acrobat, a smoking *beedi* hanging down from his betel-stained mouth.

'Can you direct us to Aasha?'

The man shrugged. His eyes bulged when he spotted the fosa in the back seat of the Jeep. The cat sat up and pressed its nose against the glass, examining the rickshaw and its owner. The man hurriedly pedalled away, narrowly missing an overcrowded tri-scooter that in turn almost ran into the gutter. Its navigator, clinging precariously to the running board, cursed loudly; he had almost been thrown off his perch where he usually stood, holding onto the side rod, banging the sides of the vehicle to warn others of its approach. The vehicle righted itself and as it passed, three village women in bright voile saris of blue, red and vermilion with the free ends draped over their heads as is customary in Northern India, stared at Anna from the back seat with kohl-lined eyes. She gave them a small wave.

A group of widows were waiting at the roadside for the traffic to pass, a restless cluster of women clad in shabby white. Their heads were shaved, as was the custom of all Hindu widows, white saris covering the yellow stubble on their skulls. In the afternoon sun, their skins had tungsten patches, their foreheads wrinkled with the years. There was something intangible about them that was common to all — a hurry in the gait, a defenceless wariness, a way of huddling together. Their shoulders drooped inside coarse cotton blouses as if the weight of ruined years rested on them. And the way their eyes and heads moved constantly suggested a nervousness more usually associated with hunted animals. They crossed the road in a dash of babble, passing the Scorpio and glaring at Samorin and Anna with suspicion. The last of them, an old woman with a slight limp, stopped and turned. She hunched over, hand shading her eyes, and peered at Samorin. He smiled and her eyes opened wide. Her companions called for her to hurry, but she broke from them and approached the Jeep with a wobbling but intent gait.

'Must be wanting money.' Samorin reached for his wallet.

The old widow came up to the car window and squinted at him. Her face was a map of lost lines. Her eyes were rheumy and blue-rimmed. Her ear lobes hung low, with gaping holes left by heavy *thodas* — the ear-pieces South Indian women used to wear. She raised a crooked, arthritic finger and scratched on the glass.

Samorin shrugged. She knocked on the glass, harshly insistent; he lowered the window and a brief gust of hot air came in.

'Captain, is that you, the *thampuran**?' she enquired in a wheezy, flat voice.

'You speak Malayalam!' Samorin exclaimed. 'You . . .'

The old woman raised a skeletal finger to her toothless mouth and grinned slyly.

* *thampuran*: feudal lord.

199

'I won't tell, I've seen you with Savitri, Captain . . .'

'Savitri! You speak my aunt's name.'

The woman gave a hollow, tubercular laugh. Blood flecked her nostrils.

'I was one of Kamala's girls, I remember you, Shekhar *thampuran* . . .'

Samorin felt his father's name in the pit of his stomach, felt a cold hand seize his throat.

'My father, you know his name . . .'

The woman's eyes suddenly grew crafty.

'Maybe you are not the captain, but you look like him for sure,' she cackled, turning away, 'only the Vampire of Cardamom Hill can tell.'

Samorin opened the door to get out, and Anna reached across to touch his arm.

'Wait . . .' he shouted.

The old widow stopped and turned.

'Leave me alone, Captain,' her voice was tired now, sounding helpless. 'I left Kamala a long time ago. Now I'm just waiting to go home with Krishna.'

'You knew my father,' he said, getting out of the Jeep and walking towards her.

'Stop playing tricks on an old woman, Captain,' she wheezed, her eyes widening. She turned away abruptly, possessed by a sudden need to escape, breaking into a buckling, clumsy run to reach her companions who were waiting under a tree down the road. Before Samorin could look back, his arm was grasped roughly from behind. He smelt sour sweat and *beedi* smoke close to his cheek.

'Troubling the old widows, are you?' A rough voice behind him asked. Samorin turned to see the pock-marked face of a policeman. The man had his right arm raised to strike, but something in Samorin's eyes stopped him. Samorin twisted his arm away, pointing at the retreating figure.

'I've to talk to her.'

'Shame on you, she is old enough to be your grand-mother,' the policeman barked. He seemed to have regained his bluster. He spat betel juice in a long thin plume of red that splashed against the railings.

'I'm asking you politely, Constable, to step aside,' Samorin said, 'before I break your face and feed it to the goats.'

A small group of urchins had collected around them. The policeman wasn't used to being talked to like that. He swung his baton threateningly and approached the Jeep.

'What is that? A panther?' he asked, peering into the Scorpio. 'You'd better come along with me to the station, you are in trouble.'

He loosened the holster flap of the service pistol at his hip. A cloud dragged itself over the morning sun. The widows were a retreating white blur, disappearing round a corner into a labyrinth of side streets. Samorin turned, but a blow glanced off his hip and he lost his balance. He rolled away from the big brown boot descending on his ribs, twisting his back into a reverse arch and somersaulting back on his feet, hands raised and fingers turned into claws, ready to descend on the man's windpipe and kill him. But Anna already had her hand around the constable's thick neck and her revolver was pressed against his temple.

'But you can't park here. Hundred rupees fine,' the man babbled.

'You move once more, and where you will be going you won't be able to collect the fine.'

Suddenly a police Jeep pulled to a halt beside them

and uniformed policemen leaped out, nervously clutching obsolete Enfield .303 rifles. A young officer, his shiny visor winking in the sun, stepped out and walked towards them, his revolver drawn. Samorin saw him come to a stop in front of Anna, his eyes sparking with sudden recognition. He holstered the revolver and saluted. Anna didn't release her grip on the policeman.

'Ma'am,' the young man said, his English faultless, 'it's OK. I'll take care of it.'

Anna let go of the man, who sank to his knees. His cap had fallen off, and his hair was wet with sweat, plastered to his skull. Anna stepped back.

'You gave a lecture at the Police Academy in my final year,' the officer said. 'I still remember your advice on friends and enemies. In Kashmir, you said, the only friends a policeman had wore uniform.'

Anna smiled a weary smile.

'That was a long time ago,' she said, slipping her gun back into its holster and gesturing to the cop whom she had attacked. 'I did not mean his kind of uniform either.'

The officer barked at the policeman, whose face was now dark with rage and puzzlement.

'See me at my office in the afternoon. Now, get lost.'

'It was not really his fault,' Samorin said. 'I met someone I thought I knew. An old widow from my village. But she seems to have vanished.'

'We'll find her, sir, we'll search all the widow shelters,' the young officer said. 'Won't you come over to the office for some lemonade? It would be a honour if the celebrated DIG Anna Khan visited us.'

'Thank you,' Anna said, 'perhaps on the way back. Have you heard of Aasha?'

The officer's eyes narrowed.

'It's actually a charitable organization, run by Dr Dubey,' Samorin interrupted.

'Oh, the painter Dhiren Das's friend?' The young man's voice revealed a dip of disappointment, as if Samorin had said something unexpectedly obscene. 'Is he a friend of yours?'

'In a manner of speaking.'

'An important man, with important friends.' The young policeman's voice was flat. 'Didn't think he could be a friend of someone like you.'

'What do you mean by that?'

He shrugged and smiled, glancing away.

'People are known to die there mysteriously, and investigations are stalled. The last time, we found a young widow dead in the fields outside Aasha. Had been living at the home.'

'And?' Anna asked.

'And nothing. Questioned Dubey, who said she had leukaemia and was depressed. And killed herself.'

'Sad. But what's odd about it?'

'OD. Cocaine. A poor widow with enough money to shoot up twenty thousand rupees' worth of cocaine? And who had no history of previous drug abuse? There are cheaper ways for widows to die in Brindaban.'

'Didn't you interrogate him further?'

'Picked him up for questioning. Before he even got off the police van, the Director General called from Delhi and asked me to release Dubey. And Dhiren Das was already waiting for me at the station to take the doctor home.'

They were directed to take the route out of the city towards the countryside. The way was pocked with potholes, and piles of rubbish swarmed with crows and flies. But the cornfields were green and the great trees that stood alongside offered shade. They spotted a sign that said Aasha, and turned into a narrow, asphalted path that ran through the corn. They passed a giant banyan tree with a cow chewing cud under its canopy and halted as a funeral procession crossed in front of them, the corpse wrapped in fresh white cloth. Its bamboo bier was festooned with marigolds and lotuses, borne aloft by men chanting 'Ram Naam Satya Hai . . .'

'An omen?' Samorin asked. 'Do you think it's one of our good doctor's patients?'

'I emailed my contact in the FBI in New York to see if they had anything on Dubey,' Anna answered. 'And they did.'

'You keep yourself busy, don't you? And did you find he murdered his patients with botulism serum while he was in America?'

She grimaced. 'Nothing so obvious. The Feds were very suspicious of him, but they couldn't prove anything. His wife died of cancer, and left everything to him. Turned out it was more than half a million dollars. The insurance company wasn't satisfied and got private investigators to go into Dubey. They found nothing on him, either.'

'He then upped and left with half a million dollars?' Samorin whistled.

'Something like that. But his credentials were impeccable.'

The gates of Aasha were painted black, set in a huge brick wall bristling with barbed wire.

'To keep them in, huh?' Samorin laughed mirthlessly and honked once.

A tall young guard came out and looked at them insolently.

'Is Dr Dubey there?'

'Who is asking?'

'We are here to see a patient, Mrs Hassan. I'm her daughter,' Anna said.

'I have no instructions about anyone wanting to meet anyone,' he said, peering into the Jeep, suddenly straightening as he saw the big cat in the back seat. His eyes filled with alarm, and he hopped back. Anna reached out and grasped his collar. He twisted around with a snarl, his hand gripping hers.

'Tell Dr Dubey that Deputy Inspector General of Police Anna Khan is here. Or I can see him in the police lock-up at the nearest station. And you, too.'

The guard's eyes were bright with fear as he opened the gates for them, fumbling and cursing under his breath. Samorin eased the Scorpio down the smooth, wide drive that wound its way through immaculate lawns bordered by carefully tended flower beds. Fountains played in the wind, and small gravel paths meandered invitingly into the shadows of cool groves. The air smelt of jasmine and lavender. A gardener in a white coat lazily dragged a long hose along, pausing to water a mass of roses, while sprinklers threw diamond drops of water in swift circles. The main building was a white, two-storeyed affair built low, as if hugging the ground. Beyond a small knoll, through a clump of trees, they could see more buildings – tiny white cottages with red roofs and a couple of two-storeyed housing blocks. Creepers festooned with fat white flowers covered the trellised front of the portico, and two huge palm trees stood sentry either side of the entrance.

'The idyllic gardens of Brindaban, at last!' Samorin said. 'Or at least the Brindaban in which Dubey is God. Sasha, stay.'

The cat yawned and winked its yellow eyes at its master. Samorin reached out and patted its smooth head. It rubbed one furry cheek against his hand.

'Kitty, kitty,' Anna murmured. Samorin laughed.

'Good to hear you laugh,' she said, adjusting her shoulder holster, tucking it under her calico vest. 'Did you really know that widow?'

Samorin frowned.

'I'm not sure. But she knew my father.'

'We'll find her.' She placed her hand on his wrist. Samorin smiled distantly. As they walked into the hospital's reception, Anna took in the set of his mouth and the smooth, unlined forehead. He seemed to imbue most things he said or did with a subtle sense of mystery.

The receptionist was a pretty young woman in a peacock-blue sari who spoke in a curious lilting shorthand.

'You have appointment?'

Anna shrugged.

'My mother-in-law is here. We have come to see her.'

'Dr Dubey tell nothing. Your good name please?'

'We're from Delhi. We've come to see Mrs Hassan. Could you please tell Dr Dubey that Anna Khan is here?'

The girl pursed her full lips and nodded her head regretfully. 'I know Mrs Hassan, good lady, kind lady, it is sad, very sad.'

Anna impatiently leaned her elbows on the polished desk. A telephone rang softly behind it and the girl turned to answer it.

'Yes, Dr Dubey,' her voice became respectful. 'No, medicine van not come in yet. Here are two . . .'

Anna leaned across and grabbed the phone from her. The receptionist looked indignant.

'You can't do that, madam . . .'

'Dr Dubey, this is Anna Khan, Deputy Inspector General of Police.' Anna spoke harshly into the phone. 'You must be the most difficult man in Brindaban to get hold of. Even for the police.'

Samorin did not catch the doctor's answer. Anna handed the phone back to the receptionist, who glared at them with an air of unsurpassed injury. Then suddenly Dr Dubey was with them, wearing a white safari suit and an expensive aftershave, his black hair brushed back, shoes polished to a mirror-like shine.

'Anna, dear Anna, why didn't you call before? Salma was here just a while ago to see Mrs Hassan.'

'So soon? I saw her in Delhi last night.'

'She wanted to see her mother suddenly, in the middle of the night. One of those urges that come only to children who love their mother the way you both do. Dhiren was coming to Brindaban and was kind enough to bring her. After all, with the new highway, it's only an hour away from Delhi.'

'Is she still here?'

'No, she left with Dhiren for his house half an hour ago, and said she'd be back. Mrs Hassan was sleeping, and I had given her a little morphine to ease her pain. Come into my study and have some coffee.'

'Thank you, no. Did she say when she would be back?' Samorin asked. The doctor turned and looked at him with mild curiosity.

'Not really. Dhiren lives next door, it's just a short walk through the trees and past the hillock to reach his

207

grounds. There's a small turnstile that separates his house from the hospital, and I'm sure Salma can find her way to her mother when she is ready. She's done so before.'

The doctor's study was large and high-roofed. A huge painting by Dhiren Das occupied most of the wall opposite his desk. It showed a tree created from people. They were entwined with each other, forming the contours of its bark, and Samorin noticed that the leaves were made of green eyes. The tree stood against a landscape that was golden and russet, and a lone eagle soared against a crepuscular sky.

'The tree of life,' Dr Dubey said. 'Ah! He's a painter with such an original imagination!'

The doctor settled into his high-backed leather chair, indicating with the graceful gesture of a perfectly manicured hand that they should sit on the leather-cushioned seats opposite. His desk was of modern design: chrome and smooth walnut, its surface, as polished as his shoes, reflected the white of the ceiling and was devoid of any paper. The screen saver on the computer on the desk was of Michelangelo's *Creation*; the animation faded out as soon as God's finger touched Adam's, and then re-appeared. An air conditioner whispered discreetly behind some fluttering palms. The white curtains were drawn back, revealing the landscaped green beyond, the *gulmohurs* and laburnums festive with flowers. The wall next to the window was lined with bookshelves, and Samorin noticed the *Lancet* and other medical journals on a table beside the sofa at the other end of the room.

Dubey opened his arms and smiled at Samorin.

'It's such an unexpected pleasure, meeting you

so soon,' he said with a pleasant little frown.

'Too soon, perhaps?'

'Oh yes, the cartoonist. I admire humour,' the doctor said, laughing loudly, as if to emphasize his point. 'Tell me, what can I do for you?'

'I'd like to see Mama,' Anna said.

Dubey picked up the phone. Samorin got up to wander around the room, taking in its discreet opulence. The breakfront cabinet in the corner was made of acacia hardwood and held some framed citations and trophies – the doctor's victory parade, he guessed. The study was expensively carpeted, displaying both a Gabbeh rug, and a Cath Kidston with its trademark European folk designs. Through the glass expanse of the window the treetops shivered in the morning breeze. The town of Brindaban they had passed through such a short while ago seemed distant and unreal, its grime and clutter a dark, unpleasant illusion. He felt the doctor's eyes follow him as he strolled across to the bookshelf, scanning the titles on the spines.

'Are you interested in medicine?' he asked.

Samorin nodded. 'Heard of Hippocrates.'

Anna stood up.

'I'd like to see Mama now, please?'

Dubey nodded and asked them to accompany him. Samorin turned to Anna.

'Do you mind if I stay here? I am not keen on hospitals. I know it sounds insensitive, but there is something about the smell that makes me feel ill.'

'Oh, it doesn't smell at all, Mr Samorin,' the doctor said. 'Our patients are looked after well. The curtains are laundered every week, there are flowers in the rooms, and paintings on the walls.'

209

'I'd rather stay, if you don't mind.'

Samorin saw Anna's eyes cloud over with puzzlement and then clear in sudden understanding. Dubey looked uneasy for a moment. Then he shrugged and asked if Samorin would like some coffee.

'There are some magazines on the table. Unless you want to look at the *Lancet*.'

'All Greek to me, I'm afraid,' Samorin said cheerfully from the sofa by the window. 'I'll pass on the coffee and just enjoy the view.'

He waited for a full five minutes after they left the room before dialling Anna's cellphone.

'Keep him out of this room for the next twenty minutes,' Samorin said. Anna's yes was curt, businesslike.

He locked the door and sat on the doctor's chair, feeling its sudden depth and softness. He tried the drawers of the desk and much to his surprise found that they were open. Smiling to himself, he rifled through the papers: nothing interesting – bills, loan application forms, various firms' pharmaceutical literature. Then a file caught his eye under the other papers, a plastic see-through folder containing a covering note that read 'Macromolecular Architecture by Dr Karen Wooley, Professor of Bioorganic Chemistry'. Samorin's mind flickered. He opened the file. It showed diagrams and chemical equations. He put it back inside the drawer and walked across to the bookshelf. There it was, a slim bound file with the name Dr Karen Wooley on its spine. *Polymer Colloids*, its title read. He put it back. He would have to come to the doctor's study again.

Later.

Outside, a group of women in white saris appeared,

walking across the grass. In the sun, their faces were serene. Their heads were not shaved, and many of them wore their hair in tight plaits. Samorin thought of the old widow who had called him by his father's name. He knew who held the secrets to her ancient, dying eyes, who would be able to translate the puzzlement in her wheezing voice. After all this was over, there would be time to unlock the mystery that lay in wait for him in a distant childhood village, peopled with ghosts in coarse linen.

Later.

On the lawn, the widows were grouped under a jacaranda. One of them stepped forward and gestured to her companions. The door opened behind Samorin.

'Yoga,' he heard Dr Dubey say. 'These are leukaemia patients. The exercise eases their pain.'

'Where is Anna?'

'She's waiting for you in the car. She's upset, seeing Mrs Hassan. It'll pass. We're giving Mrs Hassan the best of treatment.'

Anna sat in the Jeep staring straight ahead through the windscreen at the widows doing yoga on the grass, her eyes unblinking, posture rigid. The wind blew stray strands of hair on her face, but she didn't seem to notice. Samorin touched her shoulder gently. Anna smiled a small smile.

'I cannot let this pass,' she said.

'I know.'

'Mama had been sedated heavily,' Anna said. 'She thought I was Salma. She scolded me for leaving school early without waiting for Irfan.'

Samorin stroked her hair. She laid her cheek against his palm.

'It is too late for me to save Mama, but I have to get

to Salma. Get her out of Aasha, away from Dhiren Das's spell, from this death-ridden place. For Irfan's sake. He would be really angry with me if I didn't save her.'

Beneath the curve of the sky, the afternoon unfolded over Brindaban like sunlit muslin, pleated with shadows. The wind that blew across the river and through the trees held a mild coolness. Samorin took Anna's hand in his.

'The doctor is the key,' he said. 'I may have found something.'

'Let's find a hotel first,' Anna said. 'I'm tired.'

'A hotel that takes cats. Big ones.' Samorin reached out behind her and patted Sasha.

Anna laughed, but her eyes were far away.

'Yes. A hotel with a nice warm bath. Where I can listen to what you have discovered, soak and think.'

'A plan?'

'In Kashmir, one of the first survival skills learned was the art of infiltration. Tonight, we infiltrate Aasha.'

The hospital dozed in the night, hugging the landscaped hillocks furry with grass. Samorin checked the zip-drive in the pocket of his multi-purpose vest. Anna had called her young computer whizz in the Electronic Crimes Research Wing in Delhi and persuaded him to email her a hacking programme that would help them get into Dr Dubey's computer.

'Careful,' she said as they neared the edge of the trees. They had spent nearly an hour circling the perimeter of the complex until they found a low wooden gate leaning against the wall, nearly hidden in the shadow of a great pipal tree. A hand-painted sign that read THE PARADISE OF DHIREN DAS was hung on a bent copper wire. A stuffed jackdaw mounted on the gatepost guarded the entrance, its feathers ragged and torn, beak open in timeless warning.

'Creepy guy,' Anna whispered.

A guard's whistle was shrill, but far away. Samorin gestured at the path that wound its way through the trees, losing itself in the shadows of the night.

'The path to paradise,' he said, 'with one man's paradise being another's hell. The doctor said Salma had gone to Dhiren Das's house from the hospital. I'm sure you'll find her there.'

Anna nodded in the dark, her eyes troubled. 'I'll meet you at the Jeep with Salma in half an hour. Any problem, I'll text you.'

Samorin gave her a brief hug and glanced up at the sky. It looked like mackerel skin, and the clouds moved drunkenly, lazily. The air was a glass cage. Samorin ran swiftly across the grounds, keeping well in the shade of the trees until he reached the edge of the copse. As the moonlight dimmed he moved towards the doctor's window, keeping close to the ground, careful not to throw a long shadow. The window was not even locked from the outside: obviously the confident Dr Dubey wasn't expecting visitors.

'Ghosts don't need doors,' Samorin thought wryly.

Once inside the room, he bolted the door and switched on the computer. Its screen's glow illuminated the room and turned the glass table top a submarine green. Samorin slipped the hacking pro-gramme into the A-drive, the software bypassed the password and Windows 2000 came up. It took five minutes for the zip-drive to be installed, which gave him time to leaf through a few of the medical books in the doctor's study. Cell research and genetic modification were Dubey's pet subjects. There were various papers on biometrics and controlled release applications.

'Huang H., Wooley K.L., Schaefer J.,' Samorin read the names out softly. 'Determination of the Composition of Shell Cross-linked Amphiphilic Core Shell Nanoparticles and the Partitioning of Sequestered Fluorinated Guests. A mouthful indeed!'

He picked up another file.

'Hello, a South Indian! Shanmugananda Murthy K. with Ma Q., Clark C.G. Jr, Remsen E.E., Wooley K.L. Fundamental Design Aspects of Amphiphilic Shell Cross-linked Nanoparticles for Controlled Release Applications. Again Wooley!'

There were more. 'Wang M., Weinberg J.M., Wolley K.L. The Synthesis of Poly(silylester)s via AB Monomer Systems. Zhang Q., Remsen E.E., Wooley K.L. Shell Cross-linked Nanoparticles containing Hydrolytically Degradable Crystalline Core Domains.'

Wooley – the name came up everywhere. Samorin copied the hard drive of Dubey's computer into his zip-disk, shut off the machine, and looked at his watch. Ten minutes to go. The building was eerily silent. He imagined the hospital as a giant catacomb, the patients motionless in sedated torpor.

'Death with room service,' Samorin thought grimly.

He sat in the doctor's chair, and put his feet up on the polished desk. He leaned back into the plush leather, shut his eyes, and started drawing in his mind. The presences in the room came to him gradually, shyly, and his mind opened out to touch them. They migrated into the endless space behind his eyes and cast grotesque reflections – lances of steel and scalpels tipped with blood, disembodied mouths rent in screams that were never heard but in sleep . . .

The place was evil, Samorin knew then without any doubt, and full of crippled phantoms. His mind became a dark, unfurling canvas and evil inked its footprints all over it like a drunken dancer from hell. In his imagination, blood was a primitive riverforce, a hurried viscous gush through which his thoughts kayaked along, crashing and careening away from upstretched, drowning hands and bodies that floated upside down in the carmine current.

'Composition of Cross-linked Nanoparticles.' The words flashed across his mind again.

'Controlled Release Applications . . .'

'Polio shots . . .'

The demonic footprints on the canvas turned into a swarm of microbes that kept transmuting into mutant organisms, full of cunning and disguise.

Sometimes evil can be so infinitesimally tiny, he thought, and the priests are forever ranting about the unseen destroyer who is ever-present in our souls . . .

'And in our bodies, too,' a calm, cynical voice within him said, 'its form sometimes so small that even your soul can't catch it.'

A grotesque picture formed in his mind, jolting Samorin as if with electricity. He suddenly knew how Mrs Hassan was being murdered. He had to read more, delve into the maze of the doctor's twisted genius, to draw out the final matrix of its simplicity.

'*Captain Shekhar.*' A tremulous, dry whisper came to him from the shadows of another street, of another time. Samorin shook his head, the ancient art of the warrior returning instinctively to him, compelling him to turn away from the clamour that always surrounded one in battle. It was one of those moments of revelation, full of incantatory advice: 'Concentrate on the present, examine it like a stranger, observe every detail of that which is bearing down on you. Thus you can slow down time and know how to defeat your adversary.'

In the chalky blur of reality and memory, the widow shuffled away into the brushstrokes of streets turning and mating, leaving the name of his father rustling upon the ground like a skeletal leaf.

Father.

Later.

Aunt can wait.

His cellphone beeped.

Anna's text message. 'Come now to Dhiren's house.'

Dhiren Das had been watching the morning swim in through the open door of his studio, flooding the great half-finished sculpture that stood in the centre of the room. It loomed over twelve feet in height and ten feet in width, a giant slab of stone and clay. He had been working on it late into the night, only to be woken up at dawn by Salma who had driven in from Delhi, wanting to see her mother, wanting to be with him. She now lay asleep on the couch beside the window, in the shadow of the sculpture. Her face was buried in the cushions, the long copper-coloured hair tousled and hanging over the edge of the couch. One soft, full white breast with its large pink nipple was visible in the crook of her arm. She was snoring softly.

The artist looked away from her, towards the sculpture glowing in morning sun. In the magical slyness of light and shadow, the last dance of Krishna it depicted seemed to be alive. His Krishna. The forms were yet to acquire their individual characters, which he would grant them one by one, as a god gives a destiny to those waiting to be born.

Should one of them be Salma, he wondered, looking at the sleeping woman. Her red mouth was wet, and her blue-veined eyelids were crinkled and stained with mascara. He peered closer, saw the fine, violet-coloured mesh of broken capillaries on her nostrils.

The woman drinks too much, he growled to himself. He felt a rough, passing affection for her. He enjoyed sleeping with her. He touched her hair and she shifted in her sleep, rolling over and crossing her legs. She looked faintly dirty to him.

'Obviously not,' he said out loud, 'she cannot be the Lord's bride.'

He turned to look at the unfinished contours of his sculpture. In his mind's eye it was already perfect, the detail exquisite. Krishna danced in his painted, terra-cotta garden, a lithe satyr holding a flute to his bearded lips. Krishna with a beard! That was new, the blue god with a dark beard and a ponytail. On his head was an insouciant band of gold, in which a peacock feather blew back in the breeze. In the same breeze that was trapped in plaster, the trees of Arcadia bent their branches heavy with fruit. Dhiren had briefly deliber-ated on assigning nipples to the fruit, but decided against it. The widows danced around Krishna, the widows of Brindaban, whose ruined hymens were restored by worship, by the grace of the dancing monster, who was the most compassionate God of all. Krishna had slain the terrible serpent who threatened his women, had given them shelter from the storm by raising the Govardhan mountain on his forefinger. He had one true love, Radha, while he cavorted with them all. The god who had seduced the river, the god of lost loves, the doomed blue divinity, was slain by a poisoned arrow as he contemplated the destruction wreaked in the *Mahabharata*.

Radha, his eternal love, thought Dhiren Das. Who is she among the widows, these abandoned women of this city of phantoms, populated with the wraiths of husbands who prowl the dreams of their once-upon-a-time women?

Salma muttered something in her sleep, opening her eyes briefly, heavily, and smiling at him from the edge of some vision.

Suddenly he knew what this woman meant to him, this woman who always wanted him to paint her, who always wanted to be his painting. He knew her destiny.

Memories came to him in a rush, shocking him with the chaos of their arrival. They swam in his blood and burned in his eyes, they chased the heat of his breath and bound his sinews. From the spaces within him that the years in their passing had locked up, the sculpture's presence called forth forgotten, voluptuous secrets, the power of their revelations begging to be retained for ever by him. Visions of lamplight gleaming on naked skin, a young whore's wet underlip, the damp musk of a succulent darkness. The laughter of women, the rustle of their linen, the odour of passing men upon their bodies. His mother, beautiful and long-haired, wearing a white sari whose edges gleamed with gold brocade, smelling like heaven and wild basil. He remembered her waking him up, slapping his small-boy hard-on playfully, while the fragrance of coconut chutney being sautéed with curry leaves drifted from the kitchen.

Dhiren felt himself grow hard, and his breath come in short spurts. For an instant he glimpsed the soul of his masterpiece, the vision filling him with power. Salma sensed it in her sleep, anticipating the roughness of stone and wood in his sculptor's fingers, aroused by the turpentine aftersmell in their whorls, and opened her eyes wide.

'Dhiren,' she said in her hoarse, urgent voice, which he privately called the voice from hell, 'fuck me.'

He gathered her in his arms in the brown shadow of the sculpture, his embrace opening like eternity.

'Oh yes, darling,' he whispered. 'Oh yes, all the way, until the end.'

And, afterwards, having said goodbye to Salma with a tenderness he had never thought he possessed, Dhiren Das had spent the rest of the day working on his masterpiece. He was obsessed with the painstaking aspects of detail: giving final form to the figures would start only after the base tableau was completed. In the end would come the joyful play of paint, the inspired application of colour that brought it to life. It would have a soul unlike any other work of art in the world. Nothing like the silly mermaid in Denmark, nor Rodin's stone, not even the Ellora carvings, nor the Bamiyan Buddhas – none of these possessed the soul of his Farewell to Art. He felt like God, creating God in clay.

'It's time for my last bow,' he said to himself, as he wetted the plaster further to mould the undulating platform of The Lord's Great Dance with his busy fingers. 'After this, I am immortal.'

Briefly he thought of Samorin, the cartoonist's angular art and his *kalari* moves. He felt irritated, wondering what had prompted Samorin to come to his mind.

A child of privilege, Das dismissed him, but lacking that special mental edge necessary to stand apart from the multitude. Ridiculous, all that pretending to be a chaser of evil! Dhiren laughed contemptuously. But he knew his laugh also held a sense of unease, a bitterness that he had been aware of ever since his boyhood, growing in him while he had watched his opponent practise knight moves in the dawn of a wind-seared mountainside.

Watching, and learning.

Dhiren Das shook the thought away. The sculpture dominated the room. Though incomplete, it lent the atmosphere a static that its creator could feel on his skin. Limbs seemed to shift unformed and pulsed within the great womb of lime and clay – the faceless Krishna danced and played his lute while the voluptuous waists of his women moved to its tune. Their features, yet to take clear shape, sprang forth in an incandescent moment of imagination; the god's erection was full of mythical seed, and the Brindaban of legend was once again coming alive. He who had made the god with his own fingers was God.

Stumbling out of the house, intoxicated with labour and vision, Dhiren Das was unaware that Anna and Samorin were about to break into his studio. He did not see them as they walked around the sculpture, examining it, Samorin taking out his little notebook and beginning to sketch. He did not hear Anna opening and closing doors as she moved through the rooms of his house one by one, calling out for her sister-in-law. He did not see them return to their vehicle in disappointment, the policewoman carrying Salma's crumpled brown pashmina scarf, which she had discovered on the floor behind the couch. He did not know that the fosa waited patiently inside the Jeep, its primal senses anticipating the dawn long before the sky above began to lighten.

Dhiren Das was sitting in the library of his house in Delhi, sipping a congratulatory cognac, when the morning announced itself outside his window with a gentle, apologetic light. At the same moment Samorin turned the key in the ignition of the Scorpio and he and Anna began their long journey back to Delhi, and understanding.

CHAPTER THIRTEEN

At his home outside Delhi, the next day, Samorin went into seclusion with his drawing pens and art paper, drawing late into the night while the fosa patiently kept watch over its master. He hardly spoke, not even when Anna returned to visit him in the house in the wilderness, to rooms littered with unfinished sketches. The illustrations had a malignant, brooding quality to them – unfinished, screaming mouths, hands that held chisels and lutes, dancers who drank from skulls. It was as if, through his drawings, Samorin's mind was exploring the details that lay hidden in every shadow, analysing the intricate lines and crosshatch of each dark emotion and desire. Anna was becoming frustrated that there was no news of Salma; she was not at home, nor was she answering her cellphone.

'The doctor at Max Healthcare called me, unable to

find Salma,' Anna said, sitting down.' 'His fears were confirmed, Mama has leukaemia. Pretty advanced, too. I have to get her out of Aasha.'

'You can't do it without Salma,' Samorin said, 'or at least, talking to her.'

'This is typical Salma,' Anna said, 'disappearing for weeks, no news, no calls. And suddenly turning up smiling one evening on your doorstep, asking whether she couldn't come in for a drink.'

Samorin looked up at her from a drawing.

'She has done this before, has she?'

Anna shrugged.

'Why? Where does she go?'

'Ask Salma anything and you get no answers.' Anna said. 'Salma herself is one big question.'

'Maybe we are asking questions in all the wrong places,' Samorin said. 'Maybe we have to look for the answer from where it all began.'

'I don't understand.'

'I'm sure you'll find some of the answers to Salma from Dhiren. There is a connection between them I can't quite grasp,' Samorin said, 'and to get answers from Dhiren, you have to seek the source.'

'The source of Dhiren Das?'

Samorin got up. Sasha's ears pricked.

'The Village of the Widows,' he said. 'I'm going there now.'

In the taxi, riding along the familiar road from Coimbatore airport, the route leading to Aunt and home, Samorin felt a strange disquiet. The hump-backed rock, scored with political graffiti large enough to be seen from descending aeroplanes, shone in the sun, and the tiny yellow thatched roofs of cottages looked freshly washed. Here was a comforting album of landmarks subconsciously absorbed over the years: the black palmyra trees standing out against the blue sky, the endless emerald of rice paddies, thick hedges of fragrant green behind which were cool verandas where men sat and played cards, smoking cheroots and calling out to their women for more tea. But he knew that this time the journey home was somehow different. He sensed the company of unseen ghosts. He felt their shivering presences, ethereal as glinting shards of light on the wingtips of dragonflies riding the wind.

The cellphone rang. It was Anna.

'I met Dhiren, Jay. And I'm so pissed off.'

'You went to him asking for Salma? He must have loved it.'

'The bastard was so solicitous. It was he who invited me over in the morning to talk about Salma. He lectured me for an hour about the need to leave her alone. He said that we have suppressed her personality, made her dependent on Mama, Irfan and me, and how now she had to find her own soul.'

'Did he know where she was?'

'If he did, he wasn't telling. He told me her car was still parked at Aasha.'

'You should have pulled him in for questioning.'

'Thought of that, too. But it would be pointless right now, and would only put Salma off further. Do you remember Superintendent Malik, the young officer in Brindaban, who seemed disappointed we were Das's friends? Well, I made his day. I sent him a personal message to start investigating Dhiren Das.'

'What will he find that we couldn't?'

'Ah, the ever-arrogant Samorin.' He could sense the

smile in her voice in spite of the anxiety. 'I'm scared, Jay. Irfan dead. Mama dying. Now Salma has disappeared, and I don't know where to find her.'

Samorin remembered Salma's face close to him, the drunk, dark eyes smeared with fear and loss.

'What Salma would hate the most is to be alone,' Samorin said. 'I think Dhiren has given her sanctuary. But the question is, where? And why?'

'Aasha, perhaps?'

'Good hunch. The thought did cross my mind. You could make young Malik even happier by asking him to take another look around the hospital.'

'It might not be that easy. Private welfare organizations in this country have a lot of political clout, especially if they have foreign funding. We can't move until we have good enough evidence. We'll get bad press.'

'I might have some evidence for you soon,' Samorin said, pausing for a moment. 'Just need to finish some business at home and I'm back.'

'Holding out on a partner, Jay?' Anna's voice was suddenly sharp.

'No. Just need to be certain.'

'I'm not sure I like the coyness in your voice, cartoonist,' Anna said. 'But I'll tell you something that might interest you about Aasha. My Internet expert has come up with something curious. Your friend Ambassador Tsiranana is the Honorary Chairman.'

'Charles Tsiranana?' Samorin was taken aback. 'What on earth does he have to do with widows?'

'Certainly worth asking. But I can't do it officially. Maybe Dhiren roped him into it. Maybe you could play chess with him again and ask some questions.'

Anna rang off. Samorin noticed that he had crossed

the Tamil Nadu border into Kerala. He could tell by the red flags he could see through the car window. Kerala, the land of the eternal Marx, he thought, sighing.

The mention of Tsiranana intrigued him – patron of Aasha? The urbane, smiling face, the perfectly manicured fingers, the Richard James suits and the aroma of Cuban tobacco didn't go with widows at all. Charles Tsiranana was an intellectual, a man with a mind sophisticated enough to analyze St Augustine and claim that the first racist undertones in Christianity started with him. He was so well versed in Plato that he could find similarities with the philosophy in the *Upanishads*, and his tastes were sufficiently catholic to appreciate both Titian and Dhiren Das. But a man with a heart that could relate to Indian widows?

Check, Jay.

In his mind, he saw the Malagasy frown as he contemplated the unexpected move Samorin had made in sacrificing his knight and moving his bishop to threaten Tsiranana's king. They sat by the tall window of the Ambassador's study, the ivory and walnut chessboard on the Moorish tea table between them. Bach played from the quiet gloom, distant and low.

The first time he had heard Bach was on a childhood night. He had been in the cusp of a half-sleep, and the flute fluttered into his stupor like tremulous moth wings. He had followed its trail as far as Aunt's room, only to find the door locked. Behind it, the needle of the gramophone that Grandfather had bought from London exorcized the engraved notes from the record. He heard a man's low laugh and Aunt replying in an undertone, but he could not distinguish her words from the music.

It had been as if a secret opera was being performed on that arcane night, a night within a night, created by the simple act of a door shutting and barring him from a loved, familiar room. He knew there was no point in knocking, the music would become suddenly louder and the conversation would cease, and Aunt would tell him gently but firmly to go back to bed. Once, he resolved to discover the identity of the phantom who visited her, and had hidden behind the armoire facing the door. He did not know when precisely he had fallen asleep, but in the morning found himself waking in his own bed. He vaguely remembered a dream in which a tall dark man had carried him to his bedroom. And beside him, on the pillow, was the tiny model of a red Ferrari.

The Prince of Children, the myth born out of a childhood mystery. It is not known when mystery becomes a myth; perhaps when the mystery remains unsolved and finally turns into a memory. And that was how he came to associate Bach with things hermetic, painful and forbidden.

Jay Samorin suddenly recollected the music that Tsiranana loved the most, sometimes interrupting a chess game for it, rising from his seat during a difficult manoeuvre and choosing a CD from his collection.

Johann Sebastian Bach.

That itself was a manoeuvre, Samorin thought wryly. Could the Malagasy have somehow intuitively understood what would distract his opponent? It was as if he had, through some occult espionage, read Samorin's mind.

He smiled to himself at the thought of his friend, acknowledging that sometimes Tsiranana was also an opponent. And he loved him all the more for it.

'I owe you a game, Charles,' Samorin chuckled. But he couldn't quite dismiss the fact that he was troubled by Anna's revelation about Tsiranana and Aasha.

The car had passed through Palghat town and turned onto the newly asphalted road that led to Manali. Samorin noticed that some of the paddy fields were now housing estates, and neatly planted coconut groves had replaced the palmyras. The topography of childhood was being changed, the dusty crimson road running down the plains from the hills now a smooth black strip. There were walls where fences once stood. But the great banyan tree with its unbound roots still swayed in the Malabar wind, the weathered stone idols of the snake gods intact. The wind-frayed hoods of the stone serpents were smeared with crimson paste. Someone had left a lamp smoking. A man on a motorcycle passed them, driving towards the fort. There was something about the stoop of his shoulders and the curve of the back of his neck that Samorin found familiar. He asked his driver to speed up, and they drew alongside the motorcycle rider. He pulled over to the grassy roadside, turning towards the car with a frown as it came to a stop.

The face had hardly changed, though a neatly trimmed moustache now sat under a small, squat nose.

'Chami!' Samorin called his childhood friend's name in delight, getting out of the car. 'It's you, isn't it? Don't you recognize me?'

The man looked at Samorin, who could see the eyes reading him as they sparkled with pleasure.

'Thampuran . . . er . . .'

'Jay,' Samorin said firmly, putting an arm around the shoulder of his friend and shaking his hand. 'This is rich. You didn't even recognize me.'

Chami pulled his motorcycle up onto its stand and smiled. He was tall and thin like his father, and wore a white cotton shirt and blue polyester pants. They leaned against the side of the car. Chami pulled out a packet of Wills Flake and offered one to Samorin.

'This is fantastic,' Chami exclaimed, 'seeing you after all these years.'

'I do visit Aunt once in a while, though you never come to see me.'

Chami shrugged. 'You know how it is. Your aunt never really approved of me, especially after I told you vampire tales.'

'Oh yes, the Vampire of Cardamom Hill.' Samorin laughed, and then remembered the widow in Brindaban.

'The Vampire is not a joke, Thampu . . . I mean, Jay,' Chami cautioned, 'people have seen her. And the Hill belongs to the Samorin family estates, although nobody is allowed to go there, even now. Who would want to anyway, unless you want your blood sucked out and your soul damned?'

Samorin snorted.

'I thought you were too grown-up to talk such village rot. I'm going to ask Aunt to take me there this time. And you can come with me.'

Chami took a deep drag on his cigarette and threw it away. It inscribed an arc of blue smoke as it fell.

'Your aunt still doesn't like me, Jay. She thinks I was behind getting the labourers' union to create trouble at last year's harvests.'

'And were you?' Samorin asked smilingly.

'Not at all, I work in the jail now. But my college friend, Sunilan, is a labour leader now, and he is often seen with me. That idiot Madhavan Nair, who was the jail warden, must have poisoned your aunt's ears.'

'You work at the jail now? As what?'

'The records clerk. That was the advantage of being a communist student leader in my youth. I had to pay our Left Front MP only a quarter of the bribe he normally takes, for me to get the job. Old comrades and whatnot.'

Samorin did not laugh. 'I need to see you then. Urgently.'

'For what? You are seeing me here already.'

'I need to look at the records of a crime that took place in the early 70s. Just a personal obsession.'

Chami frowned, his eyes clouding.

'Your father? You should let sleeping dogs lie.'

Samorin held Chami's shoulder and forced him to look him in the eyes.

'No. Would you, if it was your father who was hanged for murder?'

Chami did not answer and shook his head slowly.

'I don't know. What is the point? It will only cause you more pain.'

'I want to know, don't you understand? I want to know everything about a father I never knew.'

'What will you learn from jail records?' Chami sounded tired.

'Everything. From the day he was arrested and brought inside, to the last day he spent on earth.'

Chami straightened up and looked his old friend in the eye.

'Tomorrow,' he said. 'Meet me tomorrow morning and I will have all the records ready for you.'

Aunt wasn't at home when he arrived. She had gone to Cochin, the servants informed him – a case in the High Court about the rescue of an unwilling widow from a prostitution ring. She would be back tomorrow at the earliest. Kamala was still around, they told him, lording it over the Village of Widows. She was the police's main suspect in the case, but her lawyer was claiming that the girl had been kidnapped by Aunt, who had called herself a social worker. Supposedly on the pretext of wanting to distribute grain, fruit and vegetables to the village, Aunt was trying to influence the poor widows to work on her estates for free.

'You mean Aunt still goes there?' Samorin asked the steward, Narayana Menon. The old man bowed his greying head, the disapproval sketched on the lines of his face.

'She is the *Thampuratti*, who can do as she pleases. I can only hint that she is feeding serpents by going there every time. But she admonishes me as a foolish old man who doesn't understand the helplessness of widows. And how dare I contradict my lady?'

Samorin asked for his things to be sent to his old room, and the estate car to be brought out. Menon had followed him to the portico.

'Yes?'

The old man cleared his throat. 'If only *Cheriya Thampuran* would talk to your aunt about Kamala.'

'What about the old widow?'

'She is poison. And one day helping these widows will only bring shame on this house.'

Samorin switched on the ignition of the Maruti Esteem, and told Menon he would be back for lunch. He was going to the municipal library.

He would search again there as he had done so many times before, looking for hidden clues in the construction of sentences and events. Gazing upon faces in grainy black-and-white photographs, he would try to read something in the stance of his father or the look in his eyes. He would strive to discover similarities, some hidden pattern in the way paragraphs were written about the trial. He would attempt to summon up the phantom voice of his mother to speak to him, to tell him about what had really happened that night. Did she have a lover, who held her naked in his arms, who made love to her the way Father had, with passion and ardour? Or was his father a covetous monster, whose greed for her lands made him sneak up on her as she slept, tired out waiting for him, dreaming of his mouth on hers and his hands on her breasts, eyes opening at the final moment of betrayal?

Samorin pored over the newspapers once more in the library – *Deshabhimani*, *Mathrubhumi*, *Malayala Manorama* and *Indian Express* – pausing again and again over the photographs of the trial, reading editorial commentaries on the murder calling for justice. He read about his father's and mother's friends and schoolfriends. He was learning about his parents from the archives of another time, an impersonal education garnered in scraps. A fighter pilot, who was retired and lived in Kanpur at the time of the trial, commented on how brave a pilot Shekhar Samorin was, and how he had taken out Pakistani tanks with the precision of a Robin Hood. A colonel in the Air Force, who was running a consultancy, said that Samorin had been exemplary as a leader, and that his men would follow him to the ends of the earth. 'They trust him, and to trust a man in the sky is more demanding than anything else. Because we are used to the ground beneath our feet.'

And that was how Father had died. Samorin closed

his eyes. In the sky, without the ground beneath his feet.

He read about Kamala fiercely proclaiming her husband's innocence, and how much he loved her and her little son, Dhiren. Remembering his past encounter with the gross mountain of flesh and the baleful eyes, he marvelled at how beautiful she looked in the pictures. He marvelled at how beautiful everyone looked at the murder trial. Father, handsome and self-assured, Mother gorgeous in silk and kohl, Aunt severe and elegant; it was as if murder had chosen its actors well that time.

He turned the pages, passing the trial and the verdict.

'The Mysterious Case of the Overworked Medic': a headline caught his eye, and a photograph of two men in uniform was displayed alongside the story. It showed Father in the company of another officer, leaning against a counter and smiling at the camera.

The news report said that because of the sudden cholera epidemic in the area, the government doctor, who also doubled as the jail doctor, was overworked. So the District Warden, Madhavan Nair, had requested Dr Pillai, who had retired from the Indian Air Force, to officiate at the hanging of Squadron Leader Shekhar Samorin. Dr Pillai was the other man in the photograph, and had served with the condemned man as the squadron's doctor.

'Can a man sign the death certificate of an officer he had served under, and loved and respected?' the writer asked. 'Is it fair on the part of the jailer to place a retired Air Force officer in such a dilemma, especially when both the District Magistrate and Collector were in hospital, felled by cholera.'

233

Should the Collector and the DM be given 'private wards' in a government hospital when people were dying of the epidemic and the official doctor was doing double shifts? the paper asked sarcastically in a front-page editorial. Did a murderer's death warrant the presence of a doctor, albeit a retired one, when he could have been conscripted to help at the hospital? The medical staff there were struggling to cope with increasing numbers of patients, who were being brought in hourly.

There were letters to the editor pleading for the warden to spare Dr Pillai since it would be traumatic for him to be involved in the case. Another correspondent wrote that the government doctor risked contracting cholera himself and should stick to jail work.

Samorin felt suddenly sick. In the slim spaces between the lines dark with printer's ink, telling stories and their tributaries, lay the unfinished foundations of his own life. In the recounting of his mother's death, in the shame of his father's ruin, and in the fierceness of Kamala's protestations, the scandal had already begun to shape his life long before he knew anything about it.

It was that shape he knew he must understand now, completely.

CHAPTER FOURTEEN

The following morning, standing in the courtyard of the great black fort Tipu Sultan had built in Palghat, Jay Samorin felt he was somehow possessed. The sun washed the towering granite walls daubed with lichen and moss, cleaning the paved stone courtyard with liquid light, pouring speckled patterns of gold inside the shadows of ancient mango trees. The fort had housed the Palghat District Jail since British times, like all of Tipu Sultan's belongings taken over after the fall of Seringapattinam.

Samorin was aware of a presence beside him as he drove to his meeting with Chami. It seemed to him that his imagination was being subtly invaded and controlled. It was as if he was seeing the day through another's eyes, as if he was seeing for the first time the looming black shoulders of the fort sunk into the hill-side, the turrets sharply defined against a pewter sky.

The act of seeing was like a memory being reborn, but he was not sure whose fragment of remembrance it was.

The moat was overgrown with fat water plants, pink and white lilies floating on the still, silent water. Once upon a time crocodiles lived there, fattened on the flesh of prisoners thrown down from the ramparts. Now the prisoners were kept securely inside the jail built by a justice more bureaucratic and even-tempered. Samorin gazed upon the low yellow building with the Indian tricolour fluttering from a flagpole inside the quadrangle, and felt an eerie familiarity. A police Jeep was parked under a huge mango tree, its branches sweeping low towards the ground before arching away, its shadow minted with sunspots. A woman was being unwillingly led to the jailer's office by two policemen, her hair in disarray, her sari dragging on the ground. Samorin locked the car door and walked towards the reception.

Every step he took seemed to echo other steps of years ago.

Somewhere there on the beaten earth of the fort, hidden among the spoor of a million passages, lost among the footprints of faceless visitors over the years, mingling with the dust of doomed arrivals and grieving departures, was the mark of his father. His father would have crossed the coins of sunlight that were scattered in the shade, would have walked across the courtyard square, inlaid with dull red brick, and climbed the seven steps that led to the long, rectangular veranda of the jail.

Prisoners looked out at Jay Samorin curiously. These were the minor offenders: pickpockets, burglars and local bullies. They would have looked at his father the

236

way they were looking at him now; half-naked men in white sarongs, clutching the iron bars that separated them from the world outside, shouting out their sneering welcomes. And Father would have inclined his head like a fallen general, conscious that he was still a warrior, a half-smile playing on his lips, his hair blowing in the breeze that rode down the Western Ghats and swept through the scented air of their estates.

'Jay,' someone called, breaking the spell. Samorin turned to see Chami. They shook hands briefly, and Chami led him inside. A garishly painted portrait of Jawaharlal Nehru smiled down from the yellow wall, his trademark rose stuck into the buttonhole of a bright blue *achkan*. His successor, Lal Bahadur Shastri, and his daughter, Indira, flanked him; her smile was carmine, teeth pointed and sharp, and the white crescent on her hair had the style and assurance of a fabled inheritance. Chami lit a cigarette, blew a smoke ring and gave a brave smile.

'Are you sure you want to see the records?'

'Yes.'

Samorin followed Chami into an ante-room that was empty except for a low table and a single rattan chair. A regulation government file lay upon the table beside a brass vase that held a bunch of dusty plastic flowers; the file looked disarmingly ugly, covered with red canvas flaps and bound with dirty white string.

'Took me a while to get hold of these,' Chami said. 'The warden keeps the records of all important prisoners in his office. A practice, I'm told, Madhavan Nair started after your father's death. One needs to fill in a special form and stuff.'

'So how did you manage?'

'Magic!' Chami winked, showing even white teeth. 'The warden's secretary is a nice girl.'

'Aha!'

'Hope to marry her some day,' Chami said with sudden seriousness. 'What about you? You married yet?'

Samorin shook his head, eager for Chami to leave him alone, keen to feel his finger on the edge of the first page he would turn. Chami lingered near the door, as if his presence guarded his childhood playmate from some dangerous knowledge that threatened to change him for ever. Then, with a sigh, he closed the door behind him, leaving Samorin to read about the last days of his father.

The records were yellow government-issue paper and held dried corpses of long-dead silverfish. The text was typed in double space on an old-fashioned Remington, and the opening page read:

Sq. Leader Shekhar Samorin, sentenced for execution, pending Appeal in Kerala High Court.

A passport-size photograph of his father, pasted on the second sheet, ambushed him – Father smiled up at him, the eyes so black and real. He tried to caress the smile on the dead lips with one finger, stroked the curly forelock and outlined the contours of the strong jaw. With a sigh, he sat on the rattan chair to read. He read slowly and carefully, sometimes turning the pages back, rereading and connecting fresh information with previous paragraphs.

Samorin learned that his father had liked to walk each day for two hours in the courtyard, a special concession granted him by the warden – the normal exercise time allowed a prisoner on death row was fifteen minutes in the morning and the same again in the evening. He learned that Father preferred black coffee from his own plantations, that this was delivered to him daily from home, and on Sundays Aunt would send him elaborate meals in a tiffin carrier. Samorin read that his father used the jail library constantly, and had asked for a fresh pack of cards so that he could play solitaire. He had one visitor almost every day and Samorin fondly traced the ink of Aunt's signature on the entry logs, ink that had dried decades ago. She was allowed fifteen minutes each time.

Savitri Thampuratti. For Cell No. 3.

Signed in by Venu Kurup.

Samorin struggled for an instant with recollection; the name Kurup was familiar. Then he remembered reading about Venu Kurup in one of the newspapers in the archives. The writer had wondered about karma and duty, and marvelled at the web of coincidence that surrounded the murder of Shyamala Samorin. The officiating physician, Dr Pillai, had served in the condemned man's squadron, like the warden, Madhavan Nair. And Venu Kurup, the jailer in charge of death row, had been his batman! The newspaper had carried this as a scoop; it seemed as if the colleagues of Shekhar Samorin, in other battles his allies, were now to be his executioners.

Samorin lit a cigarette. Was Venu Kurup alive now?

Father was the only condemned man on death row at that time, and the corridor was patrolled every night by none other than his former batman. Master and servant, prisoner and guardian.

The records noted that the lights that were meant to be kept on at all times were switched off at night on the request of the prisoner; another favour granted by the warden himself.

Small mercies, unusual irregular favours. No wonder the warden did not want the records to be available to the public.

The gallows were inspected by the prison carpenter (Fee Rs. 10) and found sturdy enough to hold Father's 72 kilos, the last count had said. He had lost only one kilo in three years. The rope (Cost Rs. 18) was bought and tested with a sack filled with wet sand, and found to be in perfect condition. A receipt was attached to the page with a rusty pin.

On the last night, Aunt had visited his father with food and fresh clothes.

Chicken biriyani and *aviyal*, the inventory read. One blue cotton shirt, one pair of dark trousers, socks and shoes. And she was accompanied by someone, whose name was not mentioned in the record.

Savitri Thampuratti plus One, signed in by Venu Kurup, 17 October 1974.

Odd. Must have been Narayana Menon, come to see the master on his last day.

Prisoner very composed, Madhavan Nair had scrawled in a note on the entry form, asked for a bottle of Laphroaig to be delivered from his personal stock. And even joked about how strong the spirit was.

Samorin smiled to himself, imagining Father sitting in his cell with Aunt and Narayana Menon, who served him the whisky in crystal tumblers from home. Did he invite his old friend and comrade, Madhavan Nair, to join them? Did he have a farewell toast to share with his former batman and attendant, Venu Kurup?

With trepidation, Samorin turned to the page that he knew would contain the details of the hanging.

It was missing.

A loose sheet of paper inserted into the file stated simply that Sq. Leader Shekhar Samorin was executed at 4 a.m. on 18 October 1974.

The death certificate was signed by Madhavan Nair himself, the District Magistrate and the Collector both being indisposed in the hospital with cholera. It was witnessed by Dr Pillai, who declared the prisoner dead and was supported by Venu Kurup (Retd IAF), Jail Guard.

The body was handed over to Savitri Thampuratti and Visitor No. 2. Her special request to let the black hood remain on the face of the dead body was respected.

Samorin remembered newspaper reports that said Father's cremation took place at Cardamom Hill and Savitri Thampuratti had not invited anyone to attend.

And then Samorin found what he was looking for.

The warden had scribbled at the bottom of the file's folder: 'Prisoner's Last Wish. If his son comes looking for him, to tell him his father was innocent.'

Samorin felt a tidal hope surge through him, lifting him and flinging him up into the freedom of an exultant sky. Father knew! He knew his son would come seeking the truth. Samorin sat back in his chair, giving himself up to the meaning of his father's final message. It ended the silence of the gallows, the dark imaginations of a distant dawn. It was the first and only thing Father had ever said to him: 'I am innocent. I did not kill your mother.'

For him that was enough. And it changed everything.

But there were too many riddles which remained unanswered in Manali – in the atmosphere of this small town, taut with its bands of loyalty, intrigue and subterfuge.

Who was the mysterious visitor who accompanied Aunt? Was it the faceless stranger in the library, whose conversation had been drowned in the fugues of Bach? Where did Kamala's husband disappear to? Why did Aunt not remove the hangman's hood?

He had to go to the Widow's Village. The greeting of a half-blind prostitute who called him by his father's name in faraway Brindaban, the inexplicable and perverse hatred of Dhiren Das, the toys left for him to find as a child, Aunt's long silences. Riddles still to be solved.

Chami looked worried as Samorin came out of the ante-chamber.

'Are you OK?'

'Never felt better. And thank you, Chami, for this.' Samorin sat and lit a cigarette, waving away the offer of tea. 'I am at peace now.'

'Tell me . . .'

'Father had left a message for me, but I'm surprised Madhavan Nair didn't tell me. I've met him often with Aunt, but he never said a word.'

Chami clapped his old friend on the shoulder. His eyes were bright and suspiciously moist.

'Oh, I'm so glad, so glad.'

Samorin went across and embraced him.

'Tell that girlfriend of yours in the warden's office that I will give her a gorgeous wedding present. Soon.'

Samorin walked down the steps into the sun. The day felt brighter, lighter. Chami called out from behind him. Samorin turned.

'What was the message that Thampuran had left for you?'

Samorin smiled.

'Freedom,' he said.

The afternoon flung its warmth like a golden parasol over the countryside and the shade of wayside trees appeared deeper and cooler as Samorin drove past on his way to the Village of the Widows. Roadside vendors selling iced drinks dozed beside their ramshackle carts, crows called out desultorily from the canopies of *ilanji* trees. The mirages wavered in the heat over the road, a shimmering curtain of watery light distorting the shapes of vehicles that passed through. *Mrigathrishna*, Aunt used to call them. A bullock cart slowly emerged from one such mirage, as if the sky were birthing it, the edges of its form blurring and burning. The *mrigathrishna* vested Samorin's journey to the village with the thrilling incandescence of mystery, transforming the ordinary into a mystical, unreal configuration.

He drove along the new road up the mountain, crossing the familiar thickets of bamboo and the hedges of wild, spicy vegetation. Purple palmyra fruit lay fallen in clusters by the roadside, upon tawny grass verges covered with shredded bamboo leaves. He skirted the marsh that stretched away to the foothills, and passed the single line of whitewashed houses, their red tiled roofs pitted with thick green moss. He glimpsed two women coming out of their homes at the approach of the car, to stand leaning provocatively against the pillars. An old woman's voice called out to them in a harsh monotone, and one of the women turned back and gave a laughing reply. Her hair was tousled and long, strung with fading jasmine, and the

243

band of her sari fell away from her blouse. A child came running out of a lane, rolling a bicycle wheel, and stopped abruptly on seeing the car. The wheel bobbed away and hit a veranda wall. Someone cursed from inside, but the child took no notice.

And so I return to the mystery of expeditions at dawn, Samorin told himself. And I will not leave without an answer.

He stopped the car and walked up the steps of the last house on the street – the first house Aunt always visited. It was the first time he had entered its portico, with its wooden pillars and low-beamed roof supported by carved wooden rafters. The veranda's ledge was paved with smooth red stone, as was the floor. He knocked on the thick wooden door studded with iron bolts and sleeves, expecting it to open and reveal the gross, malevolent bulk of Kamala. The ruins of her beautiful face came to him, distorted by loneliness and the need for revenge. But there seemed to be no-one there. Samorin gave the door a push, and called out for Kamala. It opened into silence.

The Village of Widows doesn't need protection, Samorin thought, it is a taboo land. Except for those who come to seek the pleasure of abandoned bodies and leave in the secrecy of the breaking dawn.

He stepped into a narrow, dark room that was curtained off from what seemed to be the sitting room. The curtain was printed with pictures of parakeets in cages. It smelt faintly of damp. He entered Kamala's chamber, garishly furnished with pink plastic chairs and bright red carpets. A wooden table was draped with a white lace cloth and a huge vase full of fading hibiscus flowers sat in the middle. Beside a large painting of a nautch girl, undressed and with a goblet raised to her lips, framed pictures of the god Guruvayoorappan and the goddess Lakshmi were lit up with coloured bulbs.

Whore kitsch, Samorin thought grimly as he turned to see a painting that occupied pride of place in the room. A recognizable style: early Dhiren Das showing a thoughtful Krishna gazing Narcissus-like at his own reflection in the Yamuna. The god's flute lay beside him on the grass, the peacock feather askew on his hair. Behind him, from the forest, someone was watching. Samorin could distinguish the eyes from the shadows, feeling their dark intensity – but could not tell if it was a woman or a man. Suddenly, the painted gaze was more powerful than anything else in the room, filling it. It was as if someone was trapped inside the painting, cursed by a sorcerer's spell to become an eternal witness, and the dark magic had caused the victim's life to gradually lapse into the brushstrokes of paint and turpentine, leaving only the eyes alive to watch for ever. Samorin stepped back with a small cry – below the painting, to the left of the room towards the corner, sat Kaiser.

Kaiser, the faithful dog that went missing one distant childhood afternoon.

'Kaiser.' Samorin spoke the name in wonder. In that room, the witchery of time dominated. It spun gazes and threw voices, it distorted shapes and commanded mirages.

'Kaiser!' Samorin called out but the dog did not move. He expected Kaiser to leap up, barking furiously and wagging his tail, placing his paws on Samorin's chest and licking his face. He took a step forward, watching his trusty, long-lost pet sitting in his corner, tongue hanging out, tail stretched out on the floor

245

without a twitch of recognition. His eyes were fixed on his old master.

Bemused, Samorin reached out to touch the dog. Kaiser felt hard and crusty. He knew then that it was not Kaiser at all, but a life-size replica of the dog. It was crafted with consummate skill, its lolling tongue so perfectly sculpted that it showed every serrated, nodular detail.

'Kaiser . . .' Samorin whispered, comprehension dawning slowly.

The model must have been made many years ago, as Dhiren Das began to master the laws of lime, clay and plaster. A small portion had broken off from Kaiser's front leg, revealing the clean, dry white of bone underneath. Samorin gasped.

'Hey, you!' A sharp voice whipped the air behind him and Samorin turned to see the bulk of Kamala framed by the doorway against the afternoon.

'Who are you? What do you want?'

She came closer, and her eyes widened with recognition.

'Oh, the thampuran from the House of Samorin,' her voice was soft, low and seductive, 'come looking for a girl, have you? I have plenty. Do sit down.'

Samorin shook his head in mute protest, his eyes straying to Kaiser. Kamala giggled.

'Oh, Dhiren made it himself from a dog he found.' There was pride in her voice, and a dark knowledge that lay beneath. 'Isn't he good? So talented, and you got him kicked out of school.'

Her voice had risen, and she came close to Samorin, thrusting her face into his. He could see the broken veins on her skin, the pores on her cheeks open with alcohol. Her breath was sharp and spicy. Samorin held up a hand as if in defence, but she pressed on.

'You are a murderer's son, and you cannot hide it,' Kamala snarled. 'And your family destroyed my husband and left me a widow, and turned me into a prostitute. Did you think I would let Dhiren rot the way that your bitch of an aunt wanted me to?'

'Be careful of what you say, Kamala,' Samorin warned. 'My aunt has been feeding you all these years.'

'My body was feeding me and my son. And the bodies of other widows like me. Your aunt's offerings were mere bribery.'

'Bribery for what? It was due to her that the widows didn't have to starve and sell their bodies. But you are a monster. And you created a greater monster in your son. Now I understand.'

Kamala spat at Samorin, the spittle thick and phlegmy on his face. He wiped it away in reflex, hand raised to hit her.

'Hit an old slut, just like the policemen who fuck you and then beat you. Go on, son of a murderer, break my bones.'

'Not worth it,' Samorin said, wiping his face with his handkerchief, 'you are too damned to be saved.'

The woman grabbed his collar in one fist and drew his face to her. 'Why have you come? To laugh at us with your superiority, just like your aunt did?'

'I came to look for some answers, woman. And my aunt helped you for no other reason than out of the goodness of her heart.'

'What about our children, Samorin? What about those disinherited, deserted children who languish with their abandoned mothers? Do they become pimps and thieves while your aunt brings her damned rice and vegetables once a month? Or do they all go to private schools like the privileged children of some murderers?'

'As did Dhiren. And you forget Aunt paid his fees.'

The widow cackled and spat on the floor.

'Blood money, that was what it was. For ruining me and my family.'

'How did Aunt ruin you? It was your husband who testified against my father in court.'

'Lies, all lies!' she screamed. 'Sivadas was innocent. He had to flee because the Samorins were too powerful. He ran for his life.'

The widow slumped to the floor, holding her head in her hand, rocking and wailing softly. 'He must be dead by now, my Sivadas, or hiding somewhere, an outcast in some other land. If only he knew, how proud he would be of Dhiren.'

'Well, Dhiren's famous now. And rich, too.'

Kamala looked up with a twisted smile, her eyes passionate with grief.

'He used to see you sitting in the car when your aunt came with her cursed gifts, and he would ask me in that little voice I remember so well, "Mother, who is that boy in the car? Why doesn't he come to see me? I want to play with him."'

'Why didn't you let him?'

'Play with a murderer's son? Play with the seed of a family that ruined mine? Never!'

'You have so much hate, Kamala. And I can see it in Dhiren, too.'

'Don't you say a word about him, a word, or I'll kill you,' she hissed. 'He could have been you — my son — he too could have played in the lap of his father,

248

grown up to be a master of the *kalari*, accomplished and intelligent as he is . . .'

'He does the *kalaripayattu* well,' Samorin observed drily.

'Oh yes, he does,' the widow laughed mirthlessly, 'he is Ekalavya, the outcast who is better than his master.'

The myth of Ekalavya is found in the *Mahabharata* – the story of the jungle boy who was refused a warrior's instruction by Dronacharya, the royal teacher. In secret, observing the master, he became the greatest archer in the world, better than Arjuna, who was the teacher's pet and the most accomplished archer of them all. The master insisted on *gurudakshina*, the traditional offering a guru demanded from his disciple, and ordered Ekalavya to cut off his bow-hand thumb as a sacrifice.

'But Dhiren needed to sacrifice nothing, I made sure of it. My body made sure of it.'

Samorin looked at the woman on the floor, and the tawdriness of her surroundings. He felt a stab of pain at the sight of the bone that gleamed through the plaster of Kaiser's sculpture.

'You sacrificed his soul, Kamala,' Samorin said, 'and you did it all for yourself.'

He moved swiftly past her before she could rise from the floor and launch herself at him, eyes flashing, spittle flying, pudgy hands reaching for his eyes. Her scream followed him as he walked to his car, to look for Aunt and her answers.

The evening waited for him beyond the mountains.

CHAPTER FIFTEEN

Samorin ate alone in his room that night. Aunt had not yet returned from Cochin. Outside, the wind spoke in the trees with the tongues of myriad leaves, and branches creaked like masts in a storm. Through the window, the pallid moon was fitfully obscured by the indolent passing of wispy clouds.

He poured himself a Hennessy in a balloon glass and stretched out on the planter's chair in front of the television. Anchorperson Rajdeep Sardesai's eyes looked rounder than usual, as he angrily wagged an admonishing finger at an ancient, shrunken ideologue who droned on about the need to throw multinationals out of India. Samorin flipped through the channels. Young, semi-clad women gyrated to film songs, and the hunt for Osama was still on CNN. Then he hit STAR World and suddenly there was Dhiren Das on the screen, filling it with his flamboyant presence. The long black hair, loose and freshly washed, gleamed in the studio lights, and the restless fingers constantly inscribed pictures in the air around him.

'Art has no morality,' he was saying, his white teeth flashing in a wolf-like snarl, 'Art itself is the final beauty.'

The interviewer was a pretty young woman in a black top and dangling earrings. She simpered in the artist's presence.

'Are you saying anything is permissible in art? That the artist has no duty towards the world, or society?'

Dhiren fixed her with a burning stare. 'I search for ultimate beauty in art, and pursue the debate whether art has a soul. My final work is now ready, it will be unveiled next week at the Madagascar embassy. That will explain everything.'

The scene changed to a close-up of a smiling Krishna, and Samorin sat up. The image was so sensual, so powerful that he felt its energy invade his blood. It was the first time anyone would see the god with a beard; it was black with a white streak on the chin, and the full red lips under the curving moustache dreamed of a knowledge that was complete in itself. They recalled to Samorin the power of the words those lips could utter, in a voice so harmonious that the earth itself would stop turning to listen. The lower lip contained the memory of infinite kisses: the knowledge of women's mouths, skin and nipples, and the lush, aromatic richness of their wetness. The eyes were dreamy yet sharp, as if constantly supervising creation with tender understanding. The god's hair was tied back in a ponytail.

The camera panned away, filling the screen with Dhiren's gigantic sculpture. It made Samorin gasp at the opulent beauty of its detail, the colours vibrant and complicated. The sapphire-coloured god danced on a sleeping Radha with his back to her, one foot dimpling her navel further, the other turned to raise one creamy, pink-tipped breast. The supine woman had an air of exquisite abandon; her red lips were parted, heavy blue-lidded eyes lost in the passion of an ancient, visceral vision. Her hair was spread among the flowers, a garden in itself, her arm thrown over a meek doe whose neck was bent towards the feet of the god. The doe wore a garland of chrysanthemums. The trees of Brindaban were bent in the wind, their boughs ripe with fruit that shone among the gleaming leaves and perfect branches.

The *gopis* danced naked around Krishna and Radha, and a golden moon shone out of the eye of a peacock feather in the sky. There was something frightening, something chilling about the sculpture; the puppetry of the naked dancers concealed an awkward grief, a beautiful hopelessness that was their adoration of Krishna. Radha's repose hid a doomed beauty, as if her very breath was trapped and its plumes captured in plaster by Dhiren's fingers, while Krishna watched her dreams like a sentient but merciless master.

The phone rang and Samorin switched the television off, glad for the interruption. It was Anna. There was still no news of Salma.

'We called Dr Dubey in for questioning today and it was quite a surprise,' Anna said. 'By the evening the Police Commissioner was in touch. He was contacted by the Foreign Office to go easy on the doctor.'

'Bizarre. What has the Foreign Office got to do with a medic in Brindaban?'

'Apparently it was an informal request. I believe

Charles Tsiranana asked the Foreign Secretary to see that Dubey got good treatment.'

'Aha, the game's afoot, as the Master would say. Did Dubey say whether Salma came back to the hospital?'

'No. Apparently he hasn't seen her since she visited Mama the morning we were there.'

'She'll turn up. I should be back soon, Anna. Meanwhile get Max Healthcare to run some additional tests on Mrs Hassan's blood samples. See if they contain high levels of polymers. Know any doctor who specializes in gene therapy?'

'Perhaps. But what is this about polymers? My science results in school were abysmal.'

'I'm working on a theory, but I haven't yet had the time to thoroughly explore it.'

'Really? And what do I do with a gene specialist once I find him?'

'Let him test Mrs Hassan's blood samples and see if copies of an unusual gene turn up in different tissue samples. Or copies of the same gene turn up in unexpected places.'

'OK, doc, whatever you say.'

'Anna, one more thing. Can you try to find out everything you can about Dr Karen Wooley? She is an authority on genetics and it appears Dr Dubey is an ardent admirer of her methods. It's a hunch, but one that might pay off this time.'

'Jay, you are a strange man. Profiler of evil, chess player, tortured son, *kalaripayattu* warrior with the strangest pet anyone has ever seen! And now polymers and genetics. Do I know you at all?'

'Hmmm. One of these days, you will know me better than you know yourself.'

Anna's low laugh travelled to him across the

miles, like the distant sound of bells in the wind.

'Did you find what you went looking for?' she asked.

'Some of it. But I think I am nearing the end of my search. And I'm frightened of what I will find.'

'Aren't we all? Learning the unknown is scary.'

'Hmmm. Relearning the known is even scarier.'

'Be careful, Jay.'

'I will. And you, too. I want to be back in Delhi before Dhiren unveils his *pièce de résistance*.'

'We are watching him, but he rarely steps out of his studio. We have a policewoman working undercover as a cleaning lady in his studio, and a few more under-cover cops in the guise of gardeners and watchmen prowling around the hospital. All Das seems to be doing is putting finishing touches to his masterwork. And drinking heavily.'

'No women, huh?'

'Nope. It's as if he is baiting us. I do not for one moment believe that he doesn't know we are watching him. He is playing the game.'

Anna rang off and Samorin went back to his arm-chair with a sheaf of papers and crayons. He could not draw. It was as if the power of Dhiren's sculpture he had just seen had emasculated his vision. He felt rest-less and restrained, and wished Aunt would come back soon. He wanted to feast his eyes on her beloved form, lift her in his arms despite her delighted protests, kiss the face he had loved so much since childhood. He wanted to sit her down on the chair in the library and pour her Grand Marnier in the small liqueur glass she liked, and play her favourite records. And open the windows once the wind was calm, let the moon flood into the room, heightening the yellow light from the lamps. And he wanted to speak to her about the clouds in his heart, of Anna and Salma, of Dhiren Das and his work. About Kamala's revenge, about Madhavan Nair and why he had kept Father's message secret from him all this while.

He doodled desultorily, and poured himself some more brandy. The familiar atmosphere of the room now felt oppressive, and rising. Samorin threw open the windows. The wind had subsided, and the scented night seemed to carry a hint of rain. The breeze brought the odours of spices, and a nightbird sang from the darkness. Samorin walked out of the room, switching on the lights in the sleeping house. He opened the library door and pulled the curtains; the moonlight glowed on the leather of the sofas and the chair by the window, the runelike script on the spines of books glittered. He turned on the lamp on the writing table, illuminating the square of green damask. Aunt's desk was empty save for a few papers thrust upon a spike. Bored, Samorin flicked through them. A bill caught his eye: it was for a new water heater.

Aunt had noted on it in her small neat handwriting: 'Geyser, Cardamom Hill. For Miscellaneous File.'

Samorin frowned at the paper in his hand and stood thinking for a while. Returning to his room, he pulled on a light jacket, picked up a bag and locked the door of the house behind him.

Lake Spicewater was a gigantic mirror in the moonlight, like sleeping mercury. A thin fog rose up to the sky like the soft breath of dreaming water, and wavelets sloshed at the edges of the shore with tireless rhythm. Cardamom Hill was a forbidding bulk against the pale sky. The shoreline of the lake was ringed with trees and a giant banyan bowed low into the water, the reflection of its branches undulating gently in the current. This was the lake of the Samorins – and beyond lay the island of his clan, the final resting place of his doomed father.

In silent ritual, Samorin scooped water in one cupped palm and held it against his eyes. It felt cold and fresh. The foothills began just beyond the lake. Rising up out of dark clusters of trees and rock, the family estates of the Samorins looked down into the water. A road skirted the lake, leading to the two gateless pillars that declared the ownership of the land. It was this road Samorin took, a road he remembered from his childhood when he used to accompany Aunt on her occasional visits to their holdings.

He knew that if he climbed halfway along the first hill, he would find a path that sloped away from the main road and snaked down to the lake's shore from another direction. It led to the small jetty that jutted out into the water. Narayana Menon had taught him to fish sitting on its edge. He remembered Aunt calling out sharply to them as they sat dangling their lines in the water, her voice cutting across the evening at the exact moment he had felt a tug on his line. It jolted him. He had turned in time to see her walking down to the jetty. Narayana Menon was standing up, discomfited by the sudden coldness in her voice: a harsh, finite tone that made Samorin drop the rod into the lake.

There were never any boats tied to the jetty. And after the fishing incident, Aunt had ordered it to be fenced in and locked with heavy iron chains on the gates.

Now Samorin stood at the locked gates after thirty-odd years, and remembered Aunt's warning. 'There are always spaces that are forbidden to everyone, depending on their fate. It will save you sorrow if you do not venture into them.'

The forbidden lake, the island denied to him with its lore of white wolves and vampires, and its forest mansion where his father lay.

Father of the water, Father who is an island.

Samorin stripped and quietly placed his clothes in the waterproof bag he had brought with him, and slung it around his shoulders. The water was cold as he entered it, and a gentle wave tried to heave him back. He began to swim towards the island with steady, measured strokes. The mist was thickening and a waltz of fireflies escorted his passage. He could hear the nightbirds above, crying out in harsh and abrupt tones, and the moonlight flowed through his hands as they carved the water. With each stroke, Cardamom Hill came closer, rising higher and higher into the sky, slowly encompassing the swimmer in its vast dark shadow.

In that shadow Samorin rested for a while, lying upon the white sand and letting the wind dry his body. The half-hour swim had exhausted him. Fortunately, the disciplines of *kalari* had honed his muscles and toughened his sinews, and the reserves of strength a warrior gathers within himself over the years had stood him in good stead.

He took out his clothes, and pulled on the tough walking boots he had brought. He stretched, took out a pencil torch and flung the bag over his shoulder. He began to walk around the island in search of a path that would take him into the woods. He found it at last, a narrow ochre band snaking its way up between two huge *pala* trees into the dun of the forest night. Crickets filled the air with the chatter of their wings.

257

There were movements in the darkness beside him as the woods became dense, bodies moving through thickets and bush; perhaps wild pigs or hill cats. Samorin paused as he heard a dog howl from the opposite side of the bank, its lament taken up by others from far beyond. The moon seemed to be made of melting wax as it appeared through the gaps in the treetops above.

Samorin walked slowly, inhaling the sharp and fragrant night air. There was no sign of anything human or ghostly. He had been walking for nearly a mile when the trail climbed up to a ledge that overlooked the water and veered down steeply to a clearing in the woods. Through the trees he could see the white pillars of a house.

Half-hidden by the forest, here was the mansion of the stories, the residence of the vampire.

Samorin's skin pricked. He shook himself to dispel a shiver and began to walk slowly towards the house. Leaves fell in the jungle around him, rustling in the earth, bird calls flew across the night like unintelligible signals. He reached the edge of the clearing and paused.

In the courtyard of the house was a huge *champak* tree, its branches heavy with clusters of ivory-coloured flowers perfuming the night. A marble pavilion stood in its shadow, and on a bench, with her back towards him, sat a woman in white. Fallen *champak* flowers lay around her everywhere, shifting in the wind. Her hair was long and reached down to her waist, and she was combing it slowly and sensuously. Beside her stood a tall lean man, whose hair seemed streaked with the moon. He held a single white flower in his fingers and was bending over her to place it behind her ear. She was raising her neck to his fingers, and beyond them the house gleamed white against the trees, throwing its long shadow across an immaculate lawn, coming to rest at the foot of the pavilion. A fountain sparkled on the grass, its silvery plume scattering glitterwater in the breeze.

The Vampire of Cardamom Hill. And now he knew.

Before Samorin could cry out to the woman, he heard a deep growl and turned to see two great white wolves racing towards him. As they came closer, he felt time slow down. They were huge albino Alsatians and at the tumult of their approach, the man and the woman turned too. Her dark eyes widened and her hand flew up to her mouth in horror, dropping her ivory comb. Samorin saw the man's face and an icy charge of fear tore through him – he was staring at himself – but an older, more sombre version of himself. The flower fell from the man's hands as he twisted towards the intruder, his face bearing the signs of terrible sorrow long past. The eyes held an untamed grief. The mouth was edged with lines of fierce suffering, yet the smile that had frozen on his lips as he was bending towards his demon lover held the sad tenderness of a king in exile.

Then, suddenly, Samorin felt the first dog upon him. He spun away to take the beast on his hip while his hands moved in a *kalari* arc to crush the throat of the second, but his foot caught on a stone and he fell backwards with the weight of the dogs bearing down on him, their hot and putrid breath on his face. His head hit a rock and the sky abruptly turned into a funnel of black, a whirlwind spiralling him into nothingness. Before he lost consciousness he heard the woman screaming at the dogs to stop.

It was Aunt.

CHAPTER SIXTEEN

'There are some scars one should always keep,' Father told Samorin, showing him the long, thin mark between the thumb and forefinger. 'I got this subduing an enemy.'

Samorin touched it, marvelling at the act of touching that skin, a skin that he had thought he would never feel; this was time's boon, a turn of the hourglass before the sands ran out.

The scar was rough, pain's scrawl, the skin having healed over it clumsily, as if in healing it had unfurled into itself. His eyes closed, Samorin studied the imprint with his fingertip, catching it in his memory, adding it to the many scars of the heart. His father leaned over him and kissed his brow; below the gauze bandage he had bled a little.

Later, recalling Father's voice, feeling his scar, Samorin would have the impression that he was dreaming through rippling water. When the words were clear, Father's face would become blurred and Samorin would exert his mind, recalling it from the pleats of his memory, and then the voice would become the scattered idiom of the wind.

That was how he woke up.

He lay on an unfamiliar bed in an unfamiliar room with great windows whose white linen curtains were drawn. The walls were pale and high, and a painting showed a woman smiling at something that was both wonderful and sad at the same time – a short separation, perhaps. Later, he would recognize the artist as Raja Ravi Varma. But now, Aunt sat beside him on the bed, his hand in hers, her eyes dark with worry. He smiled at her and her eyes sparkled briefly; he tried to get up, but she laid a soft, restraining palm on his chest. As his vision cleared, the details of the room came into focus and he saw the stranger in the garden standing at the foot of the bed – the stranger who had his face. The eyes were now grave and gentle, and a smile trembled on his mouth. Beside him were two others, one of whom Samorin recognized as Madhavan Nair. He did not know the other, who came over to the bed as Aunt looked at him with a question on her face, and took Samorin's pulse. His voice came from far away.

'One more day and he'll be fine. A nasty concussion and some loss of blood.'

'Dr Pillai, I am in your debt once again,' the man said.

The doctor straightened up.

'Sir, you owe me nothing.'

Samorin's eyes turned towards Madhavan Nair. 'Why didn't you tell me?' he asked, but Madhavan

Nair did not respond. His voice was a distant rumble in his ears, and he realized Nair had not heard.

The faces were blurring again, and Samorin reached for Aunt's hand. Her fingers entwined with his as sleep drew its soft shawl over him.

'For the warrior, each scar is an object of meditation. Scars teach you the art of reflection, because all wounds need not be remembered,' Father said. 'Everyone receives one wound that is the most important one in his life, that changes him for ever. When that happens, there is a shift in the nature of things. The warrior realizes that its pain is different, it is a pain that comes with knowledge. That time has changed.'

'What did you do then?'

'I became a trapper of time. The scar became my interpreter of the world.'

When he next woke, it was morning. The sun heaved against the curtains in the wind, turning the window frame into a golden rectangle. Aunt dozed in an armchair beside him, a book upside down on her lap: *Les Misérables*, Samorin noticed with mild amusement. He pulled himself against the pillows, his muscles feeling stiff and his head throbbing dully. Aunt woke, and, seeing him, gave a small cry. She came to him and sat cradling his head to her chest, covering him with her hair, her hands stroking the nape of his neck.

'Oh, my son, my child, I thought you would never wake.'

Samorin laughed weakly.

'Where am I?'

'Home.'

The door opened and the stranger came into the

room. He paused as they looked at each other, and Samorin saw that his eyes were dancing. Aunt turned to see him and smiled, holding her hand out. The stranger walked towards them, his hand grasped hers, but his eyes were on Samorin. A small smile trembled on his lips.

'How do you feel now, my son?' he asked.

The last two words came out unpractised and awkward, but there was no mistaking the deep tenderness in his voice. Aunt clasped the stranger's hand, drawing his arm around her, while she hugged Samorin close. Her cheeks were damp with tears.

'Son, my son,' she whispered, taking Samorin's hand and placing it in the man's, and holding both on her lap. 'Jay, meet your father.'

Her words wounded him and in the vulnerability of his discovery, he clutched the wound close to his heart. His hand fell away, his fists curled and held tightly to his chest as he felt his heart tear and unfold, and he knew that he had reached a bend in the road.

Then he slept.

It took Samorin two days to recover, and all that time either his father or Aunt kept vigil over him. At mealtimes, a grizzled old man he came to know later as Venu Kurup would bring him clear broths and toast, or *idiyappams* and mutton stew with chunks of browned meat floating in thick white aromatic sauce. As his appetite improved, his strength returned. The next evening, he awoke from his siesta feeling completely renewed. His father was standing by the window, looking at him. Samorin smiled at him.

'Father,' he called out, addressing him thus for the first time, 'we need to talk. I want to know everything.'

263

Father nodded. 'This evening, in the study after dinner. As you would imagine, it is a long story.'

Samorin agreed, got out of bed and went in search of Aunt.

After dinner, the three of them walked to the study. The house on the island was airy, with enclosed verandas and tall ceilings. It had been built in the 1920s by Samorin's great-grandfather, an eccentric traveller who had roamed all over the world in his youth. After learning Arabic from an old man in Marrakesh, he travelled the caravan routes across Arabia and lived with the Mongols for a while, learning to be a horseman. He spent time with Mayan tribes and learned about the true nature of gold, combining their ancient skills with the mysteries of the Arabs and the Moors. On his return from Peru, he tried in vain to cross a llama with the mules and horses on the estate. When he came back to settle in Manali, he decided to build his own residence where he could pursue his true passion, alchemy, in solitude. He would spend years with little or no contact with the outside world, cut off from it as he was by the waters of the lake. His self-imposed isolation ensured he became not much more than an eccentric memory, even for the members of his own family.

Now the study was full of old furniture and strange instruments: funnels and copper vessels with tubes, springs and contraptions, sieves made of alloys connected to pipettes and glass bowls. There were old vellum manuscripts on the shelves, books by Abramelin and treatises on the Coptic Christians, and volumes in Arabic that were carefully wrapped in cloth. A great fireplace with a baroque mantelpiece dominated one end of the room, and a circle of chairs had been laid out on the Persian rug. On the mantelpiece stood a framed black and white portrait of Aunt, her face turned shyly away from the photographer.

His father sat on the deep wingback chair nearest to the fireplace, and Aunt next to him on a chaise longue. Samorin took a chair opposite Father. There were three more chairs, empty.

'It is a long story and it has many tellers.'

The door opened, and Venu Kurup entered bearing a tray with glasses and a bottle of Laphroaig. Behind him came Madhavan Nair and the doctor. Father stood and shook hands with each of them. Kurup handed them whisky, and a glass of dark red wine to Aunt. The evening had the solemnity of a ritual, in which an arcane sect bonded by love, loyalty and murder was taking part.

'My son, Jay.' Father gestured at Samorin, addressing the men. 'I knew he would find me some day, and I had to be ready for it. Savitri brought him up like her own son, and I could not have hoped for a better mother for my child than her.'

Aunt got up and kissed Father on the cheek. He smiled at her, loving her with his eyes.

'Now he wants to know the truth, and we shall tell it to him. Then he may decide what to do with it.'

They bowed their heads in silent acknowledgement, the only sounds in the room those of glasses scraping on table tops and lighters being fired. Samorin looked at his father – he sat like a mahout guiding a dark and gigantic memory through an endless night. Father saw the questions burning in Samorin's eyes, the fear and pain that guarded them.

'I know what you want to ask me first, son,' Father

said. 'No, I did not murder your mother. But then, in a way I did kill someone: I had to murder myself.'

They are sitting in the warden's office and the blinds are drawn. Malt whisky in glass tumblers catches the light from the overhead porcelain lamps, and amber hues deepen and shift.

'The trial is not going well, I can see,' Shekhar Samorin says.

Madhavan Nair inclines his head slightly, looking at his former commander.

'You can change the course of it if you want to, you know.'

The aviator nods, sipping whisky. 'I can't and I won't. I do not want my wife's name to be sullied more than it already is. She is the mother of my son.'

'And you are his father, sir.'

Shekhar gets up and paces the room, hands in his pockets.

'Savitri has discovered a letter your wife had written to her lover on the day before her death, making an assignation. It had not been sent,' Madhavan Nair says. 'She showed it to me, and a few others she had found in Shyamala's jewellery box. And also love notes she had received from him. These will completely vindicate you.'

Shekhar's face clenches, his brow tightens at the memory.

'There has to be another way.'

'This is justice, sir.'

'Justice accompanied by honour is what I want. Savitri Thampuratti should be here. In fact, if I am not mistaken, that is probably her now.'

Footfalls sound outside in the corridor and Venu

Kurup escorts Savitri inside. She goes up to Shekhar and takes his hands in hers. 'You must ask our lawyers to produce Shyamala's papers in court,' she says.

'I do not want Jay to find out when he grows up that his mother had betrayed his father.'

'Are you comfortable with the knowledge that he will grow up thinking his father is a murderer?'

The pilot shakes his head, and lights a Camel.

'Madhavan, Savitri, there has to be another way.'

'The appeal will be heard tomorrow.'

Savitri closes her palms and prays briefly. The kohl in her eyes is smeared.

'We wait until tomorrow.'

Father paused, and the men around him shifted uneasily. Samorin was leaning forward, his chin on a fist, the unsmoked cigarette a long roll of ash in the tray.

'What happened on the night of the murder, Father?'

Father frowned, the memory hurting him again.

'I came home early, having won a bit off the good doctor here. The night was cool, I remember, and the breeze smelled of flowers. I was hungry, but wanted to have a drink with Shyamala on the veranda before we ate. She loved apple wine, and we would drink while I listened to her telling me about the goings-on in the estate – wife's talk; sometimes Savitri would join us. I plucked a rose, your mother was fond of them. Our bedroom opened onto a small private garden with its own gate and I found that the door was locked. I called out to your mother, thinking she had dozed off while waiting for me. Then I used my spare key.'

Father paused. His face had tightened in a network of lines and creases. Samorin realized that this must be a memory that waylaid him often. Sensing his anguish, Aunt came over to sit on the arm of his chair.

'I used my spare key,' the pilot continued, 'and Shyamala was there on the bed, naked. A man I did not recognize was climbing out of the window. Shyamala began to scream.'

The rose drops from his hand, his blood is ice. His limbs are numb, there is a blinding, heavy fog over his head. As he steps forward the man moves back into the room. Shyamala is screaming again, and the man takes down the rifle from the wall. Time slows.

'Wait!' The husband raises his hand. 'Who are you?'

The muzzle of the rifle blooms orange, yellow and red, a fiery hibiscus cloud that gets larger and closer and louder, and then he is riding the cloud, feeling nothing, seeing nothing.

'Your mother lay dead on the bed, half of her face blown away,' Father said, his voice low and even, 'and the side of my head was bleeding. The rifle lay on the floor beside me, and my fingers were curled around it.'

'Shyamala's lover panicked after he shot the commander,' Madhavan Nair picked up the tale. 'Thought he had killed him. And your mother was a witness. So he shot her too, thinking that whoever found them would come to the conclusion that it was a murder, followed by suicide.'

'His name was Sivadas, I met him in court later,' Father said.

'Was?' asked Samorin.

Father shrugged. Venu Kurup refilled Father's glass. 'I persuaded Savitri not to give evidence against

Shyamala.' Father's voice was heavy with sorrow. 'But that is how I met Sivadas for the first time. I recognized him as the man who shot me. He looked me in the eye and smiled at me with the knowledge that he had an alibi.'

'Kamala, his wife?'

Father nodded.

'He smiled at me with the mouth that had kissed my wife, and then I knew he had to die.'

'And . . .'

'We are warriors, Madhavan and I. In a dogfight, a warrior sometimes pretends to be stupid – a decoy move. Acting hurt, as if your plane has been damaged. And remembering that in mobility lies survival. Have you watched eagles fight? They always keep moving, zigzagging in the air. Madhavan, remember the dogfight over Kashmir in '71?'

Madhavan Nair smiled at Samorin, and began to describe the event.

'The enemy pilot was baiting me, trying to trap me, and his partner was covering him well. I dived in too soon and there I was, a sitting duck between their guns. I tried to flip my craft away, and suddenly the sky exploded beside me. I thought I was dead! But it was the commander, and he had just shot down one of them. I saw the F-16 plunge down in a tail of smoke, but the other somersaulted over me, coming up right behind with me in his gunsights.'

'I saw that Madhavan was in trouble and radioed him to act hurt, to deceive the enemy and throw him off his guard. Madhavan did a great job, rolling and weaving in the air, and it almost fooled even me. I thought he had caught some shrapnel on his fuselage from the first blast. But then the enemy pilot got too confident and close. Madhavan flipped over, and his missiles streamed at the F-16!'

Father grinned, his face suddenly boyish.

'I was flying with Madhavan that day,' Dr Pillai said mournfully. 'It was against regulations, but I had gone along for a joyride. It was meant to be just a routine patrol. Your father saved my life.'

'Like you saved mine, doctor.'

'We lost the appeal, sir,' Madhavan Nair says, coming into Shekhar Samorin's cell. The room is clean, with a table and a chair near the iron bars and a toilet in the corner. The pilot puts down the book he is reading. Dostoevsky.

'I have a plan,' he says softly.

'To move the Supreme Court and wait another two years? Then, of course, there is the President for a last appeal. Do not give up hope.'

Shekhar gestures towards the chair, asking his former comrade to sit.

'We do not appeal.'

'What? You will be hanged in less than a week! I can't do that, I will resign my job, Commander, rather than see the rope around your neck in my jail.'

'I understand the cholera epidemic is really bad in the district. And both the Collector and the DM are in the hospital.'

'Sir, with all respect, but have you lost your mind?'

'Madhavan, listen to me. I have a plan.'

'Act infirm,' Father said, looking at Samorin, 'it lulls the enemy. Act contrite and generous, as if you are acknowledging defeat.'

'Even if you are being wronged, Father?'

270

'Especially if you are being wronged. Vengeance sometimes has a disarming face.'

The car drives into the jail compound and turns onto the brick-laid path that ends at the side gate of the building. Savitri is driving, and beside her is a man. Venu Kurup opens the gate and bows slightly to Savitri.

'My lady,' he whispers. His eyes are fixed on the man with her. It is Kamala's husband, Sivadas.

'Is everything ready?' she asks.

'Yes, Thampuratti. Everything is.'

'It is the last night I will be coming to this jail,' her voice breaks. 'His things are inside the car.'

Sivadas is fidgety, shuffling his feet. Venu Kurup goes round to get the basket from the back seat of the car.

'I'm grateful for this, Sivadas. Shekhar Thampuran wants to make peace before he goes. He wants to talk to you about his wife. Does that make you uncomfortable?'

'You've paid me generously for this meeting. And also to keep my mouth shut.'

Savitri nods briefly.

Venu returns with a basket and a small suitcase. He opens his logbook and begins to make the entries.

Savitri Thampuratti plus One to meet prisoner Samorin.

One bottle of whisky. Blue shirt, trousers, shoes and fresh socks.

11.19 p.m. 17 October 1974.

'Before I saw him, I heard his footfalls in the corridor,' Father said. 'I could tell his apart from Savitri's. It

271

seemed then I had been waiting for this all my life.'

'Did you want to kill him then, Father?'

'No. First I wanted him to tell me the truth. I wanted to hear it from his own lips.'

Shekhar sees Sivadas outside his cell, standing behind Savitri. Venu Kurup takes the keys from his belt and opens the iron door. Savitri steps inside first, as if shielding Sivadas from Shekhar. Shekhar is sitting on his bed, one leg crossed over the other, his eyes thoughtful. Sivadas steps into the room, and stands as if unsure of what to do.

'We have met,' Shekhar says cryptically. The other man does not respond, his eyes blank.

'I thank you for your time,' Shekhar says, his voice weary and low. 'I requested this meeting because I wanted to leave in peace. This is not about hatred.'

Sivadas straightens up. He does not feel hatred. He does not feel anything at all but a mild pity and contempt towards this man who is going to die in a few hours, whose wife had lain with him in all her softness and heat, who now sits in front of him like a crushed shell. Sivadas pulls the chair away from the table and thumps it down opposite the pilot. Venu Kurup places the whisky on the table.

'Two glasses, please. I hope you will join me for a farewell drink.'

'If you want me to,' Sivadas says suspiciously. Behind him, Venu Kurup is already pouring the whisky.

'Cheers!' Shekhar says. He turns to Savitri and Kurup, asking them to leave. Kurup locks the door of the cell behind him. Sivadas picks up his drink gingerly and smells it.

'It's not poisoned,' Shekhar says gently, taking a sip from his glass. Sivadas drinks and makes a face. Then he tosses the contents of the glass down his throat, the way farmers drink arrack.

'Tell me about my wife,' the pilot says.

Sivadas reaches out towards the bottle of whisky and pours himself a large drink. He gulps it down. Then he pours again. And again. His eyes become dreamy, his voice is slurred. 'I was fascinated by Shyamala Thampuratti since she was a girl. I would follow her when she went with her friends to the orchards to pick green mangoes, and hide, watching her fill her skirt with them. When she grew up, I would steal red roses from the government nursery and place them by the road so that she could wear them on her way to college. But she would ignore me. She was Shyamala Thampuratti and I was just a poor boy from the village!'

The drink and the mood summon old memories: Shyamala, her black hair plaited and ribboned, *dhavani* and *pavada* billowing in the wind. Sivadas remembers her pausing underneath the tamarind tree, looking at the bunch of flowers that lay by the wayside, hears the laughter of her friends. She looks across the road and glimpses him, the flash of puzzlement in those wide dark eyes turning into understanding: she grinds the flowers under her heel. He feels rage once again, unaware of the pilot's eyes watching him in the small prison cell. Sivadas grits his teeth as he remembers another day – following Shyamala as she took a short cut through the woods alone, coming behind her and pushing her down on the grass, feeling the softness of her thighs as he grasped them, her skirt riding up. He slaps her across her face, holding her down, ripping her panties away, thrusting into her, his hand covering her mouth. Her eyes are black, huge, her teeth have grabbed the skin of his palm. And when it is over, and he pulls away from her and sits up to light a cigarette, she looks at him with a dark half-smile and says, 'Again, do it again . . .'

'What are you thinking of?' Shekhar asks him. His glass is nearly full. Sivadas laughs and pours himself more whisky.

'You aren't drinking,' he says.

'Not yet. Not until I hear the truth.'

Sivadas looks at Shekhar with a narrow gaze; it holds both cunning and triumph.

'What do you want to hear from me? That I killed your wife?'

'You tell me, Sivadas.'

'I really feel pity for you, Samorin. You will hang in a few hours, and what does it matter who killed whom? Wasn't it you who killed your wife?'

'You tell me, you were there.'

Sivadas downs the whisky in one gulp and sits back, looking at Shekhar Samorin. His eyes are glazed.

'Yes. I killed your wife.'

'I know.'

'Shot you first, and then her. Didn't want any witnesses.'

'I know. And you will hang for it.'

Sivadas lets out an incredulous laugh, but in a flash Shekhar Samorin is upon him, pinning him down. Sivadas twists and lashes out, breaking the glass, sending a shard deep into Samorin's hand. Suddenly the lights in the corridor go off and the cell is full of people. Sivadas feels groggy, the room is spinning. Someone holds him down while another ties his hands behind him, and shackles his legs to the chair.

'Welcome, Sivadas,' Samorin says gently, 'I must confess the whisky is drugged.'

There is fear in the murderer's eyes.

'You will not get away with this. What do you plan to do?'

'Think of this as a court martial. Always held in secret, the judgement passed only by the officers concerned.'

Men are standing around him: Shekhar Samorin, Jailer Madhavan Nair, Venu Kurup, Dr Pillai.

'We accuse Sivadas of murdering Shyamala Thampuratti,' Samorin says, 'members of the court, anyone for the defence?'

Silence.

'For the crime of murder, we sentence Sivadas to be hanged by the neck until dead. Gentlemen?'

Four hands go up, four heads nod grim assent. Sivadas begins to scream.

Later, days after it was declared that Squadron Leader Shekhar Samorin had been executed for the murder of his wife, one of the papers reported that he had spent his last hours screaming in jail. An enterprising reporter had talked to one of the remand prisoners, who had been released the morning after the hanging. 'It is strange that such a brave pilot, who had faced death so many times, should scream at the fear of death,' he wrote, 'but then, who can speak of the true nature of courage?'

'The cholera was what inspired me,' Father said. 'As the District Magistrate was out of action, the jail warden would have had to sign my death certificate. And with the district doctor overworked because of the epidemic, Dr Pillai could officiate for him. And Venu, my old faithful Venu, would take the drugged Sivadas to the gallows.'

'The instruction to keep the face covered was to prevent disclosure of Sivadas's identity, wasn't it?'

'Of course. It was Savitri's idea. When Sivadas was taken from the cell, he was so drugged he could hardly walk. Dr Pillai and Venu supported him by the shoulders, and his feet were dragging on the ground – I'm told he was pretty heavy.' Samorin's father permitted himself a small smile. 'In my clothes, with the hood on, the hangman did not suspect that it could have been anyone else.'

'The guards?'

'There weren't many. The few that were there had seen men on the way to the hangman act worse. They didn't want to look – to cross a condemned man's path is to bring misfortune.'

'And Father left with Aunt after receiving Sivadas's corpse,' Samorin said, 'and the cremation was at Cardamom Hill, away from the eyes of the world.'

'We gave him a good cremation.' Venu Kurup smiled without humour. 'No murderer could have hoped for a better one.'

'This is our story. Now we are waiting,' Father told Samorin.

'For what?'

'Your sentence, my son.'

Five faces turned towards him in the buttery light of the room, and Aunt's eyes were dark and anxious. Samorin met their eyes without hesitation.

'My mother was murdered. And justice was done.'

The four comrades of the secret nodded their heads.

Somewhere in the night, a dog began to howl.

CHAPTER SEVENTEEN

The Indian Airlines flight back to Delhi was late as usual. The portly, middle-aged stewardess, her hair tied back in a tight netted bun, spilled coffee on the tray and apologized indifferently. Samorin declined further service and sat back in his seat; he felt drained. The sky covered his journey and an endless, foamy moss of cloud stretched away into the misty blue azimuth of space. Higher and higher, above the flight of the falcon, above the trace of the shooting star, higher and higher until the gallows diminished into a black dot far below . . .

Now there was only the green earth beneath, patched with irregular squares of emerald fields and clumps of woodland, the shy silver of thin rivers, and then the endless pearly mosaic of cumulus.

He had spent the last few days of his convalescence in Cardamom Hill walking along its jungle paths with

Father. Sometimes Aunt would accompany them with her gun, and there would be hare or spotted doves for dinner.

'When I started my first year of exile, I could not sleep,' Father told him. 'It was Savitri who kept me together. After I got my retribution, life held no further meaning. Then Savitri would say to me, "Think about Jay. Think about your son." And it would hurt me that I couldn't see you every day, wake up with you in my arms, take you to see the great cities of the world, read you the classics and the *Mahabharata* and Whitman.'

They would sit on the white wrought-iron benches by the fountain in the afternoons, and Venu Kurup would bring foamy, cold beer.

'I would sneak out at night and come to the house to be with Savitri,' Father said. 'We would spend hours in the library talking and listening to music.'

'Of course,' Samorin gasped. 'It was you!'

Father smiled sadly.

'I would hear your little fist pound on the door and my heart would clench, but Savitri would restrain me when I would rise from my chair, ready to rush out and scoop you up in my arms. One day, there you were, at four in the morning, huddled into a little ball near the armoire. I picked you up, and you were so light. That was the first time I had touched you in four years.'

'You took me up to bed.'

'Did you like the Ferrari? And the toy planes?'

Samorin smiled, his eyes wet.

'Yes. The Prince of Children.'

'That was the only game I could play with you,' Father said, 'hiding them for you to find. And Savitri would tell me the details after you had discovered

278

them: what you said, how your voice sounded full of excitement, how your eyes sparkled.'

His face flushed, remembering.

'Each time I ventured out at night, I took fear with me as a companion,' Father said. 'Each time I took the boat out from the rushes to row over to the jetty where I knew Savitri would be waiting for me, I was afraid of being spotted. Some poacher, some fisherman out at night, some drunkard who had come to curse the sky and sob by the lake.'

'The Vampire of Cardamom Hill,' Samorin said. 'That is perhaps the strangest legend I have ever heard.'

'One day some men did come to my island,' Father said. 'Poachers. Savitri was sitting beneath the great tree that looks across the water, combing her hair. The guard dogs heard the intruders; they are trained to kill.'

Samorin smiled ruefully at the memory. Father touched him with an apology.

'I'm sorry.'

'Perhaps someone did see you,' Samorin said.

Father looked at him curiously.

'How do you know? As a matter of fact someone once did.'

After Savitri dropped him off beside the lake at daybreak, while walking towards the jetty, he stumbles upon a woman resting under the trees. She lies on the grass, her sari undone, as if someone has just left her. She smiles seductively, her face in the shadow. It is a prostitute from the village of widows. Shekhar Samorin passes swiftly, averting his face, and the woman's touch brushes him like a falling leaf.

279

'Thampuran.' Her voice is slight, hesitant.

The pilot does not answer and quickens his steps.

'I met her, you know, in Brindaban,' Samorin said. 'She called me by your name. It was what brought me here.'

'Later Savitri told me about it – bazaar gossip. The widow said she had seen my ghost and that it walks the lake, looking for revenge. That rumour was most useful, and along with the myth of the Vampire, I knew my retreat was then safe.'

Father had seen him off in the boat that Venu kept hidden inside the shed in the woods. And Aunt stood beside him as the craft pulled away into the night of the world, leaving a shimmering web of silver water in its wake, rippling a luminous farewell. And Samorin realized that for him, the world had changed for ever. He smiled.

The plane veered to the west and the stewardess offered Samorin breakfast. He refused. He leaned back and tried to sleep, but images haunted the shimmering red arc beneath his closed eyes. He pulled out his notebook and began to draw.

The pen draws by itself if you let it, Samorin had learned that long ago. The air is full of ghosts who swim in the artist's ink. Formless and voiceless, they yearn to be reborn as visions within the artist's mind. They plunder the almanac of his myths and experiences, assuming familiar forms on sheets of virgin paper. For Samorin, the act of drawing was an act of exorcism. As he sat in the plane sketching, the phantoms appeared one by one, exorcized on paper in profane haikus of evil. Kaiser guarded the Styx like

Charon — the dog's face was entirely fleshless. The riverbank was crowded with the dead mourning themselves, mostly women, silent and motionless, waiting in line for the boatman to take them across. Kaiser's skull gleamed against the dark, cross-hatched background. Tsiranana, in the form of a fat grotesque baby naked but for a collar and tie, suckled Death, his spectacles askew as his mouth puckered on one long cold wrinkled teat. The bony fingers of Death tousled his hair and its grin was surprisingly tender. The picture of Dhiren Das as Krishna was the last, and his *gopis* were all skeletons. Their skulls gaped at their god blindly, mouths open, pleading, stringy vestiges of breasts hanging loose from their ribcages. And suddenly, as he drew, in a grim epiphany, Samorin knew where Salma was.

He pressed the overhead button to summon the air hostess and ask for the airphone. He had to speak to Anna urgently.

Her voice came on the line, and his heart lurched.

'I know where Salma is,' he said. 'At Dhiren's.'

He heard her gasp at the other end of the connection. A short silence.

'Impossible, Jay. I have looked.'

'It's complicated, he has hidden her well,' he said.

'Tell me everything. From the start.'

Anna drove to Samorin's house and parked with a scream of tyres. He took her in his arms wordlessly, inhaling the freshness of her hair, the aloe vera on her cheek, the fragrance of Dior on her neck. She nestled into him, moulding her shape to his, and he could feel the length and tautness of her, the intense welcome of her limbs. He lifted her chin and kissed her clove-scented mouth, her lips sliding along his. She raised her tongue and let him explore its soft roots while her long strong fingers gripped his hair. Then, with a sigh, she laid her head against his chest, holding him tightly by the waist.

'We must hurry,' Samorin said.

'In a while, Jay, in a while. Let me just feel you back again.'

They stood in the foyer of his house, the cool kiss of marble upon their feet. Sasha padded towards them with her stealthy tread, rubbing herself against her master, her tail flicking against Anna's long legs. Samorin stooped and scratched her forehead. The big cat grunted, nuzzled against his hand, and then stood up on her hind legs to place her forepaws on his shoulders. The weight made Samorin reel back.

'Hey, I'm back, big girl,' Samorin laughed, 'and I'm not going anywhere without you, OK? Maybe one of these days, I'll take you to Cardamom Hill to meet a man I think you'll like.'

The cat placed its head on its master's shoulder, and Samorin hugged her. Sasha struggled away and resumed her four-footed stance looking rather indignant.

'Wild ones rarely like to be held, it doesn't matter how tame they become,' Samorin said. 'Let's go. Your car or mine?'

Sasha made an eager whimpering sound, pawing at the door of the Jeep.

'Easy,' Samorin laughed, opening the door of the Scorpio for her. The fosa settled her sleek length on the back seat, her tail twitching, the amber eyes speckled with saffron: patient, incurious.

'I hope you are right about Salma being at Dhiren's,'

Anna said doubtfully as the Jeep left Delhi and picked up speed on the Agra highway. 'We have gone through Brindaban with a fine toothcomb. There is not a hospital, not a widows' home, not a hotel we haven't checked. We searched the Aasha hospice, thinking that maybe Dubey had kept her under sedation. We have been watching Dhiren's house every minute, every hour. If Salma is there she must be invisible.'

Samorin barked a short humourless laugh.

'No. If my hunch is right, she is very visible.'

'Why don't you tell me, Jay? She is my sister-in-law and I have a right to know.'

Samorin looked across at her briefly. His eyes were gentle, compassionate.

'I know. But people we love sometimes decide to move beyond the comfort of our protection. Then we have to protect ourselves from them. In the end, we have to keep ourselves safe.'

'Where is she, Samorin?'

'In Brindaban, sleeping, at rest. That's all I can say, now. Unless I see her for myself, I cannot tell you. I have to know first.'

Anna's lip trembled, her shoulders shook. She made a noise inside her throat that was half a sob and half a laugh.

'Sleeping, at rest? You have a morbid sense of humour, Jay!'

'Salma is not going anywhere, Anna.'

On the way Anna spoke about the frustrating investigation into Salma's disappearance. Her voice trembled when she talked about Mrs Hassan, who had died the day before; the police had claimed the body for post-mortem. Dr Dubey had protested, and eventually had to be forcibly restrained, while Anna had taken her mother-in-law's body away in a police ambulance. In the evening the police returned to Aasha to pick Dr Dubey up for questioning, but he had disappeared.

'You can't let him get away, Anna.'

Samorin turned to look at her, and met the rage in her eyes, saw the pain in the set of her mouth. But her voice was level, calm. 'The airports, railway stations and bus terminals are being watched. We have set up roadblocks. Mama's post-mortem report came in just now.'

'Polymer in large quantities?'

'Not just polymer, but a lot of aberrational genetic matter,' Anna said. 'Our gene specialist had graduated from Washington, and had studied with Dr Wooley briefly. He knows his biometrics.'

'So what did you find?'

'Enough evidence to convict Dubey of genetic malpractice, of murder through poisoning. The same copies of the cancer DNA were everywhere. White blood corpuscles to be found in the bone marrow are there in her liver. We are examining Dubey's lab, collecting samples — we just need to find the original DNA of the cancer gene I assume the good doctor has been using.'

'Ingenious,' Samorin admitted.

'But not ingenious enough to fool you,' Anna said, rather sharply. Samorin smiled.

'Coincidence. I was left alone in his room and I prowled.'

'I was there too.'

'Evil has a pattern, Anna, and it is in its nature to reveal itself to anyone who seeks it assiduously enough. The vanity of evil never ceases to surprise me,' Samorin answered. 'But stealth and disguise are part of its basic make-up, it is a master of concealment. To find evil, always look in hidden places, especially in the mind.'

'Your philosophy disconcerts me. Is that how you guessed we'd find Salma at Dhiren's?'

Samorin nodded.

The rest of the journey was spent in silence; Anna retreated into herself, her body angled away from Samorin. But when he reached across to take her hand in his, she pressed it down on her lap, hurting him with her nails and drawing blood.

The afternoon shadows had lengthened over the lawns of the artist's studio. The undercover officer who sat in the shade of a pipal was dressed as a village hawker but his red and yellow spotted headband was too large for him, his shoes too new and he wore a watch on his wrist. He had a basket of bananas beside him that buzzed with flies.

'You call this undercover and honestly expect Das to be taken in?' Samorin grinned. Anna sighed. Her face was tense, and she beckoned the policeman to approach them. He stared at them haughtily, and Anna got out of the car to speak to him.

'Dhiren went out an hour ago,' she said, returning to the Scorpio, 'let's move.'

Samorin swung the Jeep into the gravelled driveway past the long row of *asoka* trees. The house was empty. Samorin went around the portico to the small enclosure that led to the artist's studio. The door was open and they stepped in.

He heard Anna draw in her breath as Dhiren Das's *ne plus ultra* loomed over them. The sunlight that came in through the open door and windows blazed on the sculpture, revealing every minute detail of form and colour. The bearded god appeared even more majestic and arrogant. Anna looked into his eyes and shuddered, crossing her arms, hugging herself.

'What power!' she whispered. 'It frightens me, Jay. It is as if the piece is alive, existing in some parallel reality one only has to reach across to be in. The god breathes, Jay, and the woman under him is actually dreaming.'

She took Samorin's hand.

'Look, the river could be flowing. I want to swim in it, feel the rush of water. I want to sway to his damned lute, I want to be with those women, dancing. It beckons me, Jay. I feel helpless. No wonder Salma was under this man's spell, but where is she?'

Samorin went closer to touch the sculpture, its platform well protected by brass railings. He climbed over and stood inspecting the colossal structure, running his hands across its swells and flows, his fingers lingering over the painted crevices on the lime and plaster. His eyes were closed, the lines on his face deepening in dark confirmation. He caressed the dimpled feet of the god, resting his hand on the raised breast of the sleeping woman. His palm moved over her slender shape, sweeping his touch up to her neck and caressing the line of her sleeping cheek. Gently, he stroked her eyelids, ran his fingers over the clay-matted hair and turned to Anna.

'See how she sleeps,' he whispered, sadness in his voice.

Horror widened Anna's eyes with a terrible understanding. Samorin nimbly leaped over the railings to grab the crowbar that lay near the fireplace, and swung it at the grotesque creation. As the plaster smashed away and scattered, flinging fragments of coloured earth and brittle lime in the air, Anna gasped, seeing the pallid skin of the dead woman who lay entombed within.

'Salma,' said Samorin wearily.

He opened his arms out to Anna, wanting to shelter her from the horror beneath the shattered plaster, to hush her screams and lull them into sobs. Before he could reach her the air was rent with a cry that made the grey pigeons gurgling on the roof shriek and flutter away.

'Jay Samorin!'

Dhiren Das came in through the open door, his black mane aflame with liquid sunlight – against the burning afternoon he was like a demon from an infernal forge. His hands were raised to strike down anything that stood in his way. Anna stepped forward, dropping into a fighter's crouch, but Dhiren's rage was so powerful that he swatted her aside, sending her reeling against the wall. Samorin barred his way, but Dhiren dodged him, leaping over the railings and kneeling down among the debris of his ruined work. He reached out to touch Salma's dead skin, his fingers running fond little circles over the mound of her navel. He scooped the broken pieces from the floor, sweeping them into his arms, and turned to Samorin, holding them out. His eyes blazed with hate, tears streaming down his rough cheeks.

'I'm going to squash you like an insect!'

'It's over, Dhiren,' Samorin said quietly. 'Squashing me is not going to be as easy as killing Salma.'

Dhiren's laugh was maniacal.

'If it weren't for you, she wouldn't have been dead. She would have lived for ever in my work. Look at her, the ruined Radha of an eternal Krishna,' the artist raged, his spittle spraying Samorin. 'She would have been great, but you destroyed it for her. What would she have been but an alcoholic nymphomaniac, growing old and bitter with fear and loneliness? Instead, I embalmed her in eternal art, making her soul part of Krishna and his deathless Arcadia! You, you destroyed her.'

'You tried to give evil a soul, Dhiren Das,' Samorin said, 'but the only soul evil has is death. You are nothing but a demented murderer.'

Dhiren Das lashed out with his foot, striking Samorin's thigh, the attack so unexpected and swift that it took him off guard. Dhiren closed in, his right hand a rigid spade aimed at the side of Samorin's throat. Samorin pirouetted on his heel, twisting his body sideways away from the blow. Dhiren Das now came at him, and Samorin leaned forward, grabbing his shoulder and using the attacker's own momentum to his advantage, spinning back again as Das passed and leaping to smash the ball of his foot against the sculptor's back. But Das had anticipated Samorin's move and with a wild laugh he somersaulted, meeting the foot of his opponent with his hand, seizing Samorin's ankle and twisting it hard. Samorin landed on his back, the impact like a giant fist. He rolled away on the hard earth and stood up, his eyes glossy with pain.

'*Act crippled, warrior.*' An old lesson came back to him. '*Disarm the enemy.*'

Dhiren Das laughed again, the air crackling with his manic hate.

'The master warrior is defeated by an Ekalavya! And now I'm going to kill you.'

288

Samorin knew Das, driven by hatred, was stronger. He knew he had to wait for the unguarded moment. Dhiren Das circled him, and from the corner of his eye he saw that Anna lay motionless against the wall where she had fallen.

'I'm going to make you pay for all the harm you've done so far! Here's one for Dr Dubey,' Dhiren snarled, striking out at Samorin who took the blow on his biceps, deflecting its force as he moved away towards Anna.

'I'm not finished yet. You hurt Charles Tsiranana.' Dhiren's mouth was twisted in an enraged snarl, his voice hard with contempt. 'He called you his friend!'

'Charles?' Samorin asked, circling Das, 'what about him?'

'He had a heart attack last night, while he was visiting me. Dr Dubey's disappearance had traumatized him and he drove down to see me. I took him to Aasha. I wouldn't have him anywhere else – the best doctors, the best nurses, looking after him under my own supervision. Samorin, once I'm finished with you and that bitch over there, I'll bring Charles here to see your carcass, so that he knows that the man he befriended, who betrayed him, is now dead meat. Even if I have to carry his bed myself.'

'Bodies aren't easy to hide, Dhiren.'

'Oh, my sculpture will be repaired, I assure you,' Dhiren gave a crooked smile, 'and it will just have two more souls sacrificed to art.'

For the briefest of moments, Das's eyes flickered towards the wreckage of his work, and that was all Samorin needed. He moved with the speed of the fosa, the hardened flat of his palm punching Dhiren at the base of his throat, while the other hand descended in an arc, smashing Dhiren's ribs. Das coughed and spat blood, reeling away to fall on his knees.

'Give up, Dhiren,' Samorin hissed.

The madman looked up as he knelt on all fours amongst the detritus of his art, his hair wet and matted with sweat across his face, bloody mucus dripping from his mouth. But his eyes were bright and amused. With a loud whoop, he gathered the lime, mud and plaster dust on the floor and flung it in Samorin's face, blinding him with the *poozhikadayan* – the most treacherous move in the discipline of *kalaripayattu*. Samorin yelled, the lime burning his eyes, his hands clawing at his face. Dizzy and helpless, he realized that death was about to blind him for ever. He tripped on the railings, falling on his back, and, through the agony of his eyes, he saw the hazy bulk of Dhiren Das approach. But behind him, through the open door, a long blurred form momentarily blotted out the sun. Samorin opened his swollen, weeping eyes, staring numbly as his oldest enemy towered above him, elbow bent to deliver the death blow. Then something gave a low, throaty snarl and Samorin heard Anna call out.

'Hey Dhiren! You wanted to meet the cat.'

CHAPTER EIGHTEEN

Charles Tsiranana opened his eyes to the gurgle of doves. They were pottering outside on the ledge of the window of his hospital room, snuggling against one another, rubbing their beaks and cooing their affection in their strange avian jargon. Fat leafy creepers, their tendrils shivering in the breeze, climbed along the window frame, heavy with white flowers. The curtains, too, were white and spotted with grey, held together by grey braids. The walls were creamy and soothing, and upon the white sideboard stood a crystal vase that held a bunch of fresh, bright red roses.

'Hello Charles,' Samorin said.

Startled, the Malagasy turned on his bed, almost jerking the slim plastic tube from the stand that fed him from a plastic sachet. He felt a twinge of pain and sweat beaded his forehead; Samorin leaned over and touched his arm.

'I'm sorry, old friend,' Samorin whispered gently, regretfully. Tsiranana smiled weakly.

Samorin gestured at the roses.

'I hope you like them. Anna sent them for you.'

'Where is she?' Tsiranana asked. 'I don't see her.'

'She was here with me, smoothing your pillows and arranging the flowers. She just left.' Samorin gestured at a small icebox on the side table. 'Wine, also from Anna. We are worried about you.'

'It's just a mild heart attack,' Tsiranana said. 'The doctors here are excellent. They say I should be out of hospital in a week.'

'Splendid! Then we can soon resume our chess games.'

Tsiranana did not answer. He looked at Samorin curiously. Samorin returned his gaze. He knew so well those gentle grey eyes, the laugh lines at the corners and the slender, noble arch of the brow.

'I knew you would be up and about soon. In fact, I brought our chess set with me. The same one we carried when we were travelling in Madagascar. Remember the jungle, the baobabs? Beside the fire, you and me in khakis like a couple of colonial hunters, smoking cigars and playing chess. That's when we got Sasha.'

The Malagasy nodded, his eyes careful. Samorin gestured towards the narrow teakwood box that lay beside the icebox.

'And what's a chess game with you without wine? Pouilly-Fuissé 1997. Chilled.'

Despite his wariness, Tsiranana smiled. He rubbed his palms slowly. 'Ah, my old friend! If only I could.'

Samorin spread his hands. The quiet hum of an air conditioner rimmed the silence in the room. The day was climbing towards noon, and outside the hospital window the rolling meadows of Aasha's complex were green, bright with neat, thick dams of flowers.

'Why did you do it, Charles?' Samorin asked.

'Do what?' the diplomat asked, his expression suddenly blank.

'Become an accessory to murder. Sometimes even orchestrating the killing.'

Tsiranana turned his head away from his friend, and gazed out at the matt blue of the sky. A hawk drew lazy ellipses in its heights.

'Greed? Power?' Samorin asked.

'I do not know what you are talking about, Jay.'

'So many dead, Charles. Radama, Jean Paul, the countless victims your friend the doctor dispatched. Together, you are guilty of mass murder.'

The Malagasy sighed. He opened his hands out in a gesture of mild regret. 'I wish I could smoke a cigarette.'

'Is this a game, too, Charles?'

'Ah, I love our games. We have spent many happy hours playing knight against rook, pawn against queen, sipping excellent wine. We have discussed the fragility of Nietzsche over poached salmon, and sat in the garden smoking Havanas after dinner. Have you forgotten?'

'There is also a small matter of justice, Charles, wouldn't you think?'

'Ah, justice, that delicate word! But justice is personal, Jay.'

'You shouldn't have let your mad doctor harm Mrs Hassan, Charles. You could have saved Salma from Dhiren. Then it became personal.'

'I have never personally wished pain upon them.'

'It brought Anna pain,' Samorin said, 'and when it brings her pain, it becomes personal for me.'

'Personal? How?' he asked in a small, wistful voice. 'I thought you, Samorin, were a hunter of evil. And no evil lurked in my house.'

Samorin looked at his friend with deep regret.

'Little did I know evil could have such a gentle face,' he said, 'that death could have so civilized a voice.'

'Remember Plato's cave of shadows? There is nothing called death, Jay. A little pain, an obsessive aversion to leaving your misery – that's death. But how am I supposed to have murdered all these people?'

'Are you afraid to die, Charles?'

'Regretfully, yes. I haven't shaken off the fear yet. But why are you after my poor friend Dubey? Why are you hunting him? He was driven out of America, too. Look at this hospice now! Look at the happy life the widows lead. Most of them were terribly poor, their health shattered by incessant pregnancies. Now they sleep on clean sheets, eat three times a day and their children study in the Aasha school.'

'They did not choose to become widows, Charles. You know that.'

Tsiranana raised an eyebrow.

'Their husbands all died of cancer. How do you blame Dubey for that?'

Samorin drew the small coffee table between his seat and the sickbed. He opened the chess box and laid out the pieces on the board. He brought out the Pouilly-Fuissé and two long-stemmed glasses, beaded with condensation, and opened the wine with the corkscrew of a Swiss army penknife. He poured the wine into the glasses and arranged them on either side of the chess board. Tsiranana looked perplexed, and slightly annoyed.

'This is not really funny, Samorin. I can't drink or play chess.'

Samorin moved his queen's pawn two squares forward.

'You study the board and tell me, I'll move your pieces for you.'

He raised the glass to his lips.

'To games, Charles! To the warfare of the mind.'

'The knight. Nf3 to Nc6 . . .' Tsiranana whispered, the light of battle reluctantly flaring in his eyes. Samorin could sense intense mental activity beneath the stoic demeanour of the diplomat. Tsiranana was busily analysing every move Samorin made, every word he said.

'Hmmm,' Samorin said. 'So, you were asking how Dubey could be responsible for those cancers? Ever heard of controlled release applications? Bishop to c6.'

'Sounds like a computer software package to me.'

'Oh, good analogy, bringing in viruses. Well, viruses existed long before computers, Charles. Do you know how they kill? They attach themselves to the cell walls within the body, and then penetrate the system. The passages to a cell's nucleus are guarded by shape-changing proteins that the virus tricks.'

'Ah, the Berlin Defence, Jay? That's clever. Why are you talking to a sick man about viruses, Jay?'

'Just starting to outline a profiler's theory about murder. The virus is a fantastic guerrilla; once he is inside the fort, his DNA integrates with the master plan – your genome. Once that infiltration happens, the host cell can't tell the difference, and the body even begins to manufacture virus proteins! From there the virus multiplies, and becomes legion, invading the entire body.'

'Why are you inflicting this biology lesson on me? I would have preferred some wine instead.'

'Dr Dubey is a wizard in genetics, specializing in controlled release applications. He knew enough about the dark side of gene therapy.'

'Stop this right now!' Tsiranana's face twisted in pain. 'You simply do not understand, Samorin. My wife died of cancer five years ago. As a last resort, we tried to deliver curative DNA – modifying the virus and delivering it to her genome. But the immune response triggered was so massive that it killed her. Do not talk to me about genetic research, Jay, it is humbug.'

'Maybe not. Maybe someone has invented a way to block the immune response. Dr Karen Wooley did. She created microscopic polymer containers called knedels, interestingly named after Polish matzo balls. Attach a knedel to a protein that acts as a key, fill it with the curative DNA or drugs, and presto! The warrior gene is in! The body's immune system accepts it.'

'Dubey should know the answer, why don't you ask him?' the diplomat grumbled. 'That is, if you catch him. Since he is such an expert on genetics, think of what miracles the man can accomplish!'

'Oh, he was into a lot of miracles, I assure you. Inspecting his work on cell modifications proved what a genius he is!'

'What is Dubey's crime, Jay?'

'Murder, Charles. Imagine, if the knedels could be hollowed out and filled with leukaemia genes, coated with a sugar molecule, or a few strands of amino acids to trick the proteins that guard the cell walls. Once they are in, the polymer cover dissolves and the cancer gene would integrate itself into the human genome. Knedels released in large quantities over many applications would ensure that a lot of their recipients would get cancer. Bishop to square 8. Check! You are getting careless, Charles.'

'So how is Dubey supposed to have infected people?'

'Remember the inoculation drives Aasha had? The local police station has all the statistics. Polio, cholera, hepatitis, then the booster shots that followed. The vitamin injections administered to patients. Mrs Hassan's post-mortem signed the doctor's death warrant. Dubey was a cancer factory.'

'But why, for God's sake? What was the motive?'

'Funds. With you as the chief patron, having worked with UN humanitarian agencies and as the serving envoy of a sensitive country, any outfit headed by an impressively qualified doctor whose antecedents are carefully edited and who is now tending to cancer victims and running a shelter for their widows, is bound to bleed any Christian heart.'

'Ingenious. But it can't be proved.'

'Oh believe me, Charles, it can. A simple blood test would do, indicating high polymer levels, as it did on poor Mrs Hassan. If Dubey hadn't got greedy for her money as well, this might have never come to light – I wouldn't have become involved. This is a high-profile case, Charles, and a unique one. The investigators are likely to come across the original cancer gene in the doctor's lab anytime soon. Scientists are invariably too fond of their creations to dispose of them – it's the godhood of it all. We have biotechnicians working overtime in the lab below.'

The Ambassador sighed, fingering the rim of the polished king on the board.

'But why did you do it, Charles? All those poor farmers, shopkeepers, labourers injected with death in the guise of inoculations? Why?'

Tsiranana shrugged. His eyes were suddenly weary, lost.

'At my age, I cannot afford to be sentimental. My wife Rachel is dead and the political situation in Madagascar is chaotic. The battle of the Presidents has really polarized things and, who knows, Ratsiraka could be on his way out. We were his men, people like Radama and me. If Ratsiraka goes, the old guard cannot return to Madagascar and retire to a villa in Toamasina, lying in the sun in a hammock, drinking beer, eating koba and keeping a young Creole mistress. In France, London, Italy maybe, or even in Costa Rica. But then, retirement like that needs money.'

'I know. We hacked into Aasha's transfer accounts.'

'Illegal, really, I must protest.' Tsiranana raised an eyebrow in mock outrage. Samorin laughed without humour.

'Aasha's donor accounts abroad show transfers of millions of dollars into two numbered accounts in Cayman. Radama Zafy's and yours. And we now know that the codes Jean Paul stole were used to transfer the money into another account. Yours again.'

'But how could he? He was dead. Your girlfriend shot him, remember?'

'Stansi did, on your orders. And he is away on indefinite leave, citing mental trauma as a reason. Where is he now? In Cannes? Amalfi?'

Charles Tsiranana gave a harsh laugh.

'In prison, in Madagascar. I phoned Didier Ratsiraka

and told him that Stansi had stolen the money; even sent him the codes after I emptied my account, closed it and shifted it to Panama.'

Samorin sipped his wine, his eyes hooded and watching.

'Don't you feel remorse, Charles? You and your friend Dubey killed so many. Aren't you afraid of punishment?'

'Diplomatic immunity, my friend!' Tsiranana laughed again. 'Remorse for what? Could any of those dead, with the exception of Mrs Hassan, tell Haydn from Bach? Could they discourse on Goethe or weep to *Tosca*? Could they decipher the arcane Sanskrit secrets of the *Rigveda*? On one hand rest wealth, good taste and civilization, and on the other lie ignorance and poverty, or, as in the case of Stansi, ridiculous greed. It is not as if Dubey is an indiscriminate killer without a conscience – in removing those louse-ridden husbands, he gives these women a better life.'

'Perhaps Dubey was into other kinds of genetic modification too, of more than just leukaemia cells,' Samorin warned.

Tsiranana shrugged and opened his hands out in a sophisticated, expansive gesture.

'Charles, you know the health issue that generates the biggest headlines and gets the largest amount of funding these days, don't you?'

'AIDS. I know. I have seen Africa decimated, all along the Kinhasa Highway when we were on a UN inspection tour to Botswana. It's frightening. But one day, perhaps, after the evil of poverty, violence and superstition in that continent is wiped out by the scourge, a select elite would be left to take over. No more Mobutus and Idi Amins, only civilized leaders! Imagine!'

'Imagine, instead, the AIDS virus inside knedels, modified to shorten the gestation periods to a matter of days, weeks, after inoculation,' Samorin answered.

The Ambassador's eyes gleamed briefly. Samorin caught the spark.

'You knew it all along, didn't you? The first blood samples we got from Dubey's lab were full of the modified AIDS virus. What were you guys planning: a hundred thousand deaths for a billion dollars?'

Tsiranana sighed.

'You think of me as a monster, Jay, but look at your country. Look at most of the developing world. Starving, diseased, seedy, festering with insanitary slums, corruption and poverty. If Malthus could be invoked before time, progress would be faster. The infirm and the unfortunate would be weeded out and in the atmosphere of plenty, a former Third World would become the cradle of a new civilization. We have argued the Hindu mysteries together, my friend – everything inexplicable that happens has its reason hidden behind many folds back in time. Every karma has its astral DNA, and the molecules can be traced strands and strands away.'

'And what is your karma?'

The diplomat smiled regretfully.

'I shall move to a warm coast: Lisbon, perhaps, or Rio. And spend my days reading Schopenhauer and Dante, reciting Virgil on the beach. I shall nibble at escalopes of veal to the strains of Tchaikovsky. I have lived too long in civilization not to be part of it. I shall look forward to hearing Zubin Mehta perform magic and Pavarotti sing; I shall wear snowy white shirt-fronts and play baccarat with a stoic face, and I shall miss you and our long talks and complicated chess games. I'm sorry, Jay.'

'Dhiren Das is dead, Charles,' Samorin said. 'The fosa got him when he was about to kill me. The fosa you gave me. Ironic, isn't it?'

'Ah well, the Marcus Aurelius web that entangles us all! It was inevitable. I always told Das that he had too much hate in him, especially towards you. Even in creativity, hate hinders true greatness and makes one weak. You need the civilized man's calm within to be truly powerful. Could you imagine Chopin or Einstein running around hating people and making an insufferable din?'

'Aren't you afraid of retribution and justice, Charles?'

The Malagasy grinned.

'It's a calculated chance. But I got away with it, didn't I? Look at Timur who murdered millions and died happy. Attila died in fornicatory bliss, while poor, pure Gandhi got shot dead at prayer. Karma, my boy, is the mystery of good luck.'

For the first time Jay Samorin saw contempt in Tsiranana's face and understood the colossal vanity of the man. Samorin rose from his chair.

'Checkmate, Charles,' he said gently.

Tsiranana looked up, mildly confused.

'But the game is not over yet, Jay.'

'For you it is, Charles,' Samorin said, pointing at the stand with its drip feeding into Tsiranana's arm. 'Anna was here in your room before I came, and she switched the sachets. "For Mama and Salma," she told me to tell you. Meanwhile, enjoy your guilt.'

'I have no guilt. But what sachets?'

Samorin gestured at the icebox in which the wine had been brought to Tsiranana's room.

'She told me she took a bag of saline solution containing Dr Dubey's new AIDS virus from the police lab. Highly illegal of course, stealing confiscated evidence. And while you were sleeping, she switched the sachets. Goodbye, old friend.'

Samorin turned away as Charles Tsiranana's eyes widened in horror, his mouth opening above a slack jaw.

'Wait! You don't mean . . .'

But his words were cut off as Samorin closed the door behind him and stepped into the gleaming white corridor. The embassy guard stationed at the door saluted him. A nurse hurried past him with two bottles of glucose solution and a worried expression on her face. Samorin quickened his steps, passing two doctors in the lobby poring over a sheaf of medical papers, and came out into the early winter afternoon where Anna waited for him in the sunlight.

THE END

THE TIGER BY THE RIVER
Ravi Shankar Etteth

'DAZZLES WITH ITS INTRICATE PLOTTING AND
STYLISH PROSE'
David Davidar, author of *The House of Blue Mangoes*

Swati Varma is one of modern Delhi's more blessed
inhabitants. Then one brilliant morning, when the world
seemed cleansed by the coming of the rains, the unthinkable
happens: his pregnant wife is killed in a road accident.
Devastated, Swati decides to make the pilgrimage back to the
place of his birth, Panayur, in the state of Kerala, to scatter his
beloved's ashes in the sacred waters of the Papanasini river.

Returning to this long-forgotten world, he is reunited with
Antara, a childhood companion and now caretaker of the
crumbling, ghost-filled palace that was his home. For
Panayur – still miraculously free from the religious turmoil
that threatens so much of the country – was once a
kingdom, and Swati is the direct descendant of its last
king. As the two friends talk, sharing memories and
exchanging secrets, thousands of miles away, Vel – a
cousin Swati never knew he had – sets out on a quest for
the truth about his family that will take him from America
to Berlin and, ultimately, to Panayur.

And so begins an extraordinary and healing journey. One
that will lead both Swati and Vel back through the cruel
and bloody, vibrant and myth-filled history of the kings of
Panayur to the legend that lies at its heart – the legend of
the tiger by the river . . .

Rich, seductive, and at times highly erotic, this
spellbinding novel full of mystery, magic and wonder
marks the début of a singular new literary voice.

'A HEADY MIX OF MYTHOLOGY AND MYTH-MAKING
. . . A REWARDING, ATMOSPHERIC READ, LADEN WITH
GHOSTS'
Time Out

0 552 99999 7

BLACK SWAN

A SELECTED LIST OF FINE WRITING
AVAILABLE FROM BLACK SWAN

99588 6	THE HOUSE OF THE SPIRITS	Isabel Allende	£7.99
99946 6	THE ANATOMIST	Federico Andahazi	£6.99
77105 8	NOT THE END OF THE WORLD	Kate Atkinson	£6.99
99863 X	MARLENE DIETRICH LIVED HERE	Eleanor Bailey	£6.99
77131 7	MAKING LOVE: A CONSPIRACY OF THE HEART	Marius Brill	£6.99
88879 2	GATES OF EDEN	Ethan Coen	£7.99
99990 3	A CRYING SHAME	Renate Dorrestein	£6.99
77206 2	PEACETIME	Robert Edric	£6.99
99935 0	PEACE LIKE A RIVER	Leif Enger	£6.99
99954 7	SWIFT AS DESIRE	Laura Esquivel	£6.99
77182 1	THE TIGER BY THE RIVER	Ravi Shankar Etteth	£6.99
99978 4	KISSING THE VIRGIN'S MOUTH	Donna Gershten	£6.99
77177 5	3	Julie Hilden	£6.99
77082 5	THE WISDOM OF CROCODILES	Paul Hoffman	£7.99
77109 0	THE FOURTH HAND	John Irving	£6.99
77005 1	IN THE KINGDOM OF MISTS	Jane Jakeman	£6.99
14240 9	THE NIGHT LISTENER	Armistead Maupin	£6.99
99977 6	PERSONAL VELOCITY	Rebecca Miller	£6.99
99901 6	WHITE MALE HEART	Ruaridh Nicoll	£6.99
77106 6	LITTLE INDISCRETIONS	Carmen Posadas	£6.99
77093 0	THE DARK BRIDE	Laura Restrepo	£6.99
99673 4	DINA'S BOOK	Herbjørg Wassmo	£7.99
77107 4	SPELLING MISSISSIPPI	Marnie Woodrow	£6.99